continued . . .

Hold Tight

"A thriller for the Google era." —*The New York Times*

The Woods

"A lively, fast-moving entertainment, jam-packed with the bizarre plot twists that are his stock-in-trade."
—*The Washington Post*

Promise Me

"Truly surprising." —*Entertainment Weekly*

The Innocent

"Another twist-filled triumph." —*Life*

Just One Look

"The only plausible reason for setting down this book is to make sure your front door is locked and double-bolted."
—*People*

No Second Chance
THE FIRST INTERNATIONAL
BOOK-OF-THE-MONTH CLUB® SELECTION

"Every time you think Harlan Coben couldn't get any better at uncoiling a whipsnake of a page-turner, he comes along with a new novel that somehow surpasses its predecessor."
—*San Francisco Chronicle*

Gone for Good

"This killer thriller has more twists and turns than an amusement park ride. . . . *Gone for Good* is great." —*USA Today*

Tell No One

"Pulse-pounding. . . . Coben layers secret upon secret, criss-crossing years and crime scenes." —*People*

ALSO BY HARLAN COBEN

Deal Breaker

Drop Shot

Fade Away

Back Spin

One False Move

The Final Detail

Darkest Fear

Tell No One

Gone for Good

No Second Chance

Just One Look

The Innocent

Promise Me

The Woods

Hold Tight

HARLAN COBEN

LONG LOST

A SIGNET BOOK

SIGNET
Published by New American Library, a division of
Penguin Group (USA) Inc., 375 Hudson Street,
New York, New York 10014, USA
Penguin Group (Canada), 90 Eglinton Avenue East, Suite 700, Toronto,
Ontario M4P 2Y3, Canada (a division of Pearson Penguin Canada Inc.)
Penguin Books Ltd., 80 Strand, London WC2R 0RL, England
Penguin Ireland, 25 St. Stephen's Green, Dublin 2,
Ireland (a division of Penguin Books Ltd.)
Penguin Group (Australia), 250 Camberwell Road, Camberwell, Victoria
3124, Australia (a division of Pearson Australia Group Pty. Ltd.)
Penguin Books India Pvt. Ltd., 11 Community Centre, Panchsheel Park,
New Delhi - 110 017, India
Penguin Group (NZ), 67 Apollo Drive, Rosedale, North Shore 0632,
New Zealand (a division of Pearson New Zealand Ltd.)
Penguin Books (South Africa) (Pty.) Ltd., 24 Sturdee Avenue,
Rosebank, Johannesburg 2196, South Africa

Penguin Books Ltd., Registered Offices:
80 Strand, London WC2R 0RL, England

Published by Signet, an imprint of New American Library, a division of Penguin Group (USA) Inc. Previously published in a Dutton edition.

First Signet Printing, March 2010
10 9 8 7 6 5 4 3 2 1

Copyright © Harlan Coben, 2009
Excerpt from *Caught* copyright © Harlan Coben, 2010
All rights reserved

REGISTERED TRADEMARK—MARCA REGISTRADA

Printed in the United States of America

For Sandra Whitaker,
the coolest "cuz" in the entire world

PART ONE

I

"YOU don't know her secret," Win said to me.

"Should I?"

Win shrugged.

"It's bad?" I asked.

"Very," Win said.

"Then maybe I don't want to know."

Two days before I learned the secret she'd kept buried for a decade—the seemingly personal secret that would not only devastate the two of us but change the world forever—Terese Collins called me at five a.m., pushing me from one quasi-erotic dream into another. She simply said, "Come to Paris."

I had not heard her voice in, what, seven years maybe, and the line had static and she didn't bother with hello or any preamble. I stirred and said, "Terese? Where are you?"

"In a cozy hotel on the Left Bank called d'Aubusson. You'll love it here. There's an Air France flight leaving tonight at seven."

I sat up. Terese Collins. Imagery flooded in—her Class-B-felony bikini, that private island, the sun-kissed beach, her gaze that could melt teeth, her Class-B-felony bikini.

It's worth mentioning the bikini twice.

"I can't," I said.

"Paris," she said.

"I know."

Nearly a decade ago we ran away to an island as two lost souls. I thought that we would never see each other again, but we did. A few years later, she helped save my son's life. And then, poof, she was gone without a trace—until now.

"Think about it," she went on. "The City of Lights. We could make love all night long."

I managed a swallow. "Sure, yeah, but what would we do during the day?"

"If I remember correctly, you'd probably need to rest."

"And vitamin E," I said, smiling in spite of myself. "I can't, Terese. I'm involved."

"With the nine-eleven widow?"

I wondered how she knew. "Yeah."

"This wouldn't be about her."

"Sorry, but I think it would."

"Are you in love?" she asked.

"Would it matter if I said yes?"

"Not really."

I switched hands. "What's wrong, Terese?"

"Nothing's wrong. I want to spend a romantic, sensual, fantasy-filled weekend with you in Paris."

Another swallow. "I haven't heard from you in, what, seven years?"

"Almost eight."

"I called," I said. "Repeatedly."

"I know."

"I left messages. I wrote letters. I tried to find you."

"I know," she said again.

There was silence. I don't like silence.

"Terese?"

"When you needed me," she said, "really needed me, I was there, wasn't I?"

"Yes."

"Come to Paris, Myron."

"Just like that?"

"Yes."

"Where have you been all this time?"

"I will tell you everything when you get here."

"I can't. I'm involved with someone."

That damn silence again.

"Terese?"

"Do you remember when we met?"

It had been on the heels of the greatest disaster of my life. I guess the same was true for her. We had both been pushed into attending a charity event by well-meaning friends, and as soon as we saw each other, it was as if our mutual misery were magnetic. I'm not a big believer in the eyes being the windows of the soul. I've known too many psychos who could fool you to rely on such pseudoscience. But the sadness was so obvious in Terese's eyes. It emanated from her entire being really, and that night, with my own life in ruins, I craved that.

Terese had a friend who owned a small Caribbean island not far from Aruba. We ran off that very night and told no one where we were going. We ended up spending three weeks there, making love, barely talking, vanishing and tearing into each other because there was nothing else.

"Of course I remember," I said.

"We both had been crushed. We never talked about it. But we both knew."

"Yes."

"Whatever crushed you," Terese said, "you were able to move past it. That's natural. We recover. We get damaged and then we rebuild."

"And you?"

"I couldn't rebuild. I don't even think I wanted to rebuild. I was shattered and maybe it was best to keep me that way."

"I'm not sure I follow."

Her voice was soft now. "I didn't think—check that: I still don't think—that I would like to see what my world would look like rebuilt. I don't think I would like the result."

"Terese?"

She didn't reply.

"I want to help," I said.

"Maybe you can't," she said. "Maybe there's no point."

More silence.

"Forget I called, Myron. Take care of yourself."

And then she was gone.

2

"AH," Win said, "the delectable Terese Collins. Now that's a top-quality, world-class derriere."

We sat in the rickety pullout stands in the Kasselton High School gymnasium. The familiar whiffs of sweat and industrial cleaner filled the air. All sounds, as in every similar gymnasium across this vast continent, were distorted, the strange echoes forming the audio equivalent of a shower curtain.

I love gyms like this. I grew up in them. I spent many of my happiest moments in similar airless confines with a basketball in my hand. I love the sound of the dribbling. I love the sheen of sweat that starts popping up on faces during warm-ups. I love the feel of the pebbly leather on your fingertips; that moment of neoreligious purity when your eyes lock on the front rim and you release the ball and it backspins and there is nothing else in the entire world.

"Glad you remember her," I said.

"Top-quality, world-class derriere."

"Yeah, I got that the first time."

Win had been my college roommate at Duke and was now my business partner and, along with Esperanza Diaz, my best friend. His real name was Windsor Horne Lockwood III, and he looked like it: thinning blond locks parted by a deity; ruddy complexion; handsome patrician face; golfer's V-neck burn; eyes the blue of ice. He wore overpriced khakis with a crease to rival the hair part, a blue Lilly Pulitzer blazer with a pink-and-green lining, a matching pocket hanky that puffed out like a clown's water-squirting flower.

Effete wear.

"When Terese was on TV," Win said, his snooty prep-school accent sounding as though he were explaining the obvious to a somewhat slow child, "you couldn't tell the quality. She was sitting behind the anchor desk."

"Uh-huh."

"But then I saw her in that bikini"—for those keeping score, that would be the Class-B-felony one I told you about earlier—"well, it is a wonderful asset. Wasted as an anchorwoman. It's a tragedy when you think about it."

"Like the *Hindenburg*," I said.

"Hilarious reference," Win said. "And oh so timely."

Win's expression was permanently set on haughty. People looked at Win and would see elitist, snobby, old-world money. For the most part, they'd be right. But the part where they'd be wrong . . . that could get a man seriously maimed.

"Go on," Win said. "Finish your story."

"That's it."

Win frowned. "So when do you leave for Paris?"

"I'm not going."

On the basketball court, the second quarter began. This was fifth-grade boys' basketball. My girlfriend—the term seems rather lame but I'm not sure "lady love," "significant other," or "love monkey" really apply—Ali Wilder has two children, the younger of whom played on this team. His name is Jack, and he wasn't very good. I say that not to judge or predict future success—Michael Jordan didn't start for his high school team until his junior year—but as an observation. Jack is big for his age, husky and tall, and with that often comes lack of speed and coordination. There was a plodding quality to his athleticism.

But Jack loved the game, and that meant the world to me. Jack was a sweet kid, deeply geeky in the absolute best way, and needy, as befit a boy who had lost his father so tragically and prematurely.

Ali couldn't get here until halftime and I am, if nothing else, supportive.

Win was still frowning. "Let me get this straight: You turned down spending a weekend with the delectable Ms. Collins and her world-class derriere in a boutique hotel in Paris?"

It was always a mistake talking relationships with Win.

"That's right," I said.

"Why?" Win turned toward me. He looked genuinely perplexed. Then his face relaxed. "Oh, wait."

"What?"

"She's put on weight, hasn't she?"

Win.

"I have no idea."

"So?"

"You know, so. I'm involved, remember?"

Win stared at me as if I were defecating on the court.

"What?" I said.

He sat back. "You're such a very big girl."

The game horn sounded, and Jack pulled on his goggles and lumbered toward the scorer's table with that wonderfully goofy half smile. The Livingston fifth-grade boys were playing their archrivals from Kasselton. I tried not to smirk at the intensity—not so much the kids' as the parents' in the stands. I try not to generalize but the mothers usually broke down into two groups: the Gabbers, who used the occasion to socialize, and the Harried, who lived and died each time their offspring touched the ball.

The fathers were often more troublesome. Some managed to keep their anxiety under wraps, muttering under their breath, biting nails. Other fathers screamed out loud. They rode refs, coaches, and kids.

One father, sitting two rows in front of us, had what Win and I had nicknamed "Spectator Tourette's," spending the entire game seemingly unable to stop himself from berating everyone around him out loud.

My perspective on this is clearer than most. I had been that rare commodity: the truly gifted athlete. This came as a shock to my entire family since the greatest Bolitar athletic accomplishment before I came around was my uncle Saul winning a shuffleboard tournament on a Princess Cruise in 1974. I graduated from Livingston High School as a *Parade* All-American. I was a star guard for Duke, where I captained two NCAA championship teams. I had been a first-round draft pick of the Boston Celtics.

And then, kaboom, it was all gone.

Someone yelled, "Substitution."

Jack adjusted his goggles and ran onto the court.

The coach of the opposing team pointed at Jack and shouted, "Yo, Connor! You got the new man. He's big and slow. Drive around him."

Tourette's Dad bemoaned, "It's a close game. Why are they putting him in now?"

Big and slow? Had I heard right?

I stared at the Kasselton head coach. He had highlight-filled, mousse-spiked hair and a dark goatee neatly trimmed so that he resembled an aging boy-band bass. He was tall—I'm six four and this guy had two inches on me, plus, I would guess, twenty to thirty pounds.

"'He's big and slow'?" I repeated to Win. "Can you believe the coach just yelled that out loud?"

Win shrugged.

I tried to shake it off too. Heat of the game. Let it go.

The score was tied at twenty-four when disaster struck. It was right after a time-out and Jack's team was inbounding the ball under the opposing team's hoop. Kasselton decided to throw a surprise press at them. Jack was free. The ball was passed to him, but for a moment, with the defense on him, Jack got confused. It happens.

Jack looked for help. He turned toward the Kasselton bench, the one closest to him, and Big Spiky-Haired Coach yelled, "Shoot! Shoot!" and pointed to the basket.

The wrong basket.

"Shoot!" the coach yelled again.

And Jack, who naturally liked to please and who trusted adults, did.

The ball went in. To the wrong hoop. Two points for Kasselton.

The Kasselton parents whooped with cheers and even laughter. The Livingston parents threw up their hands and moaned over a fifth grader's mistake. And then the Kasselton coach, the guy with the spiky hair and boy-band goatee, high-fived his assistant coach, pointed at Jack, and shouted, "Hey, kid, do that again!"

Jack may have been the biggest kid on the court, but right now he looked as if he were trying very hard to be as small as possible. The goofy half smile fled. His lip twitched. His eyes blinked. Every part of the boy cringed and so did my heart.

A father from Kasselton was whooping it up. He

laughed, cupped his hands into a flesh megaphone, and shouted, "Pass it to the big kid on the other team! He's our best weapon!"

Win tapped the man on the shoulder. "You will shut up right now."

The father turned to Win, saw the effete wear and the blond hair and the porcelain features. He was about to smirk and snap a comeback, but something—probably something survival basic and reptilian brained—made him think better of it. His eyes met Win's ice blues and then he lowered them and said, "Yeah, sorry. That was out of line."

I barely heard. I couldn't move. I sat in the stands and stared at the smug, spiky-haired coach. I felt the tick in my blood.

The buzzer sounded, signaling halftime. The coach was still laughing and shaking his head in amazement. One of his assistant coaches walked over and shook his hand. So did a few of the parents and spectators.

"I must depart," Win said.

I did not respond.

"Should I stick around? Just in case?"

"No."

Win gave a curt nod and left. I still had my gaze locked on that Kasselton coach. I rose and started down the rickety stands. My footsteps fell like thunder. The coach started for the door. I followed. He headed into the bathroom, grinning like the idiot he undoubtedly was. I waited for him by the door.

When he emerged, I said, "Classy."

The words "Coach Bobby" were sewn in script onto his shirt. He stopped and stared at me. "Excuse me?"

"Encouraging a ten-year-old to shoot at the wrong basket," I said. "And that hilarious line about 'Hey, kid, do it again' after you help humiliate him. You're a class act, Coach Bobby."

The coach's eyes narrowed. Up close he was big and broad and had thick forearms and large knuckles and a Neanderthal brow. I knew the type. We all do.

"Part of the game, pal."

"Mocking a ten-year-old is part of the game?"

"Getting in his head. Forcing your opponent to make a mistake."

I said nothing. He sized me up and decided that, yeah, he could take me. Big guys like Coach Bobby are sure they can take pretty much anyone. I just stared at him.

"You got a problem?" he said.

"These are ten-year-old kids."

"Right, sure, kids. What are you—one of those namby-pamby, touchy-feely daddies who thinks everyone should be equal on the court? No one should get their feelings hurt. No one should win or lose. . . . Hey, maybe we shouldn't even keep score, right?"

The Kasselton assistant coach came over. He had on a matching shirt that read "Assistant Coach Pat." "Bobby? Second half's about to start."

I took a step closer. "Just knock it off."

Coach Bobby gave me the predictable smirk and reply. "Or what?"

"He's a sensitive boy."

"Boo-hoo. If he's that sensitive, maybe he shouldn't play."

"And maybe you shouldn't coach."

Assistant Coach Pat stepped forward then. He looked at me, and that knowing smile I was all too familiar with spread across his face. "Well, well, well."

Coach Bobby said, "What?"

"Do you know who this guy is?"

"Who?"

"Myron Bolitar."

You could see Coach Bobby working the name, as if his forehead had a window and the squirrel running on the little track was picking up speed. When the synapses stopped firing, Coach Bobby's grin practically ripped the boy-band goatee at the corners.

"That big 'superstar' "—he actually made quotation marks with his fingers—"who couldn't hack it in the pros? The world-famous first-round bust?"

"The very one," Assistant Coach Pat added.

"Now I get it."

"Hey, Coach Bobby?" I said.

"What?"

"Just leave the kid alone."

The brow thickened. "You don't want to mess with me," he said.

"You're right. I don't. I want you to leave the kid alone."

"Not a chance, pal." He smiled and moved a little closer to me. "You got a problem with that?"

"I do, very much."

"So how about you and me discuss this further after the game? Privately?"

Flares started lighting up my veins. "Are you challenging me to a fight?"

"Yep. Unless, of course, you're chicken. Are you chicken?"

"I'm not chicken," I said.

Sometimes I'm good with the snappy comebacks. Try to keep up.

"I got a game to coach. But then you and me, we settle this. You got me?"

"Got you," I said.

Again with the snappy. I'm on a roll.

Coach Bobby put his finger in my face. I debated biting it off—that always gets a man's attention. "You're a dead man, Bolitar. You hear me? A dead man."

"A deaf man?" I said.

"A dead man."

"Oh, good, because if I were a deaf man, I wouldn't be able to hear you. Come to think of it, if I were a dead man, I wouldn't be able to either."

The horn sounded. Assistant Coach Pat said, "Come on, Bobby."

"Dead man," he said one more time.

I cupped my hand to my ear, hard-of-hearing style, and shouted, "What?" but he had already spun away.

I watched him. He had that confident, slow swagger, shoulders back, arms swaying a tad too much. I was going to yell out something stupid when I felt a hand on my arm. I turned. It was Ali, Jack's mother.

"What was that all about?" Ali asked.

Ali had these big green eyes and this cute, wide-open face I found fairly irresistible. I wanted to pick her up and smother her with kisses, but some might deem this the wrong venue.

"Nothing," I said.

"How did the first half go?"

"We're down by two, I think."

"Did Jack score?"

"I don't think so, no."

Ali studied my face for a moment and saw something she didn't like. I turned away and headed back up the stands. I sat. Ali sat next to me. Two minutes into the game, Ali said, "So what's the matter?"

"Nothing." I shifted on the uncomfortable bleacher.

"Liar," Ali said.

"Just getting into the game."

"Liar."

I glanced over at her, at the lovely, open face, at the freckles that shouldn't be there at this age but made her damn adorable, and saw something too. "You look a little distracted yourself."

Not just today, I thought, but for the past few weeks, things had not been great between us. Ali had been distant and troubled and wouldn't talk about it. I had been pretty busy with work myself, so I hadn't pushed it.

Ali kept her eyes on the court. "Did Jack play well?"

"Fine," I said. Then I added, "What time is your flight tomorrow?"

"Three."

"I'll drive you to the airport."

Ali's daughter, Erin, was matriculating at Arizona State. Ali, Erin, and Jack were flying out for the week to get the freshman settled.

"That's okay. I already hired a car."

"I'd be happy to drive."

"It'll be fine."

Her voice cut off any further discussions on that issue. I tried to settle back and watch the game. My pulse still raced. A few minutes later, Ali asked, "Why do you keep staring at the other coach?"

"Which coach?"

"The one with the bad cable-show dye job and Robin Hood facial hair."

"Looking for grooming tips," I said.

She almost smiled.

"Did Jack play a lot in the first half?"

"Usual amount," I said.

The game ended, Kasselton winning by three. The crowd erupted. Jack's coach, a good guy by all counts, had chosen not to play him at all in the second half. Ali was a tad perturbed by this—the coach was usually good about giving kids equal time—but she decided to let it go.

The teams disappeared into corners for the postgame spiel. Ali and I waited outside the gym door, in the school corridor. It didn't take long. Coach Bobby started toward me, the same swagger, though now his hands had tightened into fists. He had three other guys with him, including Assistant Coach Pat, all big and over-weight and not nearly as tough as they thought they were. Coach Bobby stopped about a yard short of yours truly. His three compadres spread out and folded their arms and stared at me.

For a moment no one spoke. They just gave me the hard eyes.

"Is this the part where I pee in my pants?" I asked.

Coach Bobby started with the finger again. "Do you know the Landmark Bar in Livingston?"

"Sure," I said.

"Tonight at ten. Back parking lot."

"That's past my curfew," I said. "And I'm not that kind of date. Dinner first. Maybe bring flowers."

"If you don't show"—he moved in closer with the finger—"I will find some other way to get satisfaction. You get me?"

I didn't, but before I could ask for clarification, he stomped off. His buddies followed suit. They looked back at me. I gave them all a five-finger toodle-loo wave. When one of them let his stare linger past the comfort zone, I blew him a kiss. He turned away as if he'd been slapped.

Blowing a kiss—my favorite rile-up-the-homophobe move.

I turned to Ali, saw her face, thought, *Uh-oh* . . .

"What the hell was that?"

"Something happened during the game before you got here," I said.

"What?"

I told her.

"So you confronted the coach?"

"Yes."

"Why?" she asked.

"What do you mean, why?"

"You made it worse. He's a blowhard. The kids get that."

"Jack was practically in tears."

"Then I'll handle it. I don't need your macho posturing."

"It wasn't macho posturing. I wanted him to stop picking on Jack."

"No wonder Jack didn't get to play in the second half. His coach probably saw your idiotic display and was smart enough not to fan the flames. Do you feel better now?"

"Not yet, no," I said, "but after I smash his face in at the Landmark, yeah, I think I will."

"Don't even think about it."

"You heard what he said."

Ali shook her head. "I can't believe this. What the hell is wrong with you?"

"I was sticking up for Jack."

"That's not your place. You have no right here. You're—" She stopped.

"Say it, Ali."

She closed her eyes.

"You're right. I'm not his father."

"That's not what I was going to say."

It was, but I let it go. "Maybe it's not my place, if it was about that—except that wasn't it. I would have gone after that guy even if he said it about another kid."

"Why?"

"Because it's wrong."

"And who are you to make that call?"

"What call? There's wrong. There's right. He was wrong."

"He's an arrogant ass. Some people are. That's life. Jack understands that, or he will with experience. That's part of growing up—dealing with asses. Don't you see that?"

I said nothing.

"And if my son was so gravely wounded," Ali said between clenched teeth, "who do you think you are to not tell me? I even asked why you two were talking at half-time, remember?"

"I do."

"You said it was nothing. What were you thinking—humble the little lady?"

"No, of course not."

Ali shook her head and stopped talking.

"What?" I asked.

"I let you get too close to him," she said.

I felt my heart nose-dive.

"Damn," she said.

I waited.

"For a wonderful guy who is usually so damn perceptive, you can be pretty obtuse sometimes."

"Maybe I shouldn't have gone after him, okay? But if

you'd been there when he yelled at Jack to do it again, if you'd seen Jack's face . . ."

"I'm not talking about that."

I stopped, considered. "Then you're right. I am obtuse."

I'm six four, Ali a foot shorter. She stood close and looked way up at me. "I'm not going to Arizona to get Erin settled. Or at least not just for that. My parents live there. And his parents live there."

I knew who *his* referred to—her late husband, the ghost I've learned to accept and even, at times, embrace. The ghost never leaves. I'm not sure that he ever should, though there are times I wish he would and of course that's a horrible thing to think.

"They—I mean, both sets of grandparents—want us to move out there. So we can be near them. It makes sense when you think about it."

I nodded because I didn't know what else to do.

"Jack and Erin and, heck, me too, we need that."

"Need what?"

"Family. His parents need to be part of Jack's life. They can't handle the cold weather up here anymore. Do you understand that?"

"Of course I understand."

My words sounded funny in my own ears, as if someone else were saying them.

"My parents found a place they want us to look at," Ali said. "It's in the same condo development as theirs."

"Condos are nice," I said, babbling. "Low maintenance. You pay that one monthly fee and that's it, right?"

Now she said nothing.

"So," I said, "to put it right out there, what does this mean for us?"

"Do you want to move to Scottsdale?" she asked.

I hesitated.

She put a hand on my arm. "Look at me."

I did. And then she said something I never saw coming: "We're not forever, Myron. We both know that."

A group of kids rushed past us. One bumped into me and actually said, "Excuse me." A ref blew a whistle. A horn sounded.

"Mom?"

Jack, bless his little heart, appeared around the corner. We both snapped out of it and smiled toward him. He did not smile back. Usually, no matter how awful he'd played, Jack came bounding out like a born-again puppy, offering up smiles and high fives. Part of the kid's charm. But not today.

"Hey, kiddo," I said, because I wasn't sure what to say. Lots of times I hear people in similar situations say, "Good game," but kids know that it's a lie and that they're being patronized, and that just makes it worse.

Jack ran over to me, wrapped his arms around my waist, buried his face in my chest, started to sob. I felt my heart crack anew. I stood there, cupping the back of his head. Ali was watching my face. I didn't like what I saw.

"Tough day," I said. "We all have them. Don't let it

get to you, okay? You did your best—that's all you can do." Then I added something the boy would never understand but was absolutely true: "These games aren't really that important."

Ali put her hands on her son's shoulder. He let go of me, turned to her, buried his face again. We stood there like that for a minute, until he calmed down. Then I clapped my hands and forced up a smile.

"Anyone up for ice cream?"

Jack rebounded fast. "Me!"

"Not today," Ali said. "We need to pack and get ready."

Jack frowned.

"Maybe another time," I said.

I expected Jack to give an "Awww, Mom," but maybe he heard something in her tone too. He tilted his head and then turned back to me without another word. We knuckled up—that was how we said hello and good-bye, the fist-knuckle salute—and Jack started for the door.

Ali gestured with her eyes for me to look right. I followed the gesture to Coach Bobby. "Don't you dare fight him," she said.

"He challenged me," I said.

"The bigger man steps away."

"In the movies maybe. In places filled with pixie dust and Easter Bunnies and pretty fairies. But in real life, the man who steps away is considered a big-time wuss."

"Then for me, okay? For Jack. Don't go to that bar tonight. Promise me."

"He said if I didn't show, he'd get satisfaction or something."

"He's a blowhard. Promise me."

She made me meet her eyes.

I hesitated but not for long. "Okay, I won't show."

She turned to walk away. There was no kiss, not even a buss on the cheek.

"Ali?"

"What?"

The corridor suddenly seemed very empty.

"Are we breaking up?"

"Do you want to live in Scottsdale?"

"You want an answer right now?"

"No. But I already know the answer. So do you."

3

I'M not sure how much time passed. Probably a minute or two. Then I headed out to my car. The skies were gray. A drizzle coated me. I stopped for a moment, closed my eyes, raised my face to the heavens. I thought about Ali. I thought about Terese in a boutique hotel in Paris.

I lowered my face, took two more steps—and that was when I spotted Coach Bobby and his buddies in a Ford Expedition.

Sigh.

All four of them were there: Assistant Coach Pat drove. Coach Bobby was in the passenger seat. The other two slabs of beef sat in the back. I took out my mobile phone and hit the SPEED-DIAL button one. Win answered on the first ring.

"Articulate," Win said.

That's how he always answers the phone, even when he can clearly see on the caller ID that it's me, and yes, it is annoying.

"You better circle back," I said.

"Oh," Win said, his voice kid-on-Christmas-morning happy, "goodie, goodie."

"How long will it take?"

"I'm just down the street. I suspected something like this might occur."

"Don't shoot anyone," I said.

"Yes, Mother."

My car was parked near the back of the lot. The Expedition followed slowly. The drizzle picked up a bit. I wondered what their plan was—something moronically macho, no doubt—and decided to just play it as it lays.

Win's Jag appeared and waited in the distance. I drive a Ford Taurus, aka the Chick Trawler. Win hates my car. He won't sit in it. I took out my keys and hit the remote. The car made that little ding noise and unlocked. I slipped inside. The Expedition made its big move then. It raced forward and stopped directly behind the Taurus, blocking me in. Coach Bobby jumped out first, petting his goatee. His two buddies followed.

I sighed and watched their approach in my rearview mirror.

"Something I can do for you?" I said.

"Heard your girl chewing you out," he said.

"Eavesdropping is considered rude, Coach Bobby."

"I figured maybe you'd change your mind and

wouldn't show. So I thought we could settle this now. Right here."

Coach Bobby leaned his face right into mine.

"Unless you're chicken."

I said, "Did you have tuna for lunch?"

Win's Jaguar pulled up next to the Expedition. Coach Bobby took a step back and narrowed his eyes. Win got out. The four men looked at him and frowned.

"Who the hell is he?"

Win smiled and raised his hand as if he'd just been introduced on a talk show and wanted to acknowledge the applause of the studio audience. "Nice to be here," he said. "Thank you very much."

"He's a friend," I said. "Here to even up the odds."

"Him?" Bobby laughed. His chorus joined in. "Oh, yeah, sure."

I got out of the car. Win moved a little closer to the three buddies.

Coach Bobby said, "I'm so gonna kick your ass."

I shrugged. "Take your best shot."

"Too many people around. There's a clearing in the woods right behind that field," he said, pointing the way. "No one will bother us there."

Win asked, "How, pray tell, do you know about this clearing?"

"I went to high school here. Kicked a lot of ass back there." He actually puffed out his chest as he added: "I was also captain of the football team."

"Wow," Win said in a perfect monotone. "Can I wear your varsity jacket to the prom?"

Coach Bobby pointed a beefy finger in Win's direction. "You'll be using it to soak up blood, you don't shut up."

Win tried very hard not to look overly giddy.

I thought about my promise to Ali. "We're two mature adults," I said. Each word felt like I was spitting out broken glass. "We should be above resorting to fisticuffs, don't you think?"

I looked past him toward Win. Win was frowning. "Did you really use the term 'fisticuffs'?"

Coach Bobby moved into my personal space. "You chicken?"

Again with the chicken.

But I was the bigger man—and the bigger man's the one who walks away. Sure, right.

"Yes," I said, "I'm chicken. Happy?"

"You hear that guys? He's chicken."

I winced but stayed strong. Or weak, depending on how you want to look at it. Yep, the bigger man. That was me.

I don't think I have ever seen Win look so crestfallen.

"Do you mind moving your car now so I can go?" I asked.

"Okay," Coach Bobby said, "but I warned you."

"Warned me about what?"

He was back in my personal space. "You don't want to fight, fine. But then it's hunting season on your boy out there."

I felt a rush of blood in my ears.

"What are you talking about?"

"The spastic kid who shot in the wrong basket? The rest of the season he's a target. We have a chance at a cheap shot, we take it. We see an opportunity to get in his head, we go for it."

My mouth may have dropped open. I'm not sure. I looked toward Win to make sure I heard right. Win no longer looked so crestfallen. He rubbed his hands together.

I turned back to Coach Bobby. "Are you serious?"

"Like a heart attack."

I replayed my promise to Ali, looking for a loophole. After my career-ending basketball injury I needed to prove to the world that I was just fine, thank you very much. So I attended law school—at Harvard. Myron Bolitar, the complete package—scholar-athlete, overeducated-though-debonair attorney. I had a law degree. And that meant I could find loopholes.

What had I actually promised to do here? I thought about Ali's exact words: *"Don't go to that bar tonight. Promise me."*

Well, this wasn't a bar, was it? It was a wooded area behind a high school. Sure, I might be defying the intent of the law, but not the letter. And the letter was key here.

"Let's do this," I said.

The six of us started toward the woods. Win practically skipped. About twenty yards into the trees, there was an opening. The ground was littered with cigarette butts and beer cans. High school. It never changes.

Coach Bobby took his place in the center of the opening. He lifted his right arm and beckoned for me to join him. I did.

"Gentlemen," Win said, "a moment of your time before they commence."

All eyes turned to him. Win stood with Assistant Coach Pat and the two bruisers near a large maple tree.

"I would feel remiss," Win continued, "if I failed to offer up this important advisory."

"What the hell are you babbling about?" Coach Bobby said.

"I'm not speaking to you. This advisory is for your three chums." Win's gaze traveled over their faces. "You may be tempted to step in and help Coach Bobby at some point. That will be a huge mistake. The first one of you who takes even one step in their direction will be hospitalized. Note I did not say stopped, hurt, or even harmed. Hospitalized."

They all just looked at him.

"That's the end of my advisory." He turned back toward Coach Bobby and me. "We now return you to our regularly scheduled brawl."

Coach Bobby looked at me. "This guy for real?"

But I was in the zone right now and it wasn't a good one. Rage was consuming me. That's a mistake when you fight. You need to slow things down, keep your pulse from racing, keep your adrenaline rush from paralyzing you.

Bobby looked at me, and for the first time, I saw doubt in his eyes. But now I remembered how he had laughed, how he had pointed to the wrong basket, what he'd said: *"Hey, kid, do that again!"*

I took a deep breath.

Coach Bobby put up his fists like a boxer. I did likewise, though my stance was far less rigid. I kept my knees flexed, bounced a bit. Bobby was a very big guy and local-neighborhood tough and used to intimidating opponents. But he was out of his league.

A few quick facts about fighting. One, the cardinal rule: You never really know how it is going to go. Anyone can land a lucky blow. Overconfidence is always a mistake. But the truth was, Coach Bobby had virtually no chance. I don't say this to sound immodest or repetitive. Despite what the parents in those rickety stands want to believe with their private coaches and overly aggressive third-grade travel-league schedules, athletes are mostly created in the womb. Yes, you need the hunger and the training and the practice, but the difference, the big difference, is natural ability.

Nature over nurture every time.

I had been gifted with ridiculously quick reflexes and hand-eye coordination. That's not bragging. It's like your hair color or your height or your hearing. It just is. And I'm not even talking here about the years of training I did to improve my body and to learn how to fight. But that's there too.

Coach Bobby did the predictable thing. He stepped in and threw a wild roundhouse. A roundhouse isn't an effective punch against a seasoned fighter. You learn quickly that when it counts, the shortest distance between two points is a straight line. You are better off throwing blows with that knowledge.

I slid a little to the right. Not a lot. Just enough so that I could deflect the blow with my left hand and stay close enough to counter. I stepped inside Bobby's exposed defense. Time had slowed down now. I could hit one of several soft targets.

I chose the throat.

I bent my right arm and smashed my forearm into his Adam's apple.

Coach Bobby made a squawking noise. The fight was over right there. I knew that. Or at least I should have. I should have stepped back and let him gasp to the ground.

But that mocking voice was still in my head. . . .

"Hey, kid, do that again. . . . The rest of the season he's a target. . . . We have a chance at a cheap shot, we take it. . . . Chicken!"

I should have let him fall. I should have asked him if he'd had enough and ended it that way. But the anger was out now. I couldn't harness it. I bent my left arm and began to spin full force counterclockwise. I planned on landing an elbow blow directly to the big man's face.

It would be, I realized as I spun, a devastating blow. The kind of blow that caves in the bones of a face. The kind of blow that leads to surgery and months of pain meds.

At the last second, I came just enough to my senses. I didn't stop, but I pulled back a little. Instead of landing square, my elbow careened across Bobby's nose. Blood spurted. There was a sound like someone had stepped on dried twigs.

Bobby fell hard to the ground.

"Bobby!"

It was Assistant Coach Pat. I turned toward him, put up my palms, and shouted, "Don't!"

But it was too late. Pat took a step forward, his fist cocked.

Win's body barely moved. Just his leg. He snapped a kick at Coach Pat's left knee. The joint bent sidewise, in a way it was never supposed to. Pat screamed and dropped to the dirt as though he'd been shot.

Win smiled and arched his eyebrow toward the other two men. "Next?"

Neither man did so much as breathe.

My rage dissipated all at once. Coach Bobby was on his knees now, cradling his nose as if it were a wounded animal. I looked down at him. It amazed me how much a beaten man looks like a little boy.

"Let me help you," I said.

Blood poured from his nose through his fingers. "Get away from me!"

"You need to put pressure on that. Stop the bleeding."

"I said, stay away!"

I was about to say something in my defense, but I felt a hand on my shoulder. It was Win. He shook his head as if to say, *No use*. He was right.

We left the woods without another word.

When I got home an hour later, there were two voice

mails. Both were short and very much to the point. The first was hardly a surprise. Bad news travels fast in small towns.

Ali said, "I can't believe you broke your promise."

That was it.

I sighed. Violence doesn't solve anything. Win would make a face when I said that, but the truth was, whenever I resorted to violence, which used to be fairly frequently, it never just ended there. Violence ripples and reverberates. It echoes and really never seems to go silent.

The second message on the voice mail came from Terese:

"Please come."

Any attempt at hiding the desperation was gone.

Two minutes later my cell vibrated. The caller ID told me it was Win.

"We have a small situation," he said.

"What's that?"

"Assistant Coach Pat, he of the need for orthopedic surgery?"

"What about him?"

"He is a police officer in Kasselton. A captain, in fact, though I won't ask to wear his varsity jacket to the prom."

"Oh," I said.

"Apparently they are thinking of making arrests."

"They started it," I said.

"Oh, yes," Win said, "and I'm certain that everyone

in town will take our word over a local police captain's and three lifelong residents."

He had a point.

"But I was thinking," he went on, "that we might enjoy a few weeks in Thailand whilst my attorney works this out."

"Not a bad idea."

"I know of a new gentlemen's club in Bangkok off Patpong Street. We could begin our journey there."

"I don't think so," I said.

"Such a prude. But either way, you should probably make yourself scarce too."

"That's my plan."

We hung up. I called Air France. "Any room left on tonight's flight to Paris?"

"Your name, sir?"

"Myron Bolitar."

"You're already booked and ticketed. Would you like a window or an aisle seat?"

4

I used my frequent flier miles to get an upgrade. I don't
need the free booze or better meal, but the legroom
meant a great deal to me. When I'm in coach I always get
the middle seat between two ginormous bruisers with
space issues, and in front of me, without fail, is a tiny old
lady whose feet don't even touch the ground but she has
to put her seat back as far as humanly possible, getting a
nearly sexual thrill as she hears it crunch against my
knees, tilting back far enough so that I can spend the entire flight looking for dandruff flakes in her scalp.

I didn't have Terese's phone number, but I remembered the Hotel d'Aubusson. I called and left a message
that I was on my way. I got onto the plane and jammed
the iPod buds into my ears. I quickly slipped into that
airplane half sleep, thinking about Ali, the first time I

had dated a woman with children, a widow no less, the way she turned away after she said, "We're not forever, Myron. . . ."

Was she right?

I tried to imagine life without her.

Did I love Ali Wilder? Yes.

I had loved three women in my life. The first was Emily Downing, my college sweetheart from Duke. She had ended up dumping me for my college rival from North Carolina. My second love, the closest thing I've had to a soul mate, was Jessica Culver, a writer. Jessica had also crushed my heart like it was a plastic cup—or maybe in the end I had crushed hers. It was hard to know anymore. I had loved her with everything I had, but it had not been enough. She was married now. To a guy named Stone. Stone. I kid you not.

The third, well, Ali Wilder. I had been the first man she dated after her husband died in the North Tower on 9/11. Our love was strong, but it was also calmer and more mature, and maybe love wasn't supposed to be like that. I knew the ending would sting but it wouldn't be devastating. I wondered if that too came with maturity, or if after years of getting the heart crushed, you naturally start being protective.

Or maybe Ali was right. We weren't forever. Simple as that.

There is an old Yiddish phrase I find apropos—but not by choice: "Man plans. God laughs." I am a prime example. My life was pretty much laid out for me. I was a basketball star my entire childhood, destined to be an

NBA player for the Boston Celtics. But in my very first preseason game, Big Burt Wesson slammed into me and ruined my knee. I tried gamely to come back, but there is a big difference between gamely and effectively. My career was over before I hit the parquet floor.

I was also destined to be a family man like the man I most admired in the world: Al Bolitar, my father. He had married his sweetheart, my mom, Ellen, and they moved to the suburb of Livingston, New Jersey, and raised a family and worked hard and threw barbecues in the backyard. That was supposed to be my life: supportive spouse, two-point-six children, afternoons sitting in those rickety stands watching my own offspring, a dog maybe, a rusted hoop in the driveway, visits to the Home Depot and Modell's Sporting Goods on Saturdays. You get the idea.

But here I am, north of forty now, and still unmarried with no family.

"Would you care for a beverage?" the flight attendant asked me.

I'm not much of a drinker but I asked for a scotch and soda. Win's drink. I needed something to numb me a little, help me sleep. I closed my eyes again. Back to blocking. Blocking was good.

So where did Terese Collins, the woman I was flying across an ocean to see, fit in?

I never thought of Terese in terms of love. Not like that, anyway. I thought about her supple skin and the smell of cocoa butter. I thought about the grief coming off her in waves. I thought about the way we made love on that island, two shipwrecks. When Win finally came via yacht to bring me home, I was stronger from our time together. She was not. We said our good-byes, but that hadn't been the end of us. Terese helped me when I needed it most, eight years ago, and then she vanished back into her hurt.

Now she was back.

For eight years, Terese Collins had been gone not only from me but from public view. In the nineties, she had been a popular TV personality, CNN's top anchor-woman, and then, poof, gone.

The plane landed and taxied to the gate. I grabbed my bag—no need to check luggage when it was for only a couple of nights—and wondered what awaited me. I was the third off the plane, and with my long stride I quickly took the number-one spot as we headed for the customs-and-immigration line. I had hoped to breeze through but three other flights had just landed and there was a logjam.

The line snaked through roped-off areas Disney World–style. It moved fast. The agents were mostly just waving people through, giving each passport little more than a cursory glance. When it was my turn, the female immigration officer looked at my passport, then at my face, then back at the passport, then back at me. Her eyes lingered. I smiled at her, keeping the Bolitar Charm setting on Low. I didn't want the poor woman disrobing right there at customs.

The agent turned away as if I'd said something rude. She nodded at a male agent. When she turned back to me, I figured I should up my game. Widen the smile. Turn the charm setting from Low to Stun.

"Step to the side, please," she said with a frown.

I was still grinning like an idiot. "Why?"

"My colleague will take care of your case."

"I'm a case?" I said.

"Please step to the side."

I was holding up the line and the passengers behind me were not pleased about it. I stepped to the side. The other uniformed agent said, "Please follow me."

I didn't like this, but what choice did I have? I wondered, Why me? Maybe there was a French law against being this charming because—snap—there should be.

The agent led me into a small windowless room. The walls were beige and bare. There were two hooks behind the door with hangers on them. The seats were molded plastic. There was a table in the corner. The officer took my bag and put it on the table. He started rummaging through it.

"Empty your pockets, please. Put everything in this bowl. Remove your shoes."

I did. Wallet, BlackBerry, loose change, shoes.

"I need to search you."

He was pretty thorough. I was going to make a joke about him enjoying it or maybe say a boat ride on the Bateau-Mouche would be nice before he felt me up, but I wondered about the French sense of humor. Wasn't Jerry Lewis an icon here? Maybe a sight gag would be more appropriate.

"Please sit."

I did. He left, taking the bowl with my belongings with him. For thirty minutes I sat there alone—cooling my heels, as they say. I didn't like this.

Two men stepped into the room. The first was younger, late twenties maybe, good-looking with sandy hair and that three-day growth pretty boys use to look more rugged. He wore jeans and boots and a button-down shirt with the sleeves rolled up to the start of the elbow. He leaned his back against a wall, folded his arms across his chest, and chewed a toothpick.

The second man was midfifties with oversize wire-rimmed glasses and tired gray hair that was dangerously close to a comb-over. He was drying his hands on a paper towel as he entered. His Windbreaker looked like something Members Only sold in 1986.

So much for Frenchmen and their haute couture.

The older man did the talking. "What is the purpose of your visit to France?"

I looked at him, then at the toothpick chewer, then back to him. "And you are?"

"I'm Captain Berleand. This is Officer Lefebvre."

I nodded at Lefebvre. He chewed the toothpick some more.

"Purpose of your visit?" Berleand asked again. "Business or pleasure?"

"Pleasure."

"Where will you be staying?"

"In Paris."

"Where in Paris?"

"At the Hotel d'Aubusson."

He didn't write it down. Neither of them had pen or paper.

"Will you be by yourself?" Berleand asked.

"No."

Berleand was still wiping his hands on the paper towel. He stopped, used one finger to push his glasses back up the bridge of his nose. When I still hadn't said anything else, he shrugged a "Well?" at me.

"I'm meeting a friend."

"The friend's name?"

"Is that necessary?" I asked.

"No, Mr. Bolitar, I'm nosy and am asking for no apparent reason."

The French are into sarcasm.

"The name?"

"Terese Collins," I said.

"What is your occupation?"

"I'm an agent."

Berleand looked confused. Lefebvre, it seemed, didn't speak English.

"I represent actors, athletes, writers, entertainers," I explained.

Berleand nodded, satisfied. The door opened. The first officer handed Berleand the bowl with my belongings. He put it on the table next to my bag. Then he started wiping his hands again.

"You and Ms. Collins didn't travel together, did you?"

"No, she is already in Paris."

"I see. How long do you plan on staying in France?"

"I'm not sure. Two, three nights."

Berleand looked at Lefebvre. Lefebvre nodded, peeled himself off the wall, headed for the door. Berleand followed.

"Sorry for any inconvenience," Berleand said. "I hope you have a pleasant stay."

5

TERESE Collins was waiting for me in the lobby.

She hugged me but not too hard. Her body leaned against mine for support, but again not that much, not a total collapse or anything. We were both reserved in our first greeting in eight years. Still, as we held each other, I closed my eyes and thought I could smell the cocoa butter.

My mind flashed to the Caribbean island, but mostly it flashed—let's be honest here—to the thing that truly defined us: the soul-piercing sex. That desperate clawing and shredding that makes you understand, in a totally nonsadomasochistic way, how pain—emotional pain—and pleasure not only intermingle but amplify each other. Neither of us had an interest in words or feelings or false comforts or hand-holding or even, well, reserved hugs—as if all that stuff were too tender, as if a gentle caress might pop this fragile bubble that temporarily protected us both.

Terese pulled back. She was still knee-knockingly beautiful. There had been aging, but on some women—maybe most women in this era of too much facial tucking—a little aging works.

"So what's wrong?" I asked.

"That's your opening line after all these years?"

I shrugged.

"I opened with 'Come to Paris,'" Terese said.

"I'm working on dialing back the charm," I said, "at least until I know what's wrong."

"You must be exhausted."

"I'm fine."

"I got a room for us. A duplex. Separate sleeping areas so we can have that option."

I said nothing.

"Man." Terese managed a smile. "It's so good to see you."

I felt the same. Maybe it had never been love, but it was there, strong and true and special. Ali said we weren't forever. With Terese, well, maybe we weren't everyday, but it was something—something hard to define, something you could put on a nearby shelf for years and forget about and take for granted and maybe that was how it should be.

"You knew I'd come," I said.

"Yes. And you know the same is true if you'd been the one to call."

I did. "You look great," I said.

"Come on. Let's get something to eat."

The doorman took my suitcase and sneaked an admiring glance at Terese before giving me the universal man-to-man smirk that said, *Lucky bastard*.

The Rue Dauphine is a narrow road. A white van had double-parked next to a taxi, taking up nearly the entire street. The driver of the taxi was screaming what I could only assume were French obscenities but it might have just been a particularly aggressive way of asking for directions.

We turned right. It was nine in the morning. New York City might be in full swing by that hour, but strolling Parisians were still rousing themselves from their beds. We reached the Seine River at the Pont Neuf. In the distance on our right, I could see the towers of Notre Dame Cathedral. Terese started down the river walk in that direction, past the green boxes that were famous for selling antique books but seemed more intent on pushing chintzy souvenirs. Across the river, a giant fortress with a gorgeous mansard roof rose, to quote Springsteen, bold and stark.

As we got closer to Notre Dame, I said, "Would you be embarrassed if I rounded my shoulders, dragged my left leg, and shouted, 'Sanctuary!'"

"Some might mistake you for a tourist," Terese said.

"Good point. Maybe I should buy a beret with my name stenciled on the front."

"Yeah, then you'd blend right in."

Terese still had that incredible walk, head held high, shoulders back, perfect posture. One more thing I just realized about all the women in my life: They all have great walks. I find confident walks sexy, the near prowl-like way certain women enter a room as if they already own it. You can tell a lot by the way a woman walks.

We stopped at an outdoor bistro on Saint Michel. The sky was still gray but you could see the sun fighting to take control. Terese sat and studied my face for a very long time.

"Uh, do I have something stuck in my teeth?" I asked.

Terese managed a smile. "God, I've missed you."

Her words hung in the air. I didn't know if she was doing the talking now or this city. Paris was like that. Much has been written about its beauty and splendors, and sure, that was true. Every building was a mini–architectural wonder, a feast for the eyes. Paris was like the beautiful woman who knew she was beautiful, liked the fact that she was beautiful and, ergo, didn't have to try so hard. She was fabulous and you both knew it.

But more than that, Paris makes you feel—for lack of a better term—alive. Check that. Paris makes you *want* to feel alive. You want to do and be and savor when you are here. You want to feel, simply feel, and it doesn't matter what. All sensation is heightened. Paris makes you want to cry and laugh and fall in love and write a poem and make love and compose a symphony.

Terese reached her hand across the table and took mine.

"You could have called," I said. "You could have let me know you were okay."

"I know."

"I haven't moved," I said. "My office is still on Park Avenue. I still share Win's apartment at the Dakota."

"And you bought your parents' house in Livingston," she added.

It wasn't a slip of the tongue. Terese knew about the house. She knew about Ali. Terese wanted me to know that she'd been keeping tabs on me.

"You just disappeared," I said.

"I know."

"I tried to find you."

"I know that too."

"Can you stop saying 'I know'?"

"Okay."

"So what happened?" I asked.

She took back her hand. Her eyes drifted toward the Seine. A young couple walked by us. They were fighting in French. The woman was outraged. She picked up a crushed soda can and hurled it at her boyfriend's head.

"You wouldn't understand," Terese said.

"That's worse than 'I know.'"

Her smile was so sad. "I'm damaged goods. I would have taken you down with me. I cared too much about you to let that happen."

I understood. And I didn't. "No offense but that sounds like a load of self-rationalization."

"It's not."

"So where have you been, Terese?"

"Hiding."

"From what?"

She shook her head.

"So why am I here?" I asked. "And please don't tell me it's because you missed me."

"It isn't. I mean, I did miss you. You have no idea how much. But you're right. That's not why I called."

"So?"

The waiter appeared in a black apron and white shirt. Terese ordered for both of us in fluent French. I don't speak a word of French, so for all I know she ordered me diaper rash on whole wheat.

"A week ago I got a call from my ex-husband," she said.

I hadn't even known she'd been married.

"I hadn't spoken to Rick in nine years."

"Nine years," I repeated. "That would be right around the time we met."

She looked at me.

"Don't be dazzled by my mathematical prowess," I said. "Math is one of my hidden talents. I try not to brag."

"You're wondering if Rick and I were still married when we ran off to that island," she said.

"Not really."

"You're so damn proper."

"No," I said, thinking again about the soul piercing on that island, "I'm not."

"As I can attest?"

"Again," I said, "hidden talents—I try not to brag."

"Good thing. But let me set your mind at ease. Rick and I weren't together when we met."

"So what did ex-husband Rick want?"

"He said he was in Paris. He said it was urgent I come."

"To Paris?" I asked.

"No, to Six Flags Great Adventure in Jackson, New Jersey. Of course Paris." She closed her eyes. I waited. "I'm sorry. That was uncalled-for."

"Nah, I like you snarky. What else did your ex say?"

"He told me to stay at the Hotel d'Aubusson."

"And?"

"And that's it."

I shifted in the chair. "That was the entire phone call? 'Hi, Terese. It's Rick, your ex-husband whom you haven't spoken to in nearly a decade. Come to Paris immediately, and stay at the Hotel d'Aubusson, and oh, it's urgent'?"

"Something like that."

"You didn't ask him why it was so urgent?"

"Are you being intentionally dense? Of course I asked."

"And?"

"He wouldn't tell me. He said he needed to see me in person."

"And you just dropped everything and came?"

"Yes."

"After all these years, you just . . ." I stopped. "Wait a second. You told me you were in hiding."

"Yes."

"Were you hiding from Rick too?"

"I was hiding from everyone."

"Where?"

"In Angola."

Angola? I just let that go for now. "So how did Rick find you?"

The waiter arrived. He brought two cups of coffee and what looked like an open ham-and-cheese sandwich.

"They're called Croque Monsieurs," she said.

I knew that. Open-face ham and cheese, but with a fancy name.

"Rick worked with me at CNN," she said. "He's probably the best investigative reporter in the world, but he hates being on air, so he stays behind the scenes. He tracked me down, I guess."

Terese was paler, of course, than she'd been on that sun-blessed island. The blue eyes had less sparkle, but I could still see the gold ring around each pupil. I have always preferred dark-haired women, but her lighter locks had won me over.

"Okay," I said. "Go on."

"So I did as he asked. I got here four days ago. And I haven't heard a word from him."

"You called him?"

"I don't have a number. Rick was very specific. He told me he'd contact me when I arrived. So far he hasn't."

"And that's why you called me?"

"Yes," she said. "You're good at finding people."

"If I'm so good at finding people, how come I couldn't find you?"

"Because you didn't look that hard."

That could be true.

She leaned forward. "I was there, remember?"

"I do."

She didn't add the obvious. She had helped me back then, when a life very important to me hung in the balance. Without her, I would have failed.

"You don't even know if your ex is missing," I said.

Terese didn't reply.

"He could've just been looking to exact a little payback. Maybe this is Rick's twisted idea of a joke. Or maybe whatever it was, it wasn't really that important. Maybe he changed his mind."

She just looked at me some more.

"And if he's missing, I'm not sure how I can help. Yeah, okay, I can do some stuff at home. But we're in a foreign country. I don't speak a word of the language. There's no Win to help me, no Esperanza or Big Cyndi."

"I'm here. I speak the language."

I looked at her. There were tears in her eyes. I had seen her devastated, but I had never seen her look like that. I shook my head.

"What aren't you telling me?"

She closed her eyes. I waited.

"His voice," she said.

"What about it?"

"Rick and I started dating my first year of college. We were married for ten years. We worked together nearly every day."

"Okay."

"I know everything about him, his every mood—you know what I mean?"

"I guess."

"We'd spent time in war zones. We discovered torture chambers in the Middle East. In Sierra Leone we saw things no human being should ever see. Rick knew how to keep personal perspective. He was always even, always kept his emotions in check. He hated the hyperbole that naturally came with TV news. So I have heard his voice under every kind of circumstance."

Terese closed her eyes again. "But I never heard him sound like that."

I reached my hand back across the table, but she didn't take it.

"Like what?" I said.

"There was a tremor that had never been there before. I thought . . . I thought maybe he'd been crying. He was beyond terrified—this from a man I never saw remotely scared before. He said he wanted me to be prepared."

"Prepared for what?"

Her eyes were wet now. Terese clasped her hands prayerlike, resting her fingertips on the bridge of her nose. "He said what he was going to tell me would change my entire life."

I sat back, frowned. "He used that exact phrase—change your entire life?"

"Yes."

Terese was not one for hyperbole either. I wasn't sure what to make of it.

"So where does Rick live?" I asked.

"I don't know."

"Could he live in Paris?"

"He could."

I nodded. "Did he remarry?"

"I don't know that either. Like I said, we haven't talked in a long time."

This was not going to be easy.

"Do you know if he still works for CNN?"

"I doubt it."

"Maybe you could give me a list of friends and family, something to start with."

"Okay."

Her hand shook as she picked up the coffee cup and brought it to her lips.

"Terese?"

She kept the cup up, as though using it for protection.

"What could your ex-husband possibly tell you that could change your entire life?"

Terese looked away.

Red double-decker buses flowed along the Seine, loaded up with sightseers. All the buses had this department-store ad of an attractive woman wearing an Eiffel Tower on her head. It looked ridiculous and uncomfortable. The Eiffel Tower hat appeared heavy, tottering on the woman's skull, held in place by a skimpy ribbon. The model's swan neck was bending as though in midsnap. Who thought this was a good way to advertise fashion?

Foot traffic was picking up. The girl who'd hurled the crushed can was now making out with her target. Ah, the French. A traffic officer started gesturing for a white van to stop blocking traffic. I turned and waited for Terese to answer. She put down her coffee.

"I can't imagine."

But there was a catch in her throat. A tell, if you were playing cards with her. She wasn't lying. I was pretty sure of that. But she wasn't telling me everything either.

"And there's no chance your ex is just being vindictive?"

"None." She stopped, looked off, tried to gather herself.

It was time, I knew, to take the big step. I said, "What happened to you, Terese?"

She knew what I meant. Her eyes wouldn't meet mine, but a small smile played on her lips.

"You never told me either," she said.

"Our unspoken island rule."

"Yes."

"But we're off that island now."

Silence. She was right. I had never told her what had led me to that island either—what had devastated me. So maybe I should go first.

"I was supposed to protect someone," I said. "I messed up. She died because of me. And to complicate things, I reacted badly."

Violence, I thought again. The undying echo.

"You said 'she,'" Terese said. "It was a woman you were supposed to protect?"

"Yes."

"You visited her grave site," Terese said. "I remember."

I said nothing.

It was Terese's turn now. I sat back and let her get ready. I remembered what Win had told me about her secret, about it being very bad. I felt nervous. My eyes darted about, and that was when I saw something that made me pause.

The white van.

You get used to living this way after a while. On guard, I guess. You look around and you start to see patterns and you wonder. This was the third time I had spotted the same van. Or at least I thought it was the same van. It had been outside the hotel when we left. And more to the point, the last time I saw it, the traffic cop was asking it to move.

Yet it was in the exact same place.

I turned back to Terese. She saw the look on my face and said, "What?"

"The white van may be following us."

I didn't add, "Don't look," or any of that. Terese would know better.

"What should we do?" she asked.

I thought about it. Pieces started to fall into place. I hoped that I was wrong. For a moment I imagined that this could all be over in a matter of seconds. Ex-hubby Rick was driving the van, spying on us. I go over. I open the door. I rip him out of the front seat.

I stood up and looked directly at the van's driver's-side window. No point in playing games if I was right. There was a reflection but I could still make out the unshaven face and, more to the point, the toothpick.

It was Lefebvre from the airport.

He didn't try to hide himself. The door opened and he stepped out. From the passenger side, the older agent, Berleand, stumbled into view. He pushed up his glasses and smiled almost apologetically.

I felt like an idiot. The plainclothes at the airport. That should have tipped me off. Immigration officers wouldn't be in plainclothes. And the irrelevant questioning. A stall. I should have seen it.

Both Lefebvre and Berleand reached into their pockets. I thought that they'd pull out guns, but both produced red armbands with the word "police" written on them. They slipped them up to their biceps. I looked left and saw uniformed cops heading toward us.

I did not move. I kept my hands to the sides, where they could clearly see them. I had little idea what was happening here, but this was no time for sudden moves.

I kept my eyes on Berleand's. He approached our table, looked down at Terese, and said to both of us, "Will you please come with us?"

"What's this about?" I asked.

"We can talk about that at the station."

"Are we under arrest?" I asked.

"No."

"Then we're not going anywhere until we know what this is about."

Berleand smiled. He looked at Lefebvre. Lefebvre smiled through the toothpick. I said, "What?"

"Do you think this is America, Mr. Bolitar?"

"No, but I think this is a modern democracy with certain inalienable rights. Or am I wrong?"

"We don't have Miranda rights in France. We don't have to charge you to take you in. In fact, I can hold you both for forty-eight hours on little more than a whim."

Berleand got closer to me, pushed up the glasses again, wiped his hands on the sides of his pants. "Now again I ask: Will you please come with us?"

"Love to," I said.

6

THEY separated Terese and me right there on the street.

Lefebvre escorted her to the van. I started to protest, but Berleand gave me a bored look that indicated my words would be superfluous at best. He led me to a squad car. A uniformed officer drove. Berleand slipped into the backseat with me.

"How long's the ride?" I asked.

Berleand looked at his wristwatch. "About thirty seconds."

He may have overestimated. I had, in fact, seen the building before—the "bold and stark" sandstone fortress sitting across the river. The mansard roofs were gray slate, as were the cone-capped towers scattered through the sprawl. We could have easily walked. I squinted as we approached.

"You recognize it?" Berleand said.

No wonder it had grabbed my eye before. Two armed guards moved to the side as our squad car pulled through the imposing archway. The portal looked like a mouth swallowing us whole. On the other side was a large courtyard. We were surrounded now on all sides by the imposing edifice. Fortress, yeah, that did fit. You felt a bit like a prisoner of war in the eighteenth century.

"Well?"

I did recognize it, mostly from books by Georges Simenon and because, well, I just knew it because in law-enforcement circles it was legendary.

I had entered the courtyard of 36 quai des Orfèvres—the renowned French police headquarters. Think Scotland Yard. Think Quantico.

"Soooo," I said, stretching the word out, gazing through the window, "whatever this is, it's big."

Berleand turned both palms up. "We don't process traffic violations here."

Count on the French. The police headquarters was fortress solid and intimidating and gigantic and absolutely gorgeous.

"Impressive, no?"

"Even your police stations are architectural wonders," I said.

"Wait until you see the inside."

Berleand, I quickly learned, was being sarcastic again. The contrast between the facade and what lay inside was whiplash stark. The outside had been created for the ages; the interior held all the charm and personality of a public toilet along the New Jersey Turnpike. The walls were off-white, or maybe they'd been white but had yellowed over the years. They had no paintings, no wall hangings of any kind, but enough scuff marks to make me wonder if someone had maybe run across them with dress shoes. The floors were made up of linoleum that would have been deemed too dated for tract housing in 1957.

There was no elevator as far as I could tell. We trudged up a wide staircase, the French version of a perp walk. The climb seemed to take a long time.

"This way."

Exposed wires crisscrossed the ceiling, looking like central casting for a fire hazard. I followed Berleand down a corridor. We passed a microwave oven sitting on the floor. There were printers and monitors and computers lining the walls.

"You guys moving?"

"No."

He led me to a holding cell, maybe six by six. Just one. It had glass where there might normally be bars. Two benches attached to the walls formed a V in the corner. The mattresses were thin and blue and looked suspiciously like the wrestling mats I remembered from junior high school gym class. A threadbare blanket of burnt orange, like something a bad airline had used for too long, lay folded on the bench.

Berleand spread his arm like a maître d' welcoming me to Café Maxim's.

"Where's Terese?"

Berleand shrugged.

"I want a lawyer," I said.

"And I want to take a bubble bath with Catherine Deneuve," he countered.

"Are you telling me I don't have the right to have a lawyer present during questioning?"

"That's correct. You can talk to one beforehand, but he will not be present during questioning. And I will be honest with you. It makes you look guilty. It also makes me grumpy. So I would advise against it. In the meantime, make yourself comfortable."

He left me alone. I tried to think it through, not making any rash moves. The wrestling-mat mattress was sticky and I didn't want to know from what. The smell in here was rancid—that horrible combo of sweat and fear and, uh, other bodily fluids. The stench climbed into my nostrils and hung tight. An hour passed. I heard the microwave. A guard brought me food. Another hour passed.

When Berleand came back, I was leaning against a somewhat clean spot I'd found on the glass wall.

"I trust your stay was comfortable."

"The food," I said. "I expected better food, this being a Parisian jail and all."

"I will speak to the chef personally."

Berleand unlocked the glass door. I followed him down the corridor. I expected him to take me to an interrogation room, but that wasn't the case. We stopped

in front of a door with a little sign next to it that read
GROUPE BERLEAND. I looked at him.

"Your first name is Groupe?"

"Is that supposed to be funny?"

We entered. I figured *Groupe* probably meant
"Group," and judging by what was inside the room, I
guess I was right. Six desks were crammed into an office
that wouldn't be called spacious if there had been only
one. We must have been on the top floor because the
mansard roof caused the ceiling to slant across most of
the room. I had to duck when I walked in.

Four of the six desks were currently taken by what I
assumed were other officers, part of Groupe Berleand.
There were old-fashioned computer monitors, the kind
that took up nearly half the desk space. Family pictures,
banners of favorite sports teams, a poster for Coke, a calendar with hot women—the whole atmosphere was less
a top-level police headquarters and more a muffler shop
backroom in Hoboken.

"Groupe Berleand," I said. "So you're the chief?"

"I'm a captain in the Brigade Criminelle. This is my
team. Sit."

"What, here?"

"Sure. That's Lefebvre's desk. Use his chair."

"No interrogation room?"

"You keep thinking you're in America. We conduct
all interviews in the team office."

The other officers seemed oblivious to our doings.
Two were enjoying coffees and chatting. The other typed

at his desk. I sat. There was a box of wipes on his desk. Berleand plucked one out and started with the hand cleaning again.

"Tell me about your relationship with Terese Collins," he said.

"Why?"

"Because I enjoy being up-to-date on the latest gossip." There was steel beneath the quasi-humor. "Tell me about your relationship."

"I haven't seen her in eight years," I said.

"And yet here you two are."

"Yes."

"Why?"

"She called and invited me to spend a few days in your city."

"And you just dropped everything and flew over?"

My reply was a simple eyebrow arch.

Berleand smiled. "I almost blew another French stereotype, eh?"

"You're worrying me, Berleand."

"So you came for a romantic rendezvous?"

"No."

"Then?"

"I didn't know why she wanted me to come. I just sensed that she was in trouble."

"And you wanted to help?"

"Yes."

"Did you know what she needed help with?"

"Before I arrived? No."

"And now?"

"I do, yes."

"Would you mind telling me?"

"Do I have a choice?" I asked.

"Not really, no."

"Her ex-husband is missing. He called her, said he had something urgent to discuss with her, and then he vanished."

Berleand seemed surprised by either my answer or the fact that I was being so cooperative. I had my suspicions which.

"So Ms. Collins called you to, what, help find him?"

"Exactly."

"Why you?"

"She thinks I'm good at that sort of thing."

"I thought you told me you were an agent. That you represented entertainers. How does that make you good at finding missing people?"

"My business is a rather personal one. I'm called on to do a lot of bizarre things for my clients."

"I see," Berleand said.

Lefebvre came in. He still had the toothpick. He stroked his facial growth and stood to my right and stared nails at me. Ladies and gentlemen, meet Bad Cop. I looked at Berleand as if to say, *Is this really necessary?* He shrugged.

"You care about Ms. Collins, don't you?" Berleand asked.

"Yes."

Lefebvre, playing his role to the hilt, stared more nails at me. He slowly took the toothpick out of his mouth and said, "Lying sheet!"

"Excuse me?"

"You," he said with an angry, thick French accent. "You are a lying sheeet!"

"And you," I countered, "are a lying pillowcase."

Berleand just stared at me.

"Sheet," I said. "Pillowcase. Get it?"

Berleand looked mortified. Couldn't blame him.

"Do you love Terese Collins?" he asked.

I stayed on the truth train. "I don't know."

"But you're close?"

"I haven't seen her in years."

"That doesn't change anything, does it?"

"No," I said, "I guess not."

"Do you know Rick Collins?"

For some reason, hearing him say it, I was surprised Terese took his name, but of course, they met in college. It would be natural, I guess. "No."

"Never met him?"

"Never."

"What can you tell me about him?"

"Not a damn thing."

Lefebvre put his hand on my shoulder and squeezed just a little. "Lying sheeet."

I looked back at him. "Please tell me that's not the same toothpick from the airport. Because if it is, we are talking seriously unsanitary."

Berleand said, "Is Ms. Collins correct?"

I turned back to him. "About what?"

"Are you good at finding people?"

I shrugged. "I think I know where Rick Collins is."

Berleand looked at Lefebvre. Lefebvre stood a little straighter.

"Oh? Where is he?"

"A nearby morgue," I said. "Somebody murdered him."

7

BERLEAND took me out of the Groupe Berleand office and turned right.

"Where are we going?" I asked.

He wiped his hands on his pants legs and said, "Just follow me."

We walked in a corridor with an opening that dropped down five floors. A steel net covered the space.

"What's up with the net?" I asked.

"Two years ago we brought in a terrorist suspect. A woman, as a matter of fact. When we walked her down this hallway, she grabbed one of the guards and tried to throw them both over the railing."

I looked down. It was a long drop.

"They die?"

"No, another officer grabbed them by the ankles. But now we have the netting."

He took two steps up into what appeared to be the attic. "Watch your head," Berleand said to me.

"Terrorist suspect?"

"Yes."

"You guys do terrorism?"

"Terrorism, homicide, the boundaries are no longer so clear. We do a little of everything."

He entered the attic space. I had to duck big-time now. There were clothes on a drying line. "You guys do your laundry up here?"

"No."

"So whose clothes?"

"Victims. That's where we hang them."

"You're kidding, right?"

"No."

I stopped and looked at them. A dark blue shirt was ripped and covered with bloodstains. "Do these belong to Rick Collins?"

"Follow me."

He opened a window and stepped outside onto the roof. He turned and looked back for me to follow.

Again I said, "You're kidding, right?"

"One of the great views of Paris."

"From the roof of thirty-six quai des Orfèvres?"

I stepped out onto the slate—and wow, was he right about the view. Berleand lit a cigarette, sucked in a breath so deep I thought the entire cigarette might turn to ash, released the smoke in a long stream through his nose.

"Do you often interrogate up here?"

"To be honest, this is a first," he said.

"You could threaten to push someone off."

Berleand shrugged. "Not my style."

"So why are we here?"

"We are not allowed to smoke indoors and I desperately need a cigarette."

He took another deep breath. "I used to be okay with it, you know? Smoking outside only. I would jog up and down the five flights of stairs as my way of exercising. But then I'd be so out of breath from the cigarettes."

"It would cancel each other out," I said.

"Exactly."

"You might have considered quitting."

"But then I wouldn't have a reason to run down the stairs and so I wouldn't exercise. Follow me?"

"As much as I'd like to, Berleand."

He sat down and looked out. He gestured for me to do the same. So there I was, on the roof of one of the world's most famous police stations, staring at the most breathtaking view of Notre Dame.

"And look that way."

He pointed over his right shoulder. I looked over the Seine and there it was—the Eiffel Tower. I know how touristy it is to be awestruck by the Eiffel Tower, but I just stared for a moment.

"Amazing, no?" he said.

"Next time I get arrested, I need to bring a camera."

He laughed.

"Your English is really good," I said.

"We are taught here from a young age. I also spent a semester at Amherst College in my youth and worked two years in an exchange program with Quantico. Oh, and I have the entire *Simpsons* collection on DVD in English."

"That will do it."

He took another hit from the cigarette.

"How was he murdered?" I asked.

"Shouldn't I say something like, 'Aha, how do you know he's been murdered?'"

I shrugged. "Like you said, you don't process parking violations here."

"What can you tell me about Rick Collins?"

"Nothing."

"How about Terese Collins?"

"What do you want to know?"

"She's quite beautiful," he said.

"That's what you want to know?"

"I did a little research. We have CNN over here, of course. I remember her."

"So?"

"So about a decade ago she was at the top of her profession. Suddenly she quits and there isn't a Google mention of her again. I checked. There is no sign of employment. I can't get a residence, nothing."

I didn't reply.

"Where has she been?"

"Why don't you ask her?"

"Because right now, I'm asking you."

"I told you. I haven't seen her in eight years."

"And you had no idea where she was?"

"I didn't."

He smiled and wagged his finger at me.

"What?"

"You said 'didn't.' Past tense. That implies you now know where she was."

"Your good English," I said. "It has come back to haunt me."

"So?"

"Angola," I said. "Or at least, that's what she told me."

He nodded. A police or French siren went off. The French have a different siren from the one we do—more insistent, horrible, like the love child of a cheap car alarm and the wrong-answer buzzer on *Family Feud*. We let it shatter our silence and waited for it to fade away.

I said, "You made some calls, didn't you?"

"A few."

"And?"

He didn't say anything else.

"You know I didn't kill him. I wasn't even in the country."

"I know."

"But?"

"May I offer another scenario?"

"Shoot."

"Terese Collins murdered her ex-husband," Berleand said. "She needed a way to dispose of the body—someone she could trust to help clean up the mess. She called you."

I frowned. "And when I answered, she said, 'I just killed my ex-husband in Paris. Please help me'?"

"Well, she might have just told you to fly here. She might have told you the purpose after you arrived."

I smiled. This had gone on long enough. "You know she didn't tell me that."

"How would I know that?"

"You were listening in," I said.

Berleand didn't face me then. He just kept smoking the cigarette and looked out at the view.

"When you stopped me at the airport," I continued, "you put a bug on me somewhere. My shoes maybe. Probably my cell phone."

It was the only thing that made sense. They found the body, maybe checked Rick Collins's cell phone or whatever, found out his ex-wife was in town, put a tap on her phone, saw that she called me, held me up at the airport long enough to put on a bug and start surveillance.

That was why I had been so forthcoming with Berleand—he already knew all these answers. I'd been hoping to win his trust.

"Your cell phone," he answered. "We replaced the battery with a listening device that holds the same charge. It's very new technology, quite cutting-edge."

"So you know Terese thought her ex was missing."

He tilted his head back and forth. "We know that's what she told you."

"Come on, Berleand. You heard her tone. She was genuinely distraught."

"She seemed to be," he agreed.

"So?"

He crushed out the cigarette. "You could also hear that she was holding back," Berleand said. "She's lying to you. You know it. I know it. I hoped that maybe you'd work it out of her, but you spotted the van." He thought about it. "And that's when you realized that you were bugged."

"So we're both very clever," I said.

"Or not as clever as we think."

"Have you notified his next of kin?"

"We're trying."

I aimed for subtle, but then again I thought we were somewhat past that. "Who is the next of kin?"

"His wife."

"Do you have a name?"

"Please don't push it," Berleand said.

He took out another cigarette, stuck it between his lips, let it dip down as he lit it with a hand that had done this many times before.

"There was blood found at the scene," he said. "Lots of it. Most belonged to the victim, of course. But preliminary tests tell us that there is at least one more person's blood in the mix. So we have gathered a blood sample from Terese Collins, and we will run the proper DNA test."

"She didn't do it, Berleand."

He said nothing.

"There's something else you aren't telling me," I said.

"There is a lot I'm not telling you. You, alas, are not part of Groupe Berleand."

"Can't I be deputized or something?"

He made that mortified face again. Then: "It can't be a coincidence," he said. "Him being murdered right after his ex-wife arrives."

"You heard what she told me. Her ex sounded scared. He'd probably gotten himself into some kind of mess— that's why he called her in the first place."

We were interrupted by the trill of his cell phone. Berleand unfolded it, put it to his ear, and listened. He probably made a hell of a poker player, my new friend Berleand, but something crossed his face and stayed there. He barked out something in French, clearly annoyed or puzzled. Then he went silent. After a few moments, he snapped the phone closed, stubbed out his cigarette, and stood.

"Problem?" I said.

"Take one last look." Berleand brushed off his pants with both hands. "We don't let a lot of tourists up here."

I did. Some might find it odd, this police headquarters with its spectacular view. I decided to take the moment and look out and remember why murder was such an abomination.

"Where are we going?" I asked.

"The lab received preliminary results on the DNA from the blood."

"Already?"

He shrugged a little too theatrically. "We French are about more than wine, food, and women."

"Pity. So what's it show?"

"I think," he began, ducking back inside through the window, "that we should talk to Terese Collins."

8

WE found her in the same holding cell where I'd been half an hour earlier.

Her eyes were red and swollen. When Berleand unlocked the door, all pretense of strength fled. She grabbed on to me, and I held her. She sobbed against my chest. I let her. Berleand stood there. I met his eye. He did the big shrug again.

"We are going to release you both," he said, "if you will agree to surrender your passports."

Terese pulled away, looked at me. We both nodded.

"I have a few more questions before you leave," Berleand said. "Is that okay?"

"I realize that I'm a suspect," Terese said. "Ex-wife in the same city after all these years, the phone calls between us, whatever. Doesn't matter—I just want you to nail whoever killed Rick. So ask whatever you want, Inspector."

"I appreciate your candor and cooperation." He seemed so tentative now, almost too deliberate. Something he had heard during that phone call on the roof had thrown him. I wondered what was up.

"Are you aware that your ex-husband had remarried?" Berleand asked.

Terese shook her head. "I didn't know, no. When?"

"When what?"

"Was he remarried?"

"I don't know."

"May I ask his wife's name?"

"Karen Tower."

Terese almost smiled.

"You know her?"

"I do."

Berleand nodded and did the hand rub again. I expected him to ask how she knew Karen Tower, but he let that go.

"We have some preliminary blood tests back from the lab."

"Already?" Terese looked surprised. "I just gave the sample, what, an hour ago?"

"Not on yours, no. Those will take some more time. This is the blood we found at the murder scene."

"Oh."

"Something curious."

We both waited. Terese swallowed as if she were preparing for a blow.

"Most of the blood—nearly all of it, really—belonged to the victim, Rick Collins," Berleand said. His voice was measured now, as if he were trying to wade his way through whatever he was about to tell us. "That's hardly a surprise."

We still said nothing.

"But there was another patch of blood found on the carpet, not far from the body. We're not exactly sure how it got there. Our original theory was also the most obvious: There was a struggle. Rick Collins put up a fight and injured his killer."

"And now?" I said.

"First off, we found blond hairs with the blood. Long blond hair. Like you'd find on a female."

"Females kill."

"Yes, of course."

He stopped.

"But?" I said.

"But it still seems impossible for the blood to be the killer's."

"Why's that?"

"Because, according to the DNA testing, the blood and blond hair belong to Rick Collins's daughter."

Terese didn't scream. She just let out a moan. Her knees buckled. I moved fast, grabbing her before she hit the floor. I looked a question at Berleand. He was unsurprised. He was studying her, gauging this reaction.

"You don't have children, do you, Ms. Collins?"

All color had drained from her face.

"Can you give us a second?" I said.

"No, I'm fine," Terese said. She regained her footing and looked hard at Berleand. "I have no children. But you knew that already, didn't you?"

Berleand did not reply.

"Bastard," she said to him.

I wanted to ask what was going on, but maybe this was a time for shutting up and listening.

"We haven't been able to reach Karen Tower yet," Berleand said. "But I suppose that this daughter was hers too?"

"I suppose," Terese said.

"And you, of course, knew nothing about her?"

"That's right."

"How long have you and Mr. Collins been divorced?"

"Nine years."

I'd had enough. "What the hell is going on here?"

Berleand ignored me. "So even if your ex-husband married almost immediately, this daughter really couldn't be more than, what, eight years old?"

That quieted the room.

"So," Berleand continued, "now we know that Rick's young daughter was at the murder scene and was injured. Where do you suppose she is now?"

WE chose to walk back to the hotel.

We crossed the Pont Neuf. The water was muddy green. Bells from a church pealed. People stopped on the bridge midspan and took pictures. One man asked me to snap one of him and what I guessed was his girlfriend. They snuggled in close and I counted to three and took the picture and then they asked if I minded taking one more and I counted to three again and did and then they thanked me and moved on.

Terese had not said a word.

"Are you hungry?" I asked.

"We need to talk."

"Okay."

She never broke stride across the Pont Neuf, onto the Rue Dauphine, through the hotel lobby. The concierge behind the desk offered up a very friendly "Welcome back!" but she blew past him with a quick smile.

Once the elevator doors closed, she turned to me and said, "You wanted to know my secret—what brought me to that island, why I've been on the run all these years."

"If you want to tell me," I said in a way that sounded patronizing even in my own ears. "If I can help."

"You can't. But you need to know, anyway."

We got off on the fourth floor. She opened the door to the room, let me pass, closed the door behind her. The room was average size, small by American standards, with a spiral stairway leading to what I assumed was the loft. It looked very much like what it was supposed to—a sixteenth-century Parisian home, albeit with a wide-screen TV and built-in DVD player.

Terese moved toward the window so that she was as far away from me as possible.

"I'm going to tell you something now, okay? But I want you to promise me something first."

"What?"

"Promise me you won't try to comfort me," she said.

"I'm not following."

"I know you. You'll hear this story and you'll want to reach out. You'll want to hug me or hold me or say the right thing because that's the way you are. Don't. Whatever you do, it will be the wrong move."

"Okay," I said.

"Promise me."

"I promise."

She cringed even deeper into the corner. The heck with after—I wanted to hold her now.

"You don't have to do this," I said.

"Yeah, I do. I'm just not sure how."

I said nothing.

"I met Rick during my freshman year at Wesleyan. I came in from Shady Hills, Indiana, and I was the perfect cliché—the prom queen dating the quarterback, most likely to succeed, sweet as sugar. I was that annoying, pretty girl who studied too hard and got all anxious she was going to fail and then she finishes the test early and starts putting those reinforcements in her notebook. You remember those little white things—looked like flat peppermint Life Savers?"

I couldn't help but smile. "Yes."

"I was also that pretty girl who wanted everyone to dig beneath the surface to see I was more than just pretty—but the only reason you'd want to dig was because I was pretty. You know the deal."

I did. To some this might sound immodest. It wasn't.

It was honest. Like Paris, Terese was not blind to her looks, nor would she pretend otherwise.

"So I dyed my blond hair dark so I would look smarter and went to this small liberal arts college in the Northeast. I arrived, like so many girls, with my chastity belt firmly attached and only my high school quarterback had the key. He and I were going to be the exception— we were going to make a long-distance relationship last."

I remembered those girls from my Duke days too.

"How long do you think that lasted?" she asked me.

"Two months?"

"More like one. I met Rick. He was just this whirlwind. So smart and funny and sexy in a way I had never seen before. He was the campus radical, complete with the curly hair, the piercing blue eyes, and the beard that scratched when I kissed him. . . ."

Her voice drifted off.

"I can't believe he's dead. This is going to sound corny, but Rick was such a special soul. He was genuinely kind. He believed in justice and humanity. And someone killed him. Someone intentionally ended his life."

I said nothing.

"I'm stalling," she said.

"No rush."

"Yeah, there is. I need to get this over with. If I slow down, I'll stop and I'll fall apart and you'll never get it out of me. Berleand, he probably knows this already. It's why he let me go. So let me give you the abridged version. Rick and I graduated, we got married, we worked as reporters. Eventually we ended up at CNN, me in front of the camera, Rick behind it. I told you that part already. At some stage we wanted to start a family. Or at least I did. Rick, I think, was more uncertain—or maybe he sensed what was coming."

Terese moved toward the window, gently pushed the curtain to the side, and looked out. I moved a foot closer to her. I don't know why. I just somehow needed to make that gesture.

"We had fertility problems. It's not uncommon, I'm told. Many couples have them. But when you're in the throes of it, it seems as though every woman you meet is pregnant. Fertility is also one of those problems that grows exponentially with time. Every woman I met was a mother, and every mother was happy and fulfilled and it all seemed to come so naturally. I started avoiding friends. My marriage suffered. Sex became only about procreation. You become so single-minded. I remember I did a story on unwed mothers in Harlem, these sixteen-year-old girls getting pregnant so easily, and I started to hate them because, really, was that cosmically fair?"

Her back was to me. I sat on the corner of the bed. I wanted to see her face, just part of it anyway. From my new vantage point, I was getting a sliver, maybe quarter-moon view.

"I'm still stalling," she said.

"I'm here."

"Maybe I'm not stalling. Maybe I need to tell it this way."

"Okay."

"We saw doctors. We tried everything. It was all pretty horrible. I was shot up with Pergonal and hormones and Lord knows what. It took us three years, but finally we conceived—what everyone called a medical miracle. At first, I was scared to even move. Every ache, every pang, I thought I was miscarrying. But after a while, I loved being pregnant. Doesn't that sound antifeminist? I always found those women who go on and on about their wonderful pregnancies to be so irritating, but I was as bad as any of them. I loved the rushes. I glowed. There was no nausea. Pregnancy would never happen for me again—this was my one miracle—and I relished it. The time flew by, and before I knew it, I had a six-pound, fourteen-ounce daughter. We named her Miriam after my late mother."

A cold gust blew across my heart. I knew now where this had to end.

"She would be seventeen," Terese said, her voice sounding very far away.

There are moments in your life when you feel everything inside of you go quiet and still and fragile. We just stayed there like that, Terese and I and no one else.

"I don't think a day has gone by in the last ten years when I don't try to imagine what she'd be like right now. Seventeen. Finishing up her senior year of high school. Finally past the rebellious teen years. The awkward adolescent stage would be over, and she'd be beautiful. She'd be my friend again. She'd be getting ready to start college."

Tears filled my eyes. I moved a little more to my left. Terese's eyes were dry. I started to stand. Her head snapped in my direction. No, no tears. Something worse. Total devastation, the kind that makes tears seem quaint, impotent. She held up her palm in my direction as if it were a cross and I a vampire she needed to ward off.

"It was my fault," she said.

I started shaking my head, but her eyes squeezed shut as if my gesture were too strong a burst of light. I remembered my promise and backed away and tried to make my face neutral.

"I wasn't supposed to be working that night, but at the last minute, they needed someone to anchor at eight o'clock. So I was home. We lived in London then. Rick was in Istanbul. But the eight p.m. hour—man, I wanted that coveted time period. I couldn't pass that up, now could I? Even if Miriam was asleep. Career, right? So I called a good friend—Miriam's godmother actually— and asked if I could drop her off for a few hours. She said no problem. I woke Miriam up, and I stuck her in the back of the car. The clock was ticking and I needed to be in makeup. So I drove too fast. The roads were wet. Still, we were almost there—quarter of a mile away at the most. They say you don't remember a big accident, especially when you lose consciousness. But I remember it all. I remember seeing the headlights. I spun the wheel to the left. Maybe it would have been better if I had just gone headfirst. Killed me and spared her. But, no, it was side impact. Her side. I even remember her scream. It was short, more like an intake. The last sound she ever made. I was in a coma for two weeks, but because God has a sick sense of humor, he let me live. Miriam died on impact."

Nothing.

I was afraid to move now. The room was still, as though even the walls and furniture were holding their breath. I didn't mean to, but I took a step toward her. I wonder if that's part of comforting—that it's often selfish, that the comforter often needs as much, if not more, than the comfortee.

"Don't," she said.

I stopped.

"Please leave me alone," she said. "Just for a little while, okay?"

I nodded but she wasn't looking at me. "Sure," I said, "whatever you need."

She didn't respond, but then again she had made her wishes pretty clear. So I moved to the door and let myself out.

9

I walked back out onto the Rue Dauphine, numb.

I turned left and found a spot where five streets met and sat at an outdoor café called Le Buci. Normally I liked to people-watch, but it was hard to concentrate. I thought about Terese's life. I got it now. Rebuild your life so it looks like . . . what exactly?

I took out my cell, and because I knew it would distract me, I called my office. Big Cyndi picked it up on the second ring.

"MB Reps."

The *M* stands for Myron. The *B* stands for Bolitar. The Reps is because we represent people. I came up with this name on my own and yet I managed to remain modest about my marketing skills. When we repped athletes only, I called the agency MB SportsReps. Now it is MB Reps. I will pause until the applause dies down.

"Hmm," I said. "Modern Madonna, complete with that British accent?"

"Bingo."

Big Cyndi could vocally impersonate nearly anyone or any accent. I say "vocally" because when a woman is north of six five and three hundred pounds, it is hard to get away with your killer Goldie Hawn impression in person.

"Esperanza in?"

"Please hold."

Esperanza Diaz, still best known by her professional wrestling moniker Little Pocahontas, was my business partner. Esperanza picked up the phone and said, "You getting any?"

"No."

"Then you better have a damn good reason for being there. You had meetings lined up for today."

"Yeah, sorry about that. Look, I need you to dig up all you can on Rick Collins."

"Who is he?"

"Terese's ex."

"Man, you have the weirdest romantic rendezvous."

I told her what had happened. Esperanza went quiet and I knew why. She worries about me. Win is the rock. Esperanza is the heart. When I finished explaining, she said, "So right now Terese isn't a suspect?"

"I don't know for sure."

"But it looks like a murder and a kidnapping or something?"

"I guess."

"So I'm not sure why you need to be involved. It isn't connected to her."

"Of course it's connected."

"How?"

"Rick Collins called her. He said it was urgent and it would change everything and now he's dead?"

"So what exactly do you plan on doing here? Hunt down his killer? Let that French cop do it. Either get some—or get home."

"Just do a little digging. That's all. Find out about the new wife and kid, okay?"

"Yeah, whatever. You care if I tell Win?"

"Nope."

" 'Either get some—or get home,' " she said. "That's pretty good."

"It should be a bumper sticker," I said.

We hung up. So now what? Esperanza was right. This wasn't my business. If I could somehow help Terese, okay, maybe then this would make sense. But other than to keep her out of trouble on this—other than making sure she didn't take the fall for a murder she didn't commit—I couldn't see how I could help. Berleand was not the type to railroad her.

In my peripheral vision I saw someone sit next to me at the table.

I turned and saw a man with a stubble-covered shaved

head. There were scars on the top of his skull. His skin was olive dark, and when he smiled, I saw a gold tooth that matched the gold chain dangling from his neck, urban bling-bling style. Handsome probably, in a dangerous, bad-boy way. He wore a wifebeater white tee under an unbuttoned gray short-sleeve shirt. His sweatpants were black.

"Look under the table," he said to me.

"Are you going to show me your wee-wee?"

"Look—or die."

His accent was not French—something smoother and more refined. Nearly British or maybe Spanish, almost aristocratic. I tilted my chair back and looked. He was holding a gun on me.

I left my hands on the lip of the table and tried to keep my breath steady. My eyes lifted and met his. I checked the surroundings. There was a man with sunglasses standing on the corner for absolutely no reason, trying very hard to pretend that he wasn't watching us.

"Listen to me or I will shoot you dead."

"As opposed to alive?"

"What?"

"Shoot someone dead versus shoot someone alive," I said. Then: "Never mind."

"Do you see the green vehicle on the corner?"

I did—not far from the sunglassed man who was trying not to look at us. It looked like a minivan or something. Two men sat in the front. I memorized the license plate and began to plan my next move.

"I see it."

"If you don't want to be shot, follow my instructions exactly. We are going to get up slowly, and you are going to get in the back of the vehicle. You will not make a fuss—"

And that was when I smashed the table into his face.

The moment he sat next to me I had started to consider the alternatives. Now I knew: This was a kidnapping. If I got into the vehicle, I would be cooked. Have you ever heard that when someone is missing, the first forty-eight hours are most crucial? What they don't tell you—maybe because it's so obvious—is that every second that passes makes finding the victim that much less likely.

The same works here. If they get me in the car, the chance I will be found plummets. The moment I get up and start following him to the car, my odds diminish. He isn't expecting an early strike. He figures I'm listening to him right now. I am a nonthreat. He is still working on his quasi-rehearsed speech.

So I work the element of surprise.

He had glanced away too, just for a second, to make sure the vehicle was still in place. That was all I needed. I already had my hands gripping the table. My leg muscles tightened. I exploded up like out of a power squat.

The table landed flush on his face. At the same time I turned to the side, just in case he got a shot off.

No chance.

I kept the torque in my torso and shot up and over. If there had just been Scar Head to worry about, my next step would be clear: disable him. Maim or hurt or just end his ability to fight in some way. But there were at least three other men here. My hope was that they would scatter, but I couldn't count on that.

Good thing too. Because they didn't.

My eyes searched for the gun. As I expected, he had dropped it on impact. I landed hard on top of my adversary. The table was still pressed against his face. The back of his head hit the pavement with a thud.

I went for the gun.

People screamed and scattered. I rolled off and toward the gun, picked it up, continued to roll. I made it to one knee and aimed it at the sunglassed guy, who'd been waiting on the corner.

He had a gun too.

"Freeze!" I shouted.

He raised the gun in my direction. I did not hesitate. I shot him in the chest.

The moment I pulled the trigger, I rolled toward the wall. The green minivan was racing toward me. Shots were fired. Not a handgun this time.

Machine-gun fire raking the wall.

More screams.

Oh, man, I hadn't counted on that. My calculations were all about me. There were pedestrians—and I was dealing with complete lunatics who seemed okay with hurting any and all bystanders.

I saw the first man, Scar Head, who got whacked with the table, stirring. Sunglasses was down. Blood rushed in my ears. I could hear my own breath.

Had to move.

"Stay down!" I shouted to the passing crowd, and then because you think of weird things even at times like this, I wondered how you'd say that in French or if they would be able to translate or if, hey, the machine-gun fire would clue them in.

Keeping low, I ran in the direction opposite the van's movement, toward where it had been parked. I heard a screech of tires. More gunfire. I turned the corner and kept my legs pumping. I was back on Rue Dauphine. The hotel was only about a hundred yards in front of me.

So what?

I risked a glance behind me. The van had backed up and was making the turn. I looked for a road or alley to turn down.

Nothing. Or maybe . . . ?

There was a small road on the other side of the street. I debated dodging across, but then I'd be even more exposed. The van was speeding toward me now. I saw the barrel of a weapon sticking out the window.

I was too out in the open.

My legs pumped. I kept my head low, as if that would really make me a smaller target. There were people on the street. Some figured out what was going on and dispersed. Others I bumped into, sending them sprawling.

"Get down!" I kept yelling because I had to yell something.

Another blast of gunfire. I literally felt a bullet pass over my head, could feel the air tickle my hair.

Then I heard sirens.

It was that awful French siren again, the short shrill blast, and I never thought I would so welcome that horrid sound.

The van stopped. I moved to the side and flattened myself against the wall. The van flew back in reverse, heading back to the corner. I held the gun in my hand and debated taking a shot. The van was probably too far away—and there were too many pedestrians in the way. I had already been reckless enough.

I didn't like the idea of them getting away, but I didn't want the streets riddled with more gunfire.

The back of the minivan slid open. I saw a man pop out. Scar Head was up now. There was blood on his face and I wondered if I'd broken his nose. Two days, two broken noses. Nice work if you could get paid for it.

Scar Head needed help. He looked down the street in my direction, but I was probably too far away to see. I resisted the temptation to wave. I heard the sirens again, getting closer. I turned and two police cars came toward me.

The cops jumped out and pointed weapons at me. For a moment I was surprised, ready to explain that I was the good guy here, but then it all came clear. I was holding a gun in my hand. I had shot someone.

The cops yelled something that I assume was a command to freeze and raise my hands, and I did just that. I let the weapon drop to the pavement and got on one knee. The cops ran toward me.

I looked back toward the minivan. I wanted to point it out to the cops, tell them to go after it, but I knew how any sudden move would appear. The police were shouting instructions at me, and I didn't understand any of them, so I stayed perfectly still.

And then I saw something that made me want to go for the gun again.

The minivan door was open. Scar Head was rolling in. The other man jumped in behind him and began to close the doors as the van started to move. The angle changed and for just a second—less time really, maybe half a second—I was able to see into the back of the van.

I was also a good distance away, probably seventy to eighty yards, so maybe I was wrong. Maybe I wasn't seeing what I thought I was seeing.

Panic took over. I couldn't help it—I started to stand back up. I was that desperate. I was ready to jump for the gun and start firing at the tires. But the cops were on me now. I don't know how many. Four or five. They leapt on me, pounding me back to the pavement.

I struggled and felt something sharp, probably the butt end of a club, dig into my kidney. I didn't stop.

"The green van!" I shouted.

There were too many of them. I felt my arms being twisted behind my back.

"Please"—I could hear the near-crazed fear in my voice, tried to quell it—"you have to stop them!"

But my words were having no effect. The minivan was gone.

I closed my eyes and tried to conjure back the memory of that half a second. Because what I did see in the back—or what I thought I saw—right before the van doors closed and swallowed her whole, was a girl with long blond hair.

10

TWO hours later, I was back in my stinky holding cell at 36 quai des Orfèvres.

The police questioned me for a very long time.

I kept my narrative simple and begged them to find Berleand for me. I tried to keep my voice steady as I told them to find Terese Collins at the hotel—I was worried that whoever had gone after me might be interested in her too—and mostly I repeated the van's license plate number and said that there might be a kidnap victim in the back.

First they kept me out on the street, which was odd but also made sense. I was cuffed and had two officers, one holding each elbow, with me at all times. They wanted me to point out what had happened. They walked me back to Café Le Buci on the corner. The table

was still overturned. There was a smear of blood on it.
I explained what I had done. No witness had seen Scar
Head holding the gun, of course, just my counterat-
tack. The man I had shot had been rushed off in an
ambulance, which I hoped meant he was alive.

"Please," I said for the hundredth time, "Captain
Berleand can explain everything."

If you were trying to read their body language, you'd
conclude that the cops were both skeptical of everything
I said and rather bored. But you can't judge by the body
language. I had learned that over the years. Cops are always skeptical—plus they get more information that way.
They always act like they don't believe you so you keep
talking, trying to defend and explain and blurting out
things that maybe you shouldn't.

"You need to find the van," I said again, repeating the
license plate number mantralike.

"My friend is staying at the d'Aubusson." I pointed
down the Rue Dauphine, gave Terese's name and room
number.

To all of this, the cops nodded and responded with
questions that had nothing to do with what I had just
said. I answered the questions and they continued to
stare at me as though every word out of my mouth were
a complete fabrication.

Then they dumped me back into this holding cell. I
don't think anyone had cleaned it since my last visit. Or
since de Gaulle died. I was worried about Terese. I was
also a tad worried about yours truly. I had shot a man in
a foreign country. That was provable. What was not

provable—what would be difficult, if not impossible, to corroborate—was my account of the incident.

Did I have to shoot that guy?

No question. He had a gun out.

Would he have fired at me?

You don't wait to find out. So I fired first. How would that play here in France?

I wondered if anyone else had been shot. I had seen more than one ambulance. Suppose someone innocent got hit by the machine-gun fire. That was on me. Suppose I had just gone with Scar Head. I could be with the blond girl now. Talk about terrified. What was that girl thinking and feeling, in the back of that van, probably injured since there had been blood at her father's murder scene?

Had she witnessed her father's murder?

Whoa, let's not get ahead of ourselves.

"Next time, I suggest you hire a private guide. Too many tourists try to do Paris on their own and get into trouble."

It was Berleand.

"I saw a blond girl in the back of the van," I said.

"So I heard."

"And I left Terese at the hotel," I said.

"She left about five minutes after you did."

I stayed behind the glass door, waiting for him to unlock it. He didn't. I thought about what he had just said. "Did you have us under surveillance?"

"I don't have the manpower to follow you both," he said. "But tell me: What did you make of her story about the car accident?"

"How . . . ?" Now I saw it. "You bugged our room?"

Berleand nodded. "You're not getting much action."

"Very funny."

"Or pathetic," he countered. "So what did you make of her story?"

"What do you mean what did I make of it? It's horrible."

"You believed her?"

"Of course. Who'd make up something like that?"

Something crossed his face.

"Are you telling me it's not true?"

"No, it all seems to check out. Miriam Collins, age seven, died in the accident off the A-Forty highway in London. Terese was seriously hurt. But I'm having the entire file sent to my office for review."

"Why? It was ten years ago. It doesn't have anything to do with this."

He didn't reply. He just pushed the glasses back up his nose. I felt a tad on display in this Plexiglas holding cell.

"I assume your colleagues from the crime scene filled you in on what happened," I said.

"Yes."

"You guys need to find that green van."

"We already did," Berleand said.

I moved closer to the Plexiglas door.

"The van was a rental," Berleand said. "They dumped it at CDG Airport."

"Rented with a credit card?"

"Under an alias, yes."

"You need to stop all flights out."

"Out of the largest airport in the country?" Berleand frowned. "Any other crime-stopping tips?"

"I'm just saying—"

"It's been two hours. If they flew out, they're gone."

Another cop came into the room, handed Berleand a piece of paper, and left. Berleand studied it.

"What's that?" I asked.

"Dinner menu. We're trying delivery from a new place."

I ignored Berleand's lame attempt at humor. "You know this isn't a coincidence," I said. "I saw a blond girl in the back of that van."

He was still reading the sheet of paper. "You mentioned that, yes."

"It could have been Collins's daughter."

"Doubtful," Berleand said.

I waited.

"We reached the wife," Berleand said. "Karen Tower. She's fine. She didn't even know her husband was in Paris."

"Where did she think he was?"

"I don't know all the details yet. They live in London now. Scotland Yard delivered the news. Apparently there have been some marital difficulties."

"And what about the daughter?"

"Well, that's the thing," Berleand said. "They don't have a daughter. They have a four-year-old son. He's home safe and sound with his mother."

I tried to process that one. "The DNA test showed

the blood definitely belonged to Rick Collins's daughter," I began.

"Yes."

"No doubts?"

"No doubts."

"And the long blond hair was tied to the blood?" I asked.

"Yes."

"So Rick Collins has a daughter with long blond hair," I said more to myself than him. It didn't take time to come up with an alternate scenario. Maybe it was because I was in France, supposed land of the mistress. Even the former president openly had one, hadn't he?

"A second family," I said.

Of course it wasn't just the French. There was that New York politician who got caught drunk driving on his way to visit his second family. Men have kids with their mistresses all the time. Add in Berleand's belief that there were marriage difficulties between Rick Collins and Karen Tower, and it added up. Of course, there were still major holes to fill—like why Collins would call Terese, his first wife, and tell her it was urgent to see him in Paris—but one step at a time.

I started explaining my theory to Berleand, but I could see that he wasn't buying, so I stopped the sell.

"What am I missing?" I asked.

His cell phone trilled. Again Berleand spoke in French, leaving me totally in the dark. I'd have to take a Berlitz course or something when I got home. When he hung up, he quickly unlocked the holding cell and waved

for me to come out. I did. He started down the corridor
at a hurried pace.

"Berleand?"

"Come on. I need to show you something."

We headed back into the Groupe Berleand room.
Lefebvre was there. He looked at me as if I'd just dropped
out of his worst enemy's anus. He was hooking up another monitor to the computer, flat screen and maybe
thirty inches wide.

"What's going on?" I asked.

Berleand sat at the keyboard. Lefebvre backed off.
There were two other cops in the room. They too stood
back by the wall. Berleand looked at the monitor, then at
the keyboard. He frowned. On his desk was the dis-
penser for towelettes. He pulled one out and started
wiping down the keyboard.

Lefebvre said something in French that sounded like
a complaint.

Berleand snapped something back, gesturing to the
keyboard. He finished wiping it down and then started
typing.

"The blond girl in the van," Berleand said to me.
"How old would you say she was?"

"I don't know."

"Think."

I tried, shook my head. "All I saw was long blond
hair."

"Sit down," he said.

I pulled up a chair. He opened an e-mail and down-
loaded a file.

"More video will be coming in," he said, "but this still-frame is the clearest."

"Of what?"

"Surveillance camera from the de Gaulle airport lot."

A color photograph came up—I'd expected something grainy and black-and-white, but this one was fairly clear. Tons of cars—duh, it's a parking lot—but people too. I squinted.

Berleand pointed to the upper right. "Is that them?"

The camera was unfortunately so far away that the subjects could be seen only at a great distance. There were three men. One was covering his face with something white, a shirt maybe, staving off the blood. Scar Head.

I nodded.

The blond girl was there too, but now I understood his question. From this angle—a back shot—I couldn't really tell her age but she certainly wasn't six or seven or even ten or twelve, unless she was unusually tall. She was full grown. The clothing suggested a teenager, someone young, but nowadays it is hard to know for certain.

The blonde walked between the two healthier men. Scar Head was on the far right.

"It's them," I said. Then I added: "What did we figure the daughter would have had to be? Seven or eight? The blond hair, I guess. It threw me. I overreacted."

"I'm not so sure."

I looked at Berleand. He took off his glasses, placed them on the table, and rubbed his face with both hands.

He barked out something in French. The three men, including Lefebvre, left the room. We were alone.

"What the hell is going on?" I asked.

He stopped rubbing his face and looked at me. "You are aware that no one at the café saw the other man pull a gun on you."

"Of course they didn't. It was under the table."

"Most people would have put up their hands and gone quietly. Most people would not have thought to smash the man's face with a table, grab his gun, and shoot his accomplice in the middle of the boulevard."

I waited for him to say more. When he didn't, I added: "What can I say? I'm the balls."

"The man you shot—he was unarmed."

"Not when I shot him. His cohorts took the gun when they fled. You know this, Berleand. You know I didn't just make this up."

We sat there for another minute. Berleand stared at the monitor.

"What are we waiting for?"

"Video to come in," he said.

"Of?"

"The blond girl."

"Why?"

He didn't reply. It took another five minutes. I peppered him with questions. He ignored me. Finally his e-mail dinged and a very short video from the parking lot arrived. He clicked the PLAY button and sat back.

We could see the blond girl clearer now. She was indeed a teenager—maybe sixteen, seventeen years old.

She had long blond hair. The vantage point was still from too great a distance to see the features up close, but there was something familiar about her, about the way she held her head up, the way her shoulders stayed back, the perfect posture. . . .

"We ran a preliminary DNA test on that blood sample and the blond hair," Berleand said.

The temperature in the room dropped ten degrees. I wrested my eyes away from the screen and looked at him.

"It isn't just his daughter," Berleand said, gesturing toward the blonde on the screen. "It's also Terese Collins's."

11

IT took me a while to find my voice.

"You said preliminary."

Berleand nodded. "The final DNA test will take a few more hours."

"So it could be wrong."

"Unlikely."

"But there have been cases?"

"Yes. I had one case where we grabbed a man based on a preliminary like this. It turns out it was his brother. I also know about a paternity case where a woman sued her boyfriend for child custody. He claimed that the baby wasn't his. The preliminary DNA test was a dead match—but when the lab looked closer, it turned out that it was the boyfriend's father."

I thought about it.

"Does Terese Collins have any sisters?" Berleand asked.

"I don't know."

Berleand made a face.

"What?" I said.

"You two really have a special relationship, don't you?"

I ignored the jab. "So what's next?"

"We need you to call Terese Collins," Berleand said. "So we can question her some more."

"Why don't you call her yourself?"

"We did. She won't pick up."

He handed me back my cell phone. I turned it on. One missed call. I didn't click to see who it was from just yet. There was what appeared to be junk mail, the subject reading: *When Peggy Lee sang, "Is that all there is?" was she talking about your trouser snake? Your Small Pee-Pee Needs Viagra at 86BR22.com.*

Berleand read it over my shoulder. "What does that mean?"

"One of my old girlfriends has been talking out of school."

"Your self-deprecation," Berleand said, "it's very charming."

I hit Terese's number. It rang for a while and then the voice mail picked up. I left her a message and hung up.

"Now what?"

"Do you know anything about tracing cell phone locations?" Berleand asked.

"Yes."

"And you probably know that as long as the phone is on, even if no call is being made, we can triangulate coordinates and know where she is."

"Yes."

"So we weren't worried about following Ms. Collins. We have that technology. But about an hour ago, she turned her phone off."

"Maybe she ran out of battery," I said.

Berleand frowned at me.

"Or maybe she just needed downtime. You know how hard it must have been to tell me about her car accident."

"So she—what?—turned her phone off to get away from it all?"

"Sure."

"Instead of just silencing the ringer or whatever," he went on, "Ms. Collins turned the phone all the way off?"

"You don't buy it?"

"Please. We can still run her call logs—see who called her or whom she called. About an hour ago, Ms. Collins received her only call of the day."

"From?"

"Don't know. The number bounced to some phone in Hungary and then a Web site and then we lost it. The call lasted two minutes. After that, she turned off her phone. At the time she was at the Rodin Museum. Now we have no idea where she is."

I said nothing.

"Do you have any thoughts?"

"About Rodin? I love *The Thinker*."

"You're killing me, Myron. Really."

"Are you going to hold me?"

"I have your passport. You can go, but please stay in your hotel."

"Where you can listen in," I said.

"Think of it this way," Berleand said. "If you finally get lucky, maybe I can pick up a few pointers."

The processing to release me took about twenty minutes. I started back down the quai des Orfèvres toward the Pont Neuf. I wondered how long it would take. There was a chance, of course, that Berleand already had me under surveillance, but I considered it unlikely.

Up ahead was a car with the license plate 97 CS 33.

The code, of course, couldn't have been simpler. The junk e-mail read 86 BR 22. Just add one to each one. Eight becomes a nine. B becomes a C. As I approached the car a piece of paper dropped out of the driver's-side window. The piece of paper was attached to a coin so it wouldn't blow away.

I sighed. First the overly simple code, now this. Would James Bond go so low tech?

I picked up the note.

1 RUE DU PONT NEUF, FIFTH FLOOR. TOSS PHONE IN CAR BACK WINDOW.

I did. The car took off, phone on and in tow. Let them track that. I turned right. It was the Louis Vuitton Building, the one with the glass dome on the top. The

Kenzo department store was on the bottom floor, and I felt hopelessly unhip just opening the door. I stepped into the glass elevator and saw that the fifth floor was a restaurant called Kong.

When the elevator stopped, a hostess in black greeted me. Over six feet tall and dressed in tourniquet-tight black, she looked about as fat as your average lamp cord. "Mr. Bolitar?" she said.

"Yes."

"Right this way."

She led me up a staircase that glowed fluorescent green, and into the glass dome. I would call Kong "ultrahip" but it was almost beyond that—like postmodern ultrahip. The decor was futuristic geisha. There were plasma TVs with sleek Asian women winking as you passed. The chairs were acrylic and see-through except for the printed faces of beautiful women with strange hairstyles. The faces actually glowed, as though there were a light in each one. The effect was kind of eerie.

Above my head was a giant tapestry of a geisha. The patrons were dressed like, well, the hostess—trendy and black. What made the place work, though, what pulled it all together, was the killer view of the Seine, almost as great as the one at police headquarters—and there, at the front table with the absolute best view, was Win.

"I ordered you foie gras," he said.

"Someone's going to catch on to our old trick one of these days."

"They haven't yet."

I sat across from him. "This place looks familiar."

"It was featured in a French film with François Cluzet and Kristin Scott Thomas," Win said. "They sat at this very table."

"Kristin Scott Thomas in a French film?"

"She's lived here for years and speaks fluent French."

Win knows stuff like this—I don't know how.

"Anyway," Win continued, "perhaps that's why the restaurant is causing—to remain in our French environs—déjà vu."

I shook my head. "I don't watch French films."

"Or," Win said with a deep sigh, "perhaps you recall Sarah Jessica Parker eating here in the series finale of *Sex and the City*."

"Bingo," I said.

The foie gras—goose liver for the uninitiated—arrived. I was indeed starving and dug in. I know the animal-rights people would crucify me, but I can't help it. I love foie gras. Win had red wine already poured. I took a sip. I'm no expert, but it tasted like a deity had personally squeezed the grapes.

"So I assume you now know Terese's secret," Win said.

I nodded.

"I told you it was a doozy."

"How did you learn about it?"

"It wasn't that hard to discover," Win said.

"Let me rephrase. *Why* did you learn about it?"

"Nine years ago you ran away with her," Win said.

"So?"

"You didn't even tell me you were going."

"Again I say, so?"

"You were vulnerable, so I did a background check."

"Not your place," I said.

"Probably not."

We ate some more.

"When did you arrive?" I asked.

"Esperanza called after you spoke. I turned the plane around and headed this way. When I got to your hotel, you'd just been arrested. I made some calls."

"Where is Terese?"

I figured that Win had been the one to call her to get her off the grid.

"We'll meet up with her soon enough. Fill me in."

I did. He said nothing, steepling his fingers. Win always steepled his fingers. On me it looks ridiculous. On him, with those manicured nails, it somehow works. When I finished, Win said, "Yowza."

"Nice summation."

"How much do you know about her car accident?" he asked.

"Just what I told you now."

"Terese never saw the body," Win said. "That is rather curious."

"She was unconscious for two weeks. You can't keep a body out of the ground for that long."

"Still." Win bounced his fingertips. "Didn't her now-deceased ex say that whatever he had to tell her would change everything?"

I had thought about that too. I had thought about the strange tone in his voice, his near panic.

"There has to be some other explanation. Like I said, the DNA tests are preliminary."

"You realize, of course, that the cops let you go in the hopes you'd lead them to Terese."

"I know."

"But that won't happen," Win said.

"I know that too."

"So what next?" Win asked.

That surprised me. "You're not going to try to talk me out of helping her?"

"Would it help if I did?"

"Probably not."

"It may be fun then," Win said. "And there is one more big reason to continue this quest."

"That being?"

"I'll tell you later. So where to now, kemosabe?"

"I'm not sure. I'd like to question Rick Collins's wife—she lives in London—but Berleand has my passport."

Win's cell phone chirped. He picked it up and said, "Articulate."

I hate when he says that.

He hung up. "London it is then."

"I just told you—"

Win stood. "There is a tunnel in the basement of this building. It leads to the Samaritaine Building next door. I have a car waiting. My plane is at a small airport near

Versailles. Terese is there. I have IDs for you both. Please hurry."

"What happened?"

"My big reason for wanting to continue this quest. The man you shot a few hours ago just died. The police want to pick you up for murder. I think perhaps we need to be proactive in clearing your name."

12

WHEN I told Terese about the DNA test, I expected a different reaction.

Terese and I sat in the lounge area on Win's plane, a Boeing Business Jet he'd recently purchased from a rap artist. The seats were leather and oversize. There was a wide-screen TV, a couch, plush carpeting, wood trim. The jet also had a dining room and in the back a separate bedroom.

In case you didn't figure it out, Win is loaded.

He earned his money the old-fashioned way: He inherited it. His family owned Lock-Horne Investments, still one of the leading lights on Wall Street, and Win had taken its billions and parlayed them into more billions.

The "flight attendant"—I put that in quotes because I doubt she's had much safety training—was stunning,

Asian, young, and, if I knew Win, probably very limber. Her name tag read "Mee." Her attire looked like something out of a Pan Am ad from 1968, with the tailored suit, fitted puffy blouse, even the pillbox hat.

When we started to board, Win said, "The pillbox hat."

"Yeah," I said, "it really pulls the whole look together."

"I like her to wear the pillbox hat all the time."

"Please don't go into any more details," I said.

Win grinned. "Her name is Mee."

"I read the name tag."

"As in, it's not just about you, Myron—it's about Mee. Or I enjoy having carnal knowledge alone with Mee."

I just looked at him.

"Mee and I will stay in the back so you and Terese can have some privacy."

"In the back, as in the bedroom?"

Win slapped my back. "Feel good about yourself, Myron. After all, I feel good about Mee."

"Please stop."

I boarded behind him. Terese was there. When I told her about being jumped and the ensuing shoot-out, she was obviously concerned. When I segued into the DNA test vis-à-vis her being the blond girl's mother—first using words like "preliminary" and "incomplete" to the point where I feared it might cause an eye roll—she shocked me.

She barely reacted.

"You're saying that the blood test shows I could be the girl's mother?"

In fact, the preliminary DNA test showed that she *was* the girl's mother, but maybe that was a bit much to state at this point. So I simply said, "Yes."

Again it didn't seem to be reaching her. Terese squinted as though she were having trouble hearing. There was a small and nearly imperceptible wince in the eyes. But that was about it.

"How can that be?"

I said nothing, gave a little shrug.

Never underestimate the power of denial. Terese shook it off, snapped into reporter mode, and peppered me with follow-up questions. I told her everything I knew. Her breathing grew shallow. She was trying to hold it together, so much so that I could see the quake in her lips.

But there were no tears.

I wanted to reach out and touch her, but I couldn't. I'm not sure why. So I sat there and waited. Neither of us said it, as if the very words might burst that particularly fragile bubble of hope. But it was there, the proverbial elephant in the room, and we both saw it and avoided it.

Sometimes Terese's questions seemed too pointed, anger slipping through over what perhaps her ex, Rick, had done here or maybe simply to stave off the hope. Finally she leaned back and bit down on her bottom lip and blinked.

"So where are we going now?" she asked.

"London. I thought maybe we should talk to Rick's wife."

"Karen."

"You know her?"

"Knew her, yes." She looked at me. "Remember I told you I was dropping Miriam off at a friend's house when I got in the car accident?"

"Yes." Then: "Karen Tower was that friend?"

She nodded.

The plane had reached its cruising level. The pilot made an announcement to that effect. I had a million more questions, but Terese closed her eyes. I waited.

"Myron?"

"Yes."

"We don't say it. Not yet. We both know it's here with us. But we don't voice it, okay?"

"Okay."

She opened her eyes and looked away. I understood. The moment was too raw even for eye contact. As if on cue, Win opened the bedroom door. Mee, the flight attendant, had on her pillbox hat and everything else. Win was also fully dressed and waved for me to join him in the bedroom.

"I like the pillbox hat," he said.

"So you said."

"It suits Mee."

I looked at him. He led me into the bedroom and closed the door. The room had tiger-print wallpaper with zebra-skin bedding. "You channeling your inner Elvis?"

"The rapper decorated the room. It's growing on me."

"Did you want something?"

Win pointed to the TV set. "I was watching you talk to her."

I looked up. Terese was on the screen sitting in the chair.

"That's how I knew it would be a good time for me to interject." He opened a drawer and reached in. "Here."

It was a BlackBerry cell phone.

"Your number still works—all your calls will come in, but they will be untraceable. And if they try to track you down, they'll end up someplace in southwest Hungary. By the way, Captain Berleand left you a message."

"Is it safe to call him back?"

Win frowned. "What part of 'untraceable' confuses you?"

Berleand answered on the first ring. "My colleagues want to lock you up."

"But I'm such a charming fellow."

"That's what I told them, but they're not convinced that charm trumps a murder charge."

"But charm is in such short supply." Then: "I told you, Berleand, it was in self-defense."

"So you did. And we have courts and lawyers and investigators who may eventually come to that conclusion too."

"I really don't have the time to waste."

"So you won't tell me where you are?"

"I won't."

"I find the Kong restaurant a tad touristy," he said. "Next time I will take you to this little bistro off Saint Michel that serves only foie gras. You'll love it."

"Next time," I said.

"Are you still in my jurisdiction?"

"No."

"Pity. May I request a favor?"

"Sure," I said.

"Does your new cell phone have the capability to view photographs?"

I looked at Win. He nodded. I told Berleand that it did.

"I'm sending you a photograph as we speak. Please tell me if you recognize the man in it."

I handed the phone to Win. He pressed a HOME key and then found the photograph. I took a good hard look, but I knew right away.

"It's probably him," I said.

"The man you hit with the table?"

"Yes."

"You're positive?"

"I said probably."

"Make sure."

I took a longer look. "I'm assuming this is an old photograph. The guy I hit today is at least ten years older than the one in this picture. There are changes—the head shaven, and the nose is different. But overall, I'd say I'm fairly positive."

Silence.

"Berleand?"

"I would really like you to come back to Paris."

I didn't like the way he said that.

"No can do. Sorry."

More silence.

"Who is he?" I asked.

"This is not something you can handle on your own," he said.

I looked over at Win. "I have some help."

"It won't be enough."

"You wouldn't be the first to underestimate us."

"I know who you're with. I know his wealth and reputation. It's not enough. You may be good at finding people or helping athletes in trouble with the law. But you're not equipped to handle this."

"If I were less of a tough guy," I said, "you might be scaring me right now."

"If you were less of a head case, you'd listen to me. Be careful, Myron. Stay in touch."

He hung up. I turned to Win. "Maybe we can forward this picture to someone back home, someone who can tell us who he is."

"I have a contact at Interpol," Win said.

But he wasn't looking at me. He was looking over my shoulder. I turned to follow his gaze. He was watching the TV monitor again.

Terese was there, but her resolve was gone. She was doubled over, sobbing. I tried to make out her words, but they were garbled by the anguish. Win took the remote and turned up the volume. Terese was repeating the same thing over and over, and as she slid off the couch, I finally thought I could make out what she was saying:

"Please," Terese begged to some higher power. "Please let her be alive."

13

IT was late by the time we arrived at the Claridge's hotel in the center of London. Win had rented the Davies penthouse. There were a spacious sitting room and three huge bedrooms, all with four-poster king-size beds and those wonderfully deep marble tubs and showerheads the size of manhole covers. We threw open the French windows. The terrace offered up a wonderful view of the London rooftops, but frankly I'd had my fill of views. Terese stood out there in dead-woman-walking mode. She went from numb to emotional. She was devastated, sure, but there was hope. I think hope scared her the most.

"Do you want to come back inside?" I asked.

"Give me a minute."

I'm not necessarily an expert on body language, but

every muscle in her being seemed coiled and locked in a protective stance. I waited near the French windows. Her bedroom was sunflower yellow 'n' blue. I looked at the four-poster bed, and maybe it was wrong, but I wanted to pick her up and carry her to that beautiful bed and make love to her for hours.

Okay, no "maybe." It was wrong. But . . .

When I say stuff like this out loud, Win calls me a little girl.

I stared now at Terese's bare shoulder, and I remembered a day after we had come from that island, after she came to New Jersey and helped me and she smiled, really smiled, for the first time since I had known her, and I thought that I might be falling for her. Usually I go into relationships like, well, a girl, thinking long-term. This time it sneaked up on me and she smiled and we made love differently that night, a little more tenderly, and when we were done, I kissed that bare shoulder and then she cried, also for the first time. Smiled and cried for the first time with me.

A few days later, she was gone.

Terese turned and looked at me, and it was as though she could tell what I was thinking. We finally moved into the sitting room with barrel-vaulted ceilings and crisp wooden floors. The fireplace crackled. Win, Terese, and I took our places in the plush surroundings and coldly discussed our next steps.

Terese dived right in. "We need to figure out how to exhume the body in my daughter's grave—if there is a body."

She said it just like that. No tears, no hesitation.

"We should hire a lawyer," I said.

"A solicitor," Win said, correcting me. "We're in London. We don't use the term 'lawyer,' Myron. We say solicitor."

I just looked at him, refraining from asking, *How about the term "anal douche bag"? Do we use that in London?*

"I will have my people look into it first thing in the morning."

Lock-Horne Investments had a London branch on Curzon Street.

"We should also start looking into the accident," I said. "See if we can get ahold of the police file, talk to the investigating officers, that kind of thing."

Everyone agreed. The conversation continued like this, as if we were in a boardroom launching a new product instead of wondering if Terese's daughter who had "died" in a car crash might still be alive. Crazy to even think it. Win started making calls. We found out that Karen Tower, Rick Collins's wife, still lived in the same house in London. Terese and I would go by in the morning and talk to her.

After a while, Terese took two Valiums, headed into her room, and closed the door. Win opened a cabinet. I was exhausted, what with the jet lag and the day I'd had. It was hard to think that I had landed in Paris that very morning. But I didn't want to leave the room. I love sitting with Win like this. He had a snifter of cognac in his hand. I usually favored a chocolate drink called Yoo-hoo, but tonight I stuck with Evian. We ordered up some room service munchies.

I loved the normalcy.

Mee popped her head into the room and looked at Win. He mouthed a no in her direction. Her pretty face vanished.

Win said, "It's not yet Mee time."

I shook my head.

"What specifically is your problem with Mee?"

"Mee as in the stewardess, right?"

"Flight attendant," he said—again with the terminology. "Like with solicitor."

"She looks young."

"She's almost twenty." Win gave a small laugh. "I so love when you don't approve."

"I'm not in the judging business," I said.

"Good, because I'm trying to make a point here."

"About?"

"About you and Ms. Collins on the plane. You, my dear friend, see sex as an act that requires an emotional component. I don't. For you, the act itself, no matter how physically mind-blowing, is not enough. But I view it from another perspective."

"One that usually involves several camera angles," I said.

"Good one. But let me continue. For me, the act of two people 'making love'—to use your terminology, because I'm happy with 'boink' or 'boff' or 'screw'—for me, that sacred act is wonderful. More than that, it is everything. In fact, I believe the act is at its best—at its purest, if you will—when it is all, the end-all and be-all, when there is no emotional baggage to sully it. Do you see?"

"Uh-huh," I said.

"It's a choice. That's all. You see it one way. I see it another. One is not superior to the other."

I looked at him. "Is that your point?"

"On the plane, I was watching you talk to Terese."

"So you said."

"So you wanted to hold her, didn't you? After you dropped the bombshell. You wanted to reach out and comfort her. That emotional component we just discussed."

"I'm not following."

"When you two were alone on that island, the sex was amazing and purely physical. You barely knew each other. Yet those days on the island soothed and comforted and tore into you and cured you. Now here, when the emotional has entered the picture, when you want to blend those feelings with something as physically benign as an embrace, you can't do it." Win tilted his head and smiled. "Why?"

He had a point. Why hadn't I reached out? More than that, why couldn't I?

"Because it would have hurt," I said.

Win turned away as if that said everything. It didn't. I know that there were many who concluded that Win used misogyny to protect himself, but I never really bought it. It was too pat an answer.

He checked his watch. "One more drink," Win said.

"And then I will go in the other room because—oh, you'll love this—Mee so horny."

I shook my head. The hotel phone rang. Win picked it up, talked for a moment, hung up.

"How tired are you?" he asked me.

"Why. What's up?"

"The officer who investigated Terese's automobile accident is a retired policeman named Nigel Manderson. One of my people informs me that he is currently getting soused at a pub off Coldharbour Lane, if you want to pay him a visit."

"Let's do it," I said.

14

COLDHARBOUR Lane is about a mile long in South London and joins Camberwell to Brixton. The limousine dropped us off at a rather hopping spot called the Suns and Doves near the Camberwell end. The building had a third floor that got only about halfway across the top, like someone had gotten tired and figured, Ah, hell, we won't need more space than that.

We headed about a block farther down and turned in an alley. There was a good ol'-fashioned head shop and a health-food store that was still open.

"This area has a reputation for gangs and drug dealing," Win said, as though he were a tour guide. "Thus Coldharbour Lane's nickname is—get this—Crackharbour Lane."

"Known for gangs and drug dealing," I said, "if not nickname creativity."

"What do you expect from gangs and drug dealers?"

The alley was dark and dingy and I kept thinking Bill Sikes and Fagin were lurking against the dark brick. We reached a grotty pub called the Careless Whisper. I immediately flashed to the old George Michael/Wham! song and those now-famed lyrics where the heartbroken lothario will never be able to dance again because "guilty feet have got no rhythm." Eighties deep. I figured the name had nothing to do with the song and probably everything to do with indiscretion.

But I was wrong.

We pushed open the door, and it was like walking into a past dimension. Madness's classic hit "Our House" poured out onto the streets along with two couples, both with their arms around each other, more to keep themselves upright than out of affection. The smell of sizzling sausage wafted through the air. The floor was sticky. The place was loud and jammed, and clearly whatever no-smoking law had taken effect in this country had not stretched down into this alley. I bet few laws had.

The place was New Wave, which was to say Old Wave, and proud of it. A large-screen TV showed a petulant Judd Nelson in *The Breakfast Club*. The waitresses maneuvered through the boisterous crowd clad in black dresses, bright lipstick, slicked-back hair, and nearly Kabuki whiteface. Guitars hung from around their necks. They were supposed to look like the models in that Robert Palmer "Addicted to Love" video except, well, they were rather, uh, more mature and less attractive. Like the video had been remade with the cast of *The Golden Girls*.

Madness finished telling us about their house in the middle of the street, and Bananarama came on offering to be our Venus, our fire at our desire.

Win gave me a little jab. "The word 'Venus.' "

"What?" I shouted.

"When I was young," Win said, "I thought they were singing, 'I'm your penis.' It confused me."

"Thanks for sharing."

The trappings might have been eighties New Wave, but this was still a working-class bar, where hardy men and seen-too-much women came after a full day of labor and damned if it wasn't deserved. You couldn't fake belonging here. I might be wearing jeans, but I still didn't come close to fitting in. Win, however, stuck out like a Twinkie at a health club.

Patrons—some wearing shoulder pads and thin leather ties and Terax in their hair—glared daggers at Win. It was how it always was. We know about the obvious prejudices and stereotypes and Win would be the last to ask for sympathy, but people saw him and hated him. We judge by looks—that's no surprise. People saw undeserved privilege in Win. They wanted to hurt him. It had been that way his whole life. Even I don't know the full story— Win's "origin," to use superhero lexicon—but one of those childhood beatings broke him. He didn't want to be afraid anymore. Not ever. So he used his finances and his natural gifts and spent years developing his skills. By the time we met in college, he was already a lethal weapon.

Win walked through the glares with a smile and a nod. The pub was old and run-down, and it looked almost fake, which only made it feel more authentic. The women were big and chesty with rat-nest hair. Many wore those off-one-shoulder *Flashdance* sweatshirts. One eyed Win. She had several missing teeth. There were little ribbons in her hair that seemed to add nothing, à la "Starlight"-era Madonna, and her makeup looked as though it'd been applied with paintball pellets in a dark closet.

"Well, well," she said to Win, "ain't you pretty?"

"Yes," Win said. "Yes, I am."

The bartender nodded at us as we approached. He wore a FRANKIE SAY RELAX T-shirt.

"Two beers," I said.

Win shook his head. "He means two pints of lager."

Again with the terminology.

I asked for Nigel Manderson. The bartender didn't blink. I knew this was useless. I turned and shouted out, "Which one of you is Nigel Manderson?"

A man wearing a baroque ruffled white shirt with squared-off shoulders raised his glass. He looked like he'd just walked out of a Spandau Ballet video. "Cheers, mate."

The slurred voice came from down at the end of the bar. Manderson had his hands around his drink as though it were a baby bird that had fallen out of a nest and needed protection. His eyes were rheumy. He had one of those spider veins on his nose, though it looked as if someone had stepped on the spider and squashed it.

"Nice place," I said.

"Ain't it just the maddest? It's a little rough diamond to remind me of the better times. So, now who the hell are you?"

I introduced myself and asked him if he recalled a fatal car accident from ten years ago. I mentioned Terese Collins. He interrupted me midway through.

"I don't remember," he said.

"She was a famous anchorwoman. Her child died in the accident. She was seven years old."

"I still don't remember."

"Did you have a lot of cases where seven-year-old girls ended up dead?"

He turned on his stool to face me. "You calling me a liar?"

I know his accent was legit, the real deal, but it sounded to my tin ear like Dick Van Dyke's in *Mary Poppins*. I half expected him to call me guv'nor.

I told him the intersection where the accident occurred and the make of her car. I heard a *waa-waa* sound and glanced to my left. Someone was playing a game of Space Invaders on an arcade machine.

"I'm retired," he said.

I kept at him—patiently repeating all the details I knew. The TV screen was behind him, and I confess that I love the movie *The Breakfast Club* and it was a little distracting. I don't get why I love that movie. The casting had to be a joke. A hard-core jock wrestler? How about muscle-free Emilio Estevez? A convincing tough school punk? How about Judd Nelson? I mean, Judd Nelson. Who came in second place? It would be like, to maintain the *Golden Girls* analogy, remaking a Marilyn Monroe film with Bea Arthur. And yet Nelson and Estevez worked and the movie worked and I love it and I can say every line.

After a while Nigel Manderson said, "Maybe I remember a little."

He wasn't very convincing. He finished his drink and ordered another. He watched the bartender pour and scooped it up the second it touched the sticky wood in front of him.

I looked at Win. Win's face was as usual unreadable.

The woman with the paintball makeup—hard to say an age; could have been an easy fifty or a hard twenty-five, and I wasn't counting on the latter—said to Win, "I live near here."

Win gave her the superior gaze that made people hate him. "In that alley perhaps?"

"No," she said with a big hearty laugh. Win was such a card. "I have a basement flat."

"Must be divine," Win said in a voice richly marinated in sarcasm.

"Oh, it's nothing special," Paintball said, not picking up on Win's tone. "But it's got a bed."

She pulled up on her pink 'n' purple leg warmers and winked at Win. "A bed," she repeated. In case he wasn't getting the drift.

"Sounds enchanting."

"Want to see it?"

"Madam"—Win faced her full—"I would rather have my semen removed via a catheter."

Another wink. "That a fancy way of saying yes?"

I said to Manderson, "Can you tell me about the accident?"

"Who the hell are you, anyway?"

"A friend of the driver's."

"That's a load of bull."

"Why do you say that?"

He took another deep sip. Bananarama ended. Duran Duran's classic ballad "Save a Prayer" came on. A hush fell over the bar. Someone turned down the lights as the clientele lifted lighters and started swaying as if they were at a concert.

Nigel held up his lighter too. "I'm just supposed to take your word for it—that she sent you?"

He had a point.

"And even if you were, so what? That accident was . . . How long ago did you say?"

I had said it twice. He had heard it twice. "Ten years ago."

"What would she need to know now?"

I started to ask a follow-up question but he hushed me. The lights went lower. Everyone sang that we should not say a prayer right now, but for some reason we should save it till the morning after. The morning after what? They all rocked back and forth from drink and song with their lighters still raised, and I feared with all the big hair this had to be a major fire hazard. Most patrons, including Nigel Manderson, had tears in their eyes.

This was getting us nowhere. I decided to prod a bit. "The accident didn't happen the way your report says."

He barely glanced at me. "So now you're saying I made a mistake?"

"No, I'm saying you lied and covered up the truth."

That made him stop. He lowered the lighter. So did others. He looked around, nodding at friends, looking for support. That wasn't my concern. I kept my eyes on him. Win was already checking out the competition. He was armed, I knew. He didn't show me the weapon and I know that they are supposed to be hard to come by in the UK. But Win had at least one firearm on him.

I didn't think we'd need it.

"Piss off," Manderson said.

"If you lied about something, I'm going to find out what."

"Ten years later? Good luck. Besides, I didn't have anything to do with the report. It had all pretty much been taken care of when I got there."

"What's that supposed to mean?"

"I wasn't called first, pally."

"Who was?"

He shook his head. "You said Mrs. Collins sent you?"

Suddenly he remembered the name and that she was married. "Yes."

"Well, she'd know. Or maybe ask her friend who called it in."

I let that sink in. Then: "What was her friend's name?"

"Damned if I know. Look, you want to go tilting at windmills? I just signed the report. I don't give a crap anymore. I got my pitiful pension. Nothing they can do to me. Yeah, I remember it, okay? I got to the scene. Her friend, rich girl, I don't remember her name. She called it in to someone at the top. One of my superiors was already there, a pissant maggot named Reginald Stubbs, but don't bother calling him. Cancer ate him up three years ago, thank Christ. They carted off the little girl's body. They rushed the mom to the hospital. That was all I know."

"Did you see the girl?" I asked.

He looked up from his drink. "What?"

"You said they carted off the little girl's body. Did you actually see it?"

"It was in a bag, for chrissake," he said. "But judging by the amount of blood, there wouldn't have been much to see even if I looked inside."

15

IN the morning Terese and I headed to Karen Tower's house while Win met with his "solicitors" to do some of the legal legwork, like getting the car accident's file and—man, I didn't even want to think about this—figuring out how to exhume Miriam's body.

We took a London black taxi, which compared to the rest of the world's cab services is one of life's simple pleasures. Terese looked surprisingly good and focused. I'd filled her in on my conversation with Nigel Manderson at the pub.

"You think the woman who called it in was Karen Tower?" she asked.

"Who else?"

She nodded but said no more. We drove in silence for

a few minutes; then Terese leaned forward and said, "Drop us off at the next corner."

The driver did. She started down the street. I've been to London only a few times, so it wasn't like I knew the area, but this wasn't Karen Tower's address. Terese stood on the corner. The sun was starting to get strong. She shaded her eyes. I waited.

"This is where the accident happened," Terese said.

The corner could not have been more nondescript.

"I haven't been back here."

I saw no reason that she should have been, but I said nothing.

"I came off of that exit ramp. I took it too fast. A truck floated into my lane right around there." She pointed. "I tried to turn away but . . ."

I looked around as if there might still be some telltale clue a decade later, strange skid marks or something. There was nothing. Terese started walking down the street. I caught up to her.

"Karen's house—well, I guess it's Rick and Karen's house, right?—it's down the roundabout on the left," she said.

"How do you want to handle it?"

"What do you mean?"

"Do you want me to go alone?" I asked.

"Why?"

"Maybe I can get more out of her."

Terese shook her head. "You won't. Just stay with me, okay?"

"Sure."

There were dozens of people already at the house on Royal Crescent. Mourners. I hadn't really considered that, but of course. Rick Collins was dead. People would come by to comfort the widow and pay their respects. Terese hesitated at the foot of the outside steps, but then she took my hand firmly.

When we first entered, I felt Terese stiffen. I followed her gaze to a dog—a bearded collie; I know because Esperanza has the same kind—curled up on a mat near the corner. The dog looked old and worn and wasn't moving. Terese let go of my hand and bent down to pet the dog.

"Hey, girl," she whispered, "it's me."

The dog's tail wagged as though it took great effort. The rest of the body stayed still. There were tears in Terese's eyes.

"This is Casey," she said to me. "We got her for Miriam when she was five years old."

The dog managed to lift its head. She licked Terese's hand. Terese just stayed there, on her knees. Casey's eyes were milky with cataracts. The old dog tried to get her legs under her and stand. Terese hushed her and found a spot behind the ears. The dog still twisted her head as if she wanted to look into Terese's eyes. Terese moved forward so it would be easier. The moment was tender and I felt like I was intruding.

"Casey used to sleep under Miriam's bed. She would get low and scratch her way underneath and then she'd turn around so just her head was sticking out. Like she was on guard duty."

Terese petted the dog and started to cry. I moved away, shielded them from anyone's view, gave them their time. It took Terese a few minutes to put herself back together. When she did, she took my hand again.

We headed into the living room. There was a line of maybe fifteen people waiting to pay their respects.

The whispers and stares began the moment we stepped fully into the room. I hadn't thought about it, but here was the ex-wife who had been gone for nearly a decade showing up at the home of the current wife. It would make tongues wag, I guess.

People parted and a woman dressed smartly in black—I assumed the widow—came through it. She was pretty, petite, and almost doll-like with big green eyes. A touch of Tuesday Weld, to quote a Steely Dan song. I didn't know what to expect, but her eyes seemed to light up when she saw Terese. Terese's too. The two women smiled sadly at each other, the kind of smile you give to someone you adore but wished you were seeing under better circumstances.

Karen spread her arms. The two women embraced, holding each other, staying very still. I wondered for a moment what sort of friendship these two women shared and figured that it had probably been something pretty profound.

When they finished the embrace, Karen sort of gestured with her head. The two women started out of the room. Terese reached back and grabbed my hand, so I went too. We headed into what the British probably called the "drawing room" and Karen closed the pocket doors. The two women sat on a couch as though they had done it a thousand times and knew their exact spots. No awkwardness.

Terese looked back at me. "This is Myron," she said.

I put out my hand. Karen Tower shook it with her tiny one. "I'm sorry for your loss," I said.

"Thank you." Karen turned back to Terese. "Is he your . . . ?"

"It's complicated," Terese said.

Karen nodded.

I pointed back with my thumb. "Do you guys want me to wait in the other room?"

"No," Terese said.

I stayed where I was. No one was sure how to go on, but I sure as heck wasn't going to take the lead. I stood as stoically as I could.

Karen cut right to it. "Where have you been, Terese?"

"Here and there."

"I've missed you."

"I've missed you too."

Silence.

"I wanted to reach you," Karen said. "And explain. About Rick and me."

"It wouldn't have mattered," Terese said.

"That's what Rick said. It happened slowly. You were gone. We started spending time together, for companionship. It took a long time before it became more."

"You don't need to explain," Terese said.

"Yeah, I guess not."

There was no apology in her voice, no waiting for forgiveness or understanding. They both seemed to get it.

Terese said, "I wished it ended better for you both."

"We have a son named Matthew," she said. "He's four years old."

"I heard."

"So how did you hear about the murder?"

"I was in Paris," Terese said.

That made Karen react. She blinked and backed up a bit. "That's where you've been this whole time?"

"No."

"Then I'm not sure I understand."

"Rick called me," Terese said.

"When?"

Terese filled her in on Rick's emergency phone call. Karen's face, already something of a death mask, lost even more color.

"Rick told you to come to Paris?" Karen asked.

"Yes."

"What did he want?"

"I was hoping you might know," Terese said.

Karen shook her head. "We haven't been talking much lately. We were going through a pretty bad spell. Rick had become withdrawn. I was kind of hoping it was just because he was onto a big story. You know how he got then?"

Terese nodded. "How long had he been like that?"

"Three, four months now—since his father died."

Terese stiffened. "Sam?"

"I figured you knew."

"No," Terese said.

"In the winter, yeah. He took a bottle of pills."

"Sam committed suicide?"

"He was sick, something terminal. He kept it from us, for the most part. Rick didn't know how bad it had gotten. I guess it got bad at the end, so he decided to speed up the inevitable. Rick went into a funk, but then he started in on some big new investigation. He would disappear for weeks at a time. When I asked where he was, he'd snap and then he'd be sweet, but he wouldn't tell me. Or he'd lie about it."

Terese was still trying to get her bearings.

"Sam was such a sweet man," Terese said.

"I really never got to know him too well," Karen said. "We only visited him a couple of times, and he'd gotten too ill to come over here."

Terese swallowed, tried to get herself back on track. "So Sam commits suicide, and Rick buries himself in his work."

"Something like that, yeah."

"And he wouldn't tell you what he was investigating?"

"No."

"Did you ask Mario?"

"He wouldn't say."

I didn't ask who Mario was. I figured Terese would fill me in later.

Terese continued now, back on a roll. "Do you have any idea what it was Rick was working on?"

Karen studied her friend. "How well hidden were you, Terese?"

"Pretty well."

"Maybe that's what he was working on. Trying to find you."

"It wouldn't have taken him months."

"You're sure?"

"And even if that's what he was doing, why would he?"

"I'm trying not to be a jealous wife here," Karen said. "But I would think something like a father killing himself might make you question your life choices."

Terese made a face. "You think . . . ?"

Karen shrugged.

"No chance," Terese said. "And even if you thought Rick was trying to—I don't know—connect or woo me back, why would he tell me it was an emergency?"

Karen thought about that. "Where were you when he reached you?"

"In a remote spot in northwest Angola."

"And when he said it was urgent, you dropped everything and came, right?"

"Yes."

Karen spread her hands as if that answered everything.

"He wasn't lying to get me to Paris, Karen."

Karen did not look convinced. She had looked sad before we entered. Now she looked deflated. Terese glanced back at me. I nodded.

It was time to kick this up a notch.

Terese said, "We need to ask you about the accident."

The words hit Karen like a stun gun. Her eyes shot up, and they looked dazed now, out of focus. I'd wondered about the use of the word "accident," if she would understand what Terese meant. Clearly she did.

"What about it?"

"You were there. At the scene, I mean."

Karen didn't reply.

"Were you?"

"Yes."

Terese seemed a little startled by the answer. "You never told me that."

"Why would I tell you? Strike that—when would I tell you? We never talked about that night. Not ever. You woke up. It wasn't like I was going to say, 'Hi. How are you feeling? I was at the scene.'"

"Tell me what you remember."

"Why? What difference could it make now?"

"Tell me."

"I love you, Terese. I always will."

Something changed. I could see it in her body language. A stiffening of the spine maybe. The best friend was slipping away. An adversary was coming to the surface.

"I love you too."

"I don't think a day goes by that I don't still think about you. But you left. You had your reasons and your pain, and I got it. But you left. I made a life with this man. We were having problems, but Rick was my whole world. Do you get that?"

"Of course."

"I loved him. He was the father of my son. Matthew is only four. And someone murdered his father."

Terese just waited.

"So we're in mourning right now. I'm dealing with that. I'm dealing with trying to keep my life together and protecting my child. So I'm sorry. I'm not going to talk about a car accident from ten years ago. Not today."

She stood. It all made sense and yet something in her tone sounded oddly hollow.

"I'm trying to do the same," Terese said.

"What?"

"I'm trying to protect my child."

Karen had the stun-gun look again. "What are you talking about?"

"What happened to Miriam?" Terese asked.

Karen studied Terese's face. Then she turned to me, as if I might offer a glimmer of sanity. I kept my gaze steady.

"Did you see her that night?" Terese asked.

But Karen Tower didn't reply. She opened those pocket doors and vanished into a pack of mourners.

16

WHEN Karen left the drawing room, I walked around to the desk.

"What are you doing?"

"Snooping," I said.

The desk was rich mahogany with a gold letter opener that doubled as a magnifying glass. Slit envelopes stood vertically in antique holders. I didn't feel great about this, but I didn't feel terrible about it either. I took out my BlackBerry. The one Win gave me had a pretty good camera feature. I started opening envelopes and taking pictures.

I found credit card statements. I didn't have time to go through them all, but all I would need was the account numbers anyway. There were phone bills (that interested me) and energy bills (that didn't). I opened the drawers and started riffling through the contents.

"What are you looking for?" Terese asked.

"An envelope that says 'BIG CLUE INSIDE.'"

I was hoping for a miracle, of course. Something about Miriam. Pictures maybe. Short of that, I had the bills, the credit card, the phone numbers. We should be able to get some information from that. I hoped to find a day planner, but there was none.

I stumbled across a few photographs of people I assumed were Rick, Karen, and their son, Matthew.

"Is this Rick?" I asked.

She nodded.

I didn't know what to make of him. He had a prominent nose, blue eyes, and dirty blond hair that landed someplace between wavy and unruly. A man can't help it—he sees an ex, he sizes him up. I started to do that and then I made myself stop. I put the pictures back where I found them and continued my search. No more pictures. No blond daughter he'd kept hidden for years. No old photographs of Terese.

I turned and saw the laptop on the matching credenza.

"How much more time do you think we have?" I asked.

"I'll stand guard by the door."

I flipped on the MacBook. It came up in seconds. I clicked on the iCal icon on the bottom. His daybook came up. Nothing in the past month. On the right, there was only one to-do note. It read:

OPAL

HHK

4714

I had no idea what that meant, but the priority was listed as *High*.

"What?" Terese said.

I read off the to-do and asked her if she had any idea what it meant. She didn't. Time was still a factor here. I debated e-mailing the iCal contents to Esperanza, but that might get noticed. Then again, so what? Win, of course, had several anonymous e-mail addresses. I sent copies of the data on both the calendar and address book to him. Then I went into the sent file and deleted them so no one would see.

Ain't I clever?

Here I was, rummaging through the belongings of a man who'd recently been murdered while his widow and son mourned in the other room. I felt quite the hero. Maybe on the way out, I should kick good ol' Casey.

"Who is the Mario you two talked about?" I asked her.

"Mario Contuzzi," Terese said. "He was Rick's best friend and assistant producer. They worked on everything together."

I looked up his name in Address Book. Bingo. I plugged both his home and cell number into my phone.

Again with the clever.

"Do you know where Wilsham Street is?" I asked.

"It's walking distance. Does Mario still live there?"

I nodded and dialed Mario's home phone number. A man with an American accent answered and said, "Hello?" I hung up.

"He's home," I said.

I hope the amateur detectives out there are taking notes.

"We should head over."

I quickly opened up iPhoto. There were plenty of pictures but nothing that stood out. I couldn't e-mail all of them out. That would take forever. The pictures were normal, which is to say heartbreaking. Karen looked happy next to her man. Rick looked happy too. Their faces beamed as they held their son. IPhoto has this feature that allows you to put the cursor over an event and the pictures fly by in a rapid slide show. I watched the MATTHEW IS BORN! event and FIRST BIRTHDAY and a few others. Again heartbreakingly normal.

I stopped at one very recent shot under DAD'S SOCCER FINALS. Rick and Matthew were in matching Manchester United soccer uniforms. Rick had a big smile and held his son close to his side. The sweat was dripping off him. You could almost tell that he was out of breath and ecstatic about it. Four-year-old Matthew huddled against him, wearing goalie gear—the oversize gloves and that little black eye makeup—and trying to look serious, and I thought that this kid would now grow up without that smiling father and I thought about Jack, another boy who had to grow up without his father—and I thought about my own father, how much I loved and still needed him, and then I closed the file.

We slipped toward the front door without saying good-bye. I looked behind me and spotted little Matthew slumped in a chair in the corner. He was wearing a dark suit.

Four-year-olds don't belong in dark suits. Four-year-olds belong in goalie uniforms next to their dads.

MARIO Contuzzi answered the door without asking who it was. He was thin and wiry and reminded me of a Weimaraner dog. He jabbed a narrow face in Terese's direction.

"You have some nerve."

"Nice to see you too, Mario."

"I just got a call from a friend at Karen's. He says you popped in unannounced. Is that true?"

"Yes."

"What were you thinking?" Mario's head snapped toward me. "And why would you bring this ass wipe, of all people?"

"Do I know you?" I asked.

Mario wore those tortoiseshell glasses I always thought were trying too hard. He was wearing suit pants and a white dress shirt that he had been in the midst of buttoning. "I don't have time for this. Please leave."

"We need to talk," Terese said.

"Too late."

"What's that supposed to mean?"

He spread his arms. "You left, Terese—remember? You had your reasons, maybe. That's fine. Your choice.

But you left, and now that he's dead, you finally want to have a little chitchat? Forget it. I have nothing to say to you."

"That was a long time ago," she said.

"Precisely my point. Rick waited for you to come back. Did you know that? For two years, he waited. You were distraught and depressed—we all understood that—but that didn't stop you from shacking up with Mr. Basketball here."

He pointed at me with his thumb. I was Mr. Basketball here.

"Rick knew about that?" Terese asked.

"Of course. We thought you were devastated, vulnerable maybe. We kept an eye on you. I think Rick hoped you'd come back. Instead you go off to some little island for a private orgy with Hoop Head."

He pointed at me with the thumb again. Now I was Hoop Head.

Terese said, "You were following me?"

"We were keeping an eye on you, yes."

"For how long?"

He didn't reply. Suddenly his sleeve needed to be unrolled.

"How long, Mario?"

"We always knew where you were. I'm not saying we discussed it anymore, and you've been at that refugee center for the past six years, so it's not like we checked all the time. But we knew. That's why I'm surprised to see you with Bozo the SuperJock here. We thought you dumped this meathead years ago."

He waved his thumb in my face again.

"Mario?" I said.

He looked at me.

"Point that thumb at me again and it will end up midcolon."

"Physical threats from the big man on campus," he said, a smirk splitting the narrow face. "It's like I'm back in high school."

I was about to get into it with him, but I didn't think that would help. "We have some questions for you," I said.

"And I'm supposed to answer them? You don't get it, do you? She was married to my best friend, and then she shacks up with you on some deserted island. You know how that made him feel?"

"Bad?" I said.

That stopped him. He turned back to Terese. "Look, I don't mean to come on like a raging ass, but you don't belong here. Rick and Karen had a good thing. You gave this up long ago."

I looked at Terese. She was trying very hard to hold it together.

"Did he blame me?" she asked.

"For what?"

She said nothing.

Mario's shoulders deflated along with, I assumed, his anger. His voice softened. "No, Terese, he never blamed you. Not for any of it, okay? I did, I guess, for the leaving-him part—and, yeah, that's not my place. But he never blamed you, not for a second."

She said nothing.

"I have to get ready," Mario said. "I'm helping Karen with the arrangements. Arrangements. Like it's a choral piece. What a dumb-ass word."

Terese still seemed a little dazed, so I stepped in. "Do you have any thoughts on who might have killed him?"

"What are you, Bolitar, some kind of cop now?"

"We were in Paris when he was killed," I said.

He turned toward Terese. "You saw Rick?"

"I never got the chance."

"But he called you?"

"Yes."

"Damn." Mario closed his eyes. He still hadn't invited us in, but I sort of pressed myself into the doorway, and he stepped back. I expected a bachelor pad—I'm not sure why—but there were toys on the floor and a Pack 'n Play in the corner. Empty baby bottles were lined up on the counter.

"I married Ginny," he said to Terese. "You remember her?"

"Of course. I'm glad to hear you're happy, Mario."

He took a beat, reassessing, calming down. "We have three kids. We keep saying we're going to buy a bigger place, but we like it here. And real estate is ridiculous in London."

We stood there.

"So Rick called you," Mario said to Terese.

"Yes."

He shook his head.

I broke the silence. "Was there anybody who'd want to kill Rick?"

"Rick was one of the best investigative reporters in the world. He pissed off a lot of people."

"Anybody specific?"

"Not really, no. I still don't get what this has to do with either one of you."

I wanted to explain, but I knew that we didn't have the time. "Could you just humor us for another moment?"

"Humor you? Like this is funny?"

Terese said, "Please, Mario. It's important."

"Because you say it is?"

"You know me," she said. "You know if I'm asking, it's important."

He thought about that.

"Mario?"

"What do you want to know?"

"What was Rick working on?" she asked.

He looked off, his upper teeth working his lower lip. "A few months ago he started investigating a charitable entity called Save the Angels."

"What about them?"

"Frankly, I'm not sure. They started out as an evangelical group, a classic right-to-life group, protesting abortion clinics, Planned Parenthood, stem cell research, the whole deal. But they broke away. He was obsessed with learning all he could about them."

"What did he find?"

"Not much that I could see. The money structure

seemed a little odd. We couldn't trace it down. Basically they were against abortion, against stem cell research, and really into adoptions. Truth was, I thought they seemed like a pretty solid group. I don't want to get into a pro-life versus pro-choice argument, but I think both sides would agree that adoption is a viable alternative. That seems to be the direction they headed. Instead of firebombing clinics, Save the Angels worked on getting unwanted pregnancies to term and getting the kids adopted."

"And Rick was interested in them?"

"Yes."

"Why?"

"I don't know."

"What made him start looking into them?"

"Again, I can't say for sure." His voice sort of died away.

"But you have a thought."

"It started when he went home after his father died." Mario turned to Terese. "You know about Sam?"

"Karen told me."

"Suicide," he said.

"He was ill?"

Mario nodded. "Huntington's."

Terese looked shocked. "Sam had Huntington's disease?"

"Surprised, huh? He kept it hidden, I guess, but when it got bad, well, he didn't want to go through that. Took the easy way out."

"But . . . how . . . I never knew."

"Neither did Rick. Or Sam, for that matter, until the end."

"How is that possible?"

"You know anything about Huntington's?" Mario asked.

She nodded. "I did a story on it. It's strictly hereditary. One of your parents has to have it. If they do, you have a one-in-two chance of contracting it."

"Exactly. The theory is, Sam's father—Rick's grandfather—had it, but he died in Normandy, before the illness would have taken effect. So Sam had no idea."

"Did Rick get tested?" Terese asked.

"I don't know. He didn't even tell Karen the whole story—just that his father found out he had a terminal illness. But anyway, he stayed over in the USA for a while. I think he was going through his father's things, settling the estate. That was when he stumbled onto this Save the Angels charity."

"How?"

"No idea."

"You said they're against stem cell research. Was that somehow related to Huntington's?"

"Could be, but Rick mostly had me run through their finances. Follow the money. That's the old motto. Rick wanted to know everything he could about it, and the people who ran it—until he told me to get off the story."

"He gave up?"

"No. He just wanted me to stop. Not him. Just me."

"Do you know why?"

"Not really. He came by and took all my files, and then he said something really weird." Mario looked first at Terese, then back at me. "He said, 'You need to be careful. You have a family.'"

We waited.

"So I said the obvious: 'So do you.' But he just shook it off. I could see he was totally unnerved. Terese, you knew how he was. Nothing scared him."

She nodded. "He was that way on the phone with me."

"So I try to get him to talk to me, open up. He won't. He hurries out and I don't hear anything else from him. Ever. And then I get the call today."

"Any clue where those files are now?"

"He usually kept copies at the office."

"It might help if we could see them."

Mario just stared at her.

"Please, Mario. You know I wouldn't ask if it wasn't important."

He was still annoyed, but he did seem to get it. "Let me go look around for them first thing in the morning, okay?"

I looked over at Terese. I wasn't sure how hard we pushed now. This man seemed to know Rick Collins as well as anyone. It was her call.

"Has Rick talked about Miriam much recently?" she asked.

Mario looked up. He took his time, and I expected an expansive answer. But all he said was, "No."

We waited for him to elaborate. He didn't.

"I think," Terese said, "that there's a chance that Miriam is still alive."

If Mario Contuzzi knew something about it, then the guy had to be a psychopath. I'm not saying that people can't lie and act and fool you. I have seen it done too many times by some all-time greats. The way the all-time greats do it is to either fool themselves into believing that the lie is the truth or they are true, honest-to-goodness psychopaths. If Mario suspected that Miriam was alive, he fit into one of those two camps.

He made a face as though he had heard wrong. His voice had an angry edge. "What are you talking about?"

But saying it out loud had drained Terese. I took over. Trying to sound somewhat sane as I told him about the blood samples and the blond hair. I didn't tell him about seeing her on the video or any of that. This was too hard to believe as it was. The best way to present it was with scientific evidence—DNA testing—not my intuition based on her walk on a grainy surveillance video.

For a long time he said nothing.

Then: "The blood test has to be wrong."

We both said nothing.

"Or . . . wait. They think you killed Rick, right?"

"They originally thought Terese had a hand in it, yes," I said.

"What about you, Bolitar?"

"I was in New Jersey when he was murdered."

"So they think Terese did it—is that it?"

"Yes."

"And you know how cops are. They play mind games. What better mind game than this—telling you your dead daughter might still be alive?"

Now I made a face. "How would that help land her for his murder?"

"How am I supposed to know? But, I mean, come on, Terese. I know you want this. Hell, I want this. But how can it possibly be?"

"'Once you eliminate the impossible, whatever remains, no matter how improbable, must be the truth,'" I said.

"Sir Arthur Conan Doyle," Mario said.

"Yep."

"You ready to go that far, Bolitar?"

"I'm ready to go out as far as I need to."

17

WHEN we were a block away, Terese said, "I need to visit Miriam's grave."

We found another cab and rode in silence. When we got to the fenced cemetery, we stopped at the gate. Cemeteries always have a fence and gate. What exactly were they protecting?

"Do you want me to wait out here?" I asked.

"Yes."

So I stayed outside the gates, as though afraid to trample sacred ground, which, I guessed, I would have been. I kept Terese in sight for reasons of safety, but when she bent down on her knees, I turned away and started to walk. I thought about what must have been going through her mind, what images were running through her head. This, I assure you, wasn't a good idea, so I called Esperanza back in New York.

It took her six rings to answer.

"There's a time change, dummy."

I looked at my watch. It was five a.m. in New York. "Oops," I said.

"What now?"

I decided to open big. I told Esperanza about the DNA and the blond girl.

"It's her daughter?"

"Apparently."

"That," Esperanza said, "is seriously messed up."

"It is."

"So what do you need from me?"

"I took a bunch of pictures—credit card bills, phone, whatever—and e-mailed them over," I said. "Oh, and there's some weird thing about opals or something in the to-dos."

"Opals like the stones?"

"No idea. Might be code."

"I'm terrible at codes."

"Me too, but maybe something will click. Anyway, let's start figuring out what Rick Collins was up to. Also his father committed suicide." I gave her his name and location. "Maybe we can look into that."

"Into a suicide?"

"Yes."

"Look into it for what?"

"See if there was anything suspicious. I don't know."

There was silence. I started walking. "Esperanza?"

"I like her."

"Who?"

"Margaret Thatcher. Who are we talking about? Terese, dopey. And you know me. I hate all your girl-friends."

I thought about it. "You like Ali," I said.

"I do. She's a good person."

"Do I hear a 'but'?"

"But she's not for you."

"Why not?"

"There are no intangibles," she said.

"What does that mean?"

"What made you a great athlete?" Esperanza asked. "Not a good athlete. I'm talking about pro level, first-team collegiate All-American, all that."

"Skill, hard work, genetics."

"Lots of guys have those. But what separates you— what divides the greats from the almosts—is the intan-gibles."

"And Ali and I?"

"No intangibles."

I heard a baby crying in the background. Esperanza's son, Hector, was eighteen months old.

"He still doesn't sleep through the night," Esperanza said, "so you can imagine how thrilled I am about your call."

"Sorry."

"I'll get on it. Take care of yourself. Tell Terese to hang tough. We'll figure this out."

She hung up. I stared at the phone. Usually Win and

Esperanza hate when I get involved in stuff like this. All of a sudden the reluctance was gone. I wondered about that.

Across the street, a man with sunglasses, black Chuck Taylor high-tops, and a green T-shirt strolled without a care. My Spidey senses started tingling. His hair was close-cropped and dark. So was his skin—what we call Semitic, which I often confuse with Latino or Arabic or Greek or, heck, Italian.

He turned the corner and vanished. I waited to see if he reappeared. He didn't. I looked around to see if someone else had now entered the scene. Several people walked by but no one else set off my Spidey senses.

When Terese came back she was dry-eyed.

"Should we grab a cab?" she asked.

"Do you know this area?"

"Yes."

"Is there a subway station nearby?"

I could almost hear Win saying, *"In London, Myron, we call it the tube or the underground."*

She nodded. We walked two blocks. She led the way.

"I know this sounds like the most idiotic question known to mankind," I began, "but are you okay?"

Terese nodded. Then: "Do you believe in anything supernatural?"

"Meaning?"

"Ghosts, spirits, ESP, any of that."

"No. Why? Do you?"

She didn't answer the question directly. "That was

only the second time I've visited Miriam's grave," she said.

I put my credit card in the ticket-buying machine and let Terese press the right buttons.

"I hate it there. Not because it makes me sad. But because I don't feel anything. You would think that all that misery, all the tears that have been shed there— Have you ever stopped and thought about that at a graveyard? How many people have cried. How many people have said final good-byes to loved ones. You'd think—I don't know—that all that human suffering would swirl up in tiny particles and form some sort of negative cosmic sensation. A tingle in the bones maybe, a cold prickle on the back of the neck, something."

"But you never felt it," I said.

"Never. The whole idea of burying the dead and putting a stone marker over their remains . . . it seems like a waste of space, like something held over from a superstitious era."

"Yet," I said, "you wanted to go back today."

"Not to pay my respects."

"Then what?"

"This is going to sound nuts."

"Go for it."

"I wanted to come back to see if maybe something changed in the past decade. To see if this time I could feel something."

"That doesn't sound so nuts."

"Not 'feel' like that. I'm not saying this right. I thought coming back here might help us."

"In what way?"

Terese kept walking. "Here's the thing. I figured . . ." She stopped, swallowed.

"What?" I said.

She blinked into the sunlight. "I don't believe in the supernatural either—but you know what I do believe in?"

I shook my head.

"I believe in the maternal bond. I don't know how else to say it. I'm her mother. That's the most powerful link known to mankind, right? A mother's love for her child trumps all. So I should feel *something*, one way or the other. I should be able to stand by that gravestone and know if my own daughter is alive or not. You know what I mean?"

My gut reaction was to offer up some patronizing pap like "How could you?" or "Don't beat yourself up about it," but I stopped myself before uttering the inane. I have a son, at least biologically. He's grown now and doing his second tour overseas—this one in Kabul. I worry about him all the time—and while I don't believe it's possible, I keep thinking I would know if something bad happened to him. I will feel it or imagine a chilly gust inside my chest or some nonsense like that.

I said, "I know what you mean."

We headed down an escalator that seemed to go forever. I glanced behind me. No sign of Sunglasses Man.

"So what now?" Terese asked.

"We head back to the hotel. You start looking at what we found at Karen's. Think about that opal code—see where that leads you. Esperanza will e-mail you whatever she gets. Something happened to Rick recently—something that made him change his life and reach out to you. The best thing to do right now is figure out who killed him, why, and what he was working on the last few months. So you need to go through his stuff, see what jumps out at you."

"What did you think of our conversation with Karen?" Terese asked me.

"You two were close, right?"

"Yes, very."

"Then I will put it politely: I don't think Karen was being totally forthcoming. You?"

"Before today I would have said I would trust her with my life," Terese said. "But you're right. She's lying about something."

"Any idea what?"

"No."

"Let's maybe go back and try something else. Tell me everything you remember about the accident."

"You think I'm holding back?"

"Of course not. But now that you've heard all this new stuff, I'm wondering if anything about that night is striking you as different."

"No, nothing." She looked out the window, but there was only the blur of the tunnel. "I've spent the past decade trying to forget that night."

"I understand."

"You don't understand. I've replayed that night in my head every single day for the past ten years."

I said nothing.

"I have looked at that night from every angle. I have pondered every what-if—if I had driven slower, taken a different route, left her at home, hadn't been so damn ambitious, everything. There is nothing more to remember."

We got off the train and headed forward toward the exit.

When we entered the lobby, my phone vibrated. Win sent the following text:

BRING TERESE TO THE PENTHOUSE. THEN GO TO
ROOM 118. ALONE.

Then two seconds later, Win added:

PLEASE REFRAIN FROM TEXTING BACK SOME WITTY
ALBEIT HOMOPHOBIC COMEBACK VIS-À-VIS THE
"ALONE" COMMENT.

Win was the only person I knew who was more verbose in texts than in person. I took Terese up to the penthouse. There was a laptop with Internet access. I pointed to it. "Maybe you can start digging into this Save the Angels charity."

"Where are you going?" she asked.

"Downstairs. Win wants to talk to me."

"I can't go?"

"He said alone."

"I'm not really sure I like that idea," Terese said.

"Neither am I, but I find it's better not to question him."

"How crazy is he?"

"Win is sane. He is just overly rational. He sees things in black and white." Then I added: "He tends to be more of an ends-justify-means sort of guy."

"His means can be pretty extreme," she said.

"Yes."

"I remember that from when I helped you find that donor."

I said nothing.

"Win isn't trying to spare my feelings, is he?"

"Win and sparing a woman's feelings," I said, making a scale with my hands. "I don't think that's a factor."

"You'd better go."

"Yep."

"Will you tell me what happens?"

"Probably not. If Win wants to keep something from you, it's for the best. You have to trust that, I guess."

She nodded and stood. "I'm going to wash up and then hit the Internet."

"Okay."

She started for the bedroom. I reached for the door to the corridor.

"Myron?"

I turned toward her. She stood facing me full. She was beautiful and vulnerable and strong, and she stood like she was readying to take a blow, and I wanted to jump in the way and protect her.

"What?" I asked.

"I love you," Terese said.

She said it just like that. Facing me full, beautiful and vulnerable and strong. Something in my chest rose and took flight. I stood there, frozen, the gift of speech temporarily taken away from me.

"I know the timing sucks and I don't want it to interfere with what we're doing now. But either way, if Miriam is alive or if this is all some horrible practical joke, I want you to know: I love you. And when this is over, however it turns out, I want more than anything to give you and me a try."

I opened my mouth, closed it, opened it again. "I'm kinda with someone."

"I know. I guess my timing double-sucks. But that's okay. If you love her, then that's that. If you don't, I'm here."

Terese didn't wait for a response. She turned and opened the bedroom door and vanished inside.

18

I staggered to the elevator.

How had that Snow Patrol song put it a couple of years back? Those three words, they say so much—they're not enough.

Baloney. They were enough.

I thought about Ali in Arizona. I thought about Terese standing there and telling me that she loved me. Terese was probably right—the best response was to not let it interfere. But it was there. And it was gnawing at me.

The blinds were drawn in room 118.

I reached for the light switch and then thought better of it. Win sat in a plush chair. I could hear the clink of ice in whatever he was drinking. Alcohol never seemed to affect Win, but this was awfully early.

I sat across from him. We have been friends for a very long time. We met as college students at Duke University. I remember seeing his photograph in the freshman face book the first day I arrived on campus. The entry listed him as Windsor Horne Lockwood III from some obnoxious-sounding prep school on the Main Line in Philadelphia. He had the perfect hair and the haughty expression. My father and I had just lugged up all my stuff to my fourth-floor walk-up. Typical of my father. He drove me to North Carolina from New Jersey, never bitching once, insisting on carrying the heaviest items himself, and we sat down and took a break, and I started paging through the face book, and I pointed to Win's picture and said, "Hey, Dad, look at this guy. I bet I never even see him in my four years."

I was wrong, of course.

For a long time I felt Win was indestructible. He had killed many, but none who didn't seem to deserve it, and, yes, I know how disturbing it is to say that. But age has a way of creeping up on all of us. What seems eccentric and edgy when you're in your twenties or thirties turns into something closer to pathetic at forty.

"It will be difficult to get permission to exhume the body," Win began. "We have no cause of action."

"How about the DNA test?"

"The French authorities won't release the results. I also tried the most direct route—a bribe."

"No takers?"

"Not yet. There will be, but it will take some time, which it seems we don't have."

I thought about it. "You have a suggestion?"

"I do."

"I'm listening."

"We bribe gravediggers. We do it ourselves tonight under the cover of darkness. We only need a small sample. We send it to our lab, compare the DNA with Terese's"—he raised his glass—"and we're done."

"Ghoulish," I said.

"And effective."

"Do you think there's a point?"

"Meaning?"

"We know how the result is going to turn out."

"Do tell."

"I heard the tone in Berleand's voice. He may have talked about premature and inconclusive, but we both know. And I saw that girl on that surveillance video. Okay, not her face and it was at a distance. But she had her mother's walk, if you know what I mean."

"How about her mother's derriere?" Win asked. "Now that would be solid evidence."

I just looked at him.

He sighed. "Mannerisms are often more of a tell than facial features or even height," he said. "I get it."

"Yes."

"You and your son have that," Win said. "When he sits down, he shakes his leg like you do. He has your motion—the way your fingertips come off the ball—on the jump shot, if not your result."

I don't think Win had ever mentioned my son before.

"We still need to do this," I said. I thought again about that Sherlock Holmes axiom about eliminating the impossible. "At the end of the day, the most obvious answer is still some kind of mistake in Berleand's DNA test. We need to know for certain."

"Agreed."

I hated the idea of violating a grave, of course, especially of someone who'd been taken so young. I would run it by Terese, but she had made it pretty clear how she felt about ashes to ashes. I told Win to go ahead.

"Is that why you wanted to see me alone?" I asked.

"No."

Win took a deep sip, rose, filled his glass. He didn't bother offering me any. He knew I couldn't handle hard liquor. Though I'm six four and nearly 220 pounds, I handle booze about as well as a sixteen-year-old girl sneaking into her first mixer.

"You saw the video of the blond girl at the airport," he said.

"Yes."

"And she was with the man who attacked you. The one in the photograph."

"You know this."

"I do."

"So what's wrong?"

Win pressed a button on his cell phone and raised it to his ear. "Please join us."

The door from the connecting room opened. A tall woman in a dark blue power suit entered. She had raven black hair and big shoulders. She blinked, put a hand to her eyes, and said, "Why are the lights so low?"

She had a British accent. This being Win, I figured that the woman was, well, Mee-like, if you will. But that wasn't the case. She moved across the room and took the open seat.

"This," Win said, "is Lucy Probert. She works at Interpol here in London."

I said something inane, like "Nice to meet you." She nodded and studied my face as though it were a modern painting she didn't quite get.

"Tell him," Win said.

"Win forwarded me the photograph of the man whom you assaulted."

"I didn't assault him," I said. "He pulled a gun on me."

Lucy Probert waved that away as if it were so much flotsam. "My division at Interpol works international child trafficking. You probably think it's a pretty sick world out there, but trust me, it's sicker than you can imagine. The crimes that I deal with— Well, it boggles the mind what people can dream up to do to the most vulnerable. In our battles against this depravity, your friend Win has been an invaluable ally."

I looked over at said friend and as usual his face gave away nothing. For a long time, Win had been—for lack of a better term—a vigilante. He would go out late at night and walk the most dangerous streets of New York or Philadelphia in hopes of being attacked so that he could maim those who would prey on the perceived weak. He would read about a pervert who'd gotten off on a technicality or some wife beater who'd gotten his wife to clam up, and he would pay them what we called "Night Visits." There was one case of a pedophile the police knew had kidnapped a girl but couldn't get to talk. They were forced to release him. Win paid him a Night Visit. He talked. The girl was found, already dead. No one knows where the pedophile is now.

I thought that maybe Win had stopped or at least slowed down, but now I realized that hadn't been the case. He had started taking more overseas trips. He had been an "invaluable ally" in the fight against child trafficking.

"So when Win asked me for a favor," Lucy went on, "I did it. This seemed like a pretty innocuous request anyway—to run the photo Captain Berleand sent you through the system and come up with an ID. Routine, right?"

"Right."

"It was not. We have plenty of ways at Interpol to identify people from photographs. There's facial recognition software, for example."

"Miss Probert?"

"Yes."

"I don't really need a technology lesson."

"Wonderful, because I have neither the time nor inclination to give you one. My point is, such requests are fairly routine at Interpol. I put the photograph into the system before I left for the day, figuring the computer would work on it overnight and spew out an answer. Is that simplifying matters enough for you?"

I nodded, realizing that I'd be wrong to interrupt. She was clearly agitated and I hadn't helped.

"So when I arrived at work this morning, I expected to have an identity to report back to you. But that wasn't the case. Instead—how shall I put this politely?—all forms of intestinal waste hit the proverbial fan. Someone had gone through my desk. My computer had been accessed and searched. Don't ask me how I know—I know."

She stopped and started searching through her bag. She found a cigarette and put it in her mouth. "You damn Americans and your antismoking crusade. If one of you says anything about no-smoking rules . . ."

Neither of us did.

She lit up, took a deep breath, let it go.

"In short, that photograph was classified or top secret or fill in your own terminology."

"Do you know why?"

"Why it was classified?"

"Yes."

"No. I am fairly high up on the Interpol food chain. If it was over my head, it is ultrasensitive. Your photograph sent warning bells right to the top. I was summoned to Mickey Walker's office—the big boss in London. I haven't been honored by an audience with Mickey in two years. He called me in and sat me down and wanted to know where I'd got the photograph and why I'd made this request."

"What did you tell him?"

She looked over at Win, and I knew the answer.

"That I'd received a tip from a reliable source that the man in the photograph might be involved in trafficking."

"And he asked you for the name of the source?"

"Of course."

"And you gave it to him?"

Win said, "I would have insisted."

"There was no choice," she said. "They would have found out anyway. If they went through my e-mails or phone records, they might have been able to track it down."

I looked at Win. Again no reaction. She was wrong—they wouldn't have been able to track it down, but I understood where she was coming from. This was clearly something big. To not cooperate would be career suicide and maybe worse. Win would have been right to insist she put it on us.

"So now what?"

"They wish to talk to me," Win said.

"Do they know where you are?"

"Not yet, no. My solicitor informed them I would voluntarily come in within the hour. We are checked in here under an assumed name, but if they try hard enough, they will find us here."

She looked at her watch. "I better head back."

I thought about the Sunglasses Man who'd set off my Spidey senses. "Is there any chance one of your people is following me?"

"I would doubt it."

"You're under heavy suspicion," I said. "How do you know they didn't follow you here?"

She looked at Win. "Is he a dope or just a sexist?"

Win considered that. "A sexist."

"I'm an agent for Interpol. I took precautions."

But not enough precautions so as not to get caught in the first place. I kept that thought to myself. It wasn't fair. She couldn't have known how putting that picture in the system would blow up.

We all rose. She shook my hand and kissed Win's cheek. Win and I settled back into our seats after she left.

"What are you going to tell Interpol?" I asked.

"Is there any reason to lie?"

"Not that I can see."

"So I tell them the truth—for the most part. My dear friend—that would be you—was attacked by this man in Paris. I wanted to know who he was. We cover for Lucy by saying I lied to her and said the man was involved in child trafficking."

"Which for all we know is a possibility."

"True."

"Do you mind if I tell Terese about this?"

"As long as you leave Lucy's name out of it."

I nodded. "We need to get an ID on this guy."

I walked Win down to the Claridge's rather spectacular lobby. No violin quartet played concertos in the foyer, but they should have. The decor was modern British Upper Crust, which is to say a hybrid of Old English and art deco, done in a style both relaxed enough for jeans-clad tourists and yet haughty enough to imagine that certain chairs and maybe the molding on the ceiling were thumbing their collective nose at you. I liked it. After Win left, I started for the elevator when something made me pull up.

Black Chuck Taylor high-tops.

I moved toward the elevators, stopped, and patted my pockets. I turned back with a confused expression on my face, as though I had just realized that I had misplaced something. Myron Bolitar, Method Actor. I used the opportunity to glance surreptitiously at the man with the black Chuck Taylor high-tops.

No sunglasses. Blue Windbreaker now. A baseball cap that hadn't been there at the cemetery. But I knew. It was my guy. And he was good. People have a tendency to remember very little. Guy with sunglasses and close-cropped hair. Throw a cap on, a Windbreaker over your T-shirt—no one will notice you unless they're looking hard.

I had almost missed it, but now I knew for sure: I was being followed. My boy from the graveyard was back.

There were several ways to play this, but I was not in the mood to be coy. I walked down a narrow corridor toward the rooms they used for meetings and conferences. It was a Sunday, so they were empty. I folded my arms, leaned against the coatroom, and waited for my man to make an appearance.

When he did—five minutes later—I grabbed him by the shirt and pulled him into the coatroom. "Why are you following me?"

He looked at me confused.

"Is it my strong chin? My hypnotic blue eyes? My shapely ass? By the way, do these pants make me look fat? Tell me the truth."

The man stared for another second, maybe two, and then he did what I had done earlier: He just attacked.

He led with a palm strike toward my face. I blocked it. He spun and threw an elbow. Fast. Faster than I'd anticipated. The blow landed on the left side of my chin. I turned my head to lessen the impact, but I could still feel my teeth rattle. He kept the attack going, throwing another blow, then a side kick, then a fist to the body. The body shot landed the hardest, on the bottom of the rib cage. It would hurt. If you ever watch boxing on TV, even casually, you will hear every announcer say the same things: Body shots accumulate. The opponent will feel them in the late rounds. That's true and it's not. Body shots also hurt right now. They make you cringe and lower your defenses.

I was in trouble.

Part of my brain started berating myself—stupid to do this without a weapon or Win as backup. Most of my brain, however, had kicked into survival mode. Even the most seemingly innocent fight—at a bar, a sporting event, whatever—will make your adrenaline go haywire because your body knows what maybe your mind doesn't want to accept: This is about survival. You could very well die.

I fell to the ground and rolled away. The coatroom was small. This guy knew what he was doing. He stayed on me, trying to rain down foot stomps, chasing me. He landed a kick to my head; stars exploded like something out of a cartoon. I debated yelling for help, anything to get him to stop.

I rolled a second or so more, noticed his timing. I left my gut open, hoping he would go for it with a kick. He did. As he started to cock his knee, I reverse-rolled toward him, bent at the waist, got my hands ready. The kick landed in ye olde breadbasket, but I was ready for it. I clamped his foot against my body with both hands and rolled hard. He had two choices. Fall quickly to the ground or have his ankle bone snap like a dried twig.

He knew to throw blows as he fell, but for the most part they were incffcctive.

We were both on the ground. I was hurt and dazed, but I had two major advantages now. One, I still had his foot, though I could feel that grip loosening. Two, now that we were on the ground, well, size became important—and I mean that in a clean way. I was holding his leg with both hands. He tried to punch his way through. I moved closer to him, ducking my head into his chest. When an opponent is throwing punches, most people think that they should give the guy some distance. But it's just the opposite. You put your face into his chest and smother his power. That was what I did here.

He tried to box my ears, but that required both hands, leaving him vulnerable. I lifted my head hard and fast and caught him under the chin. He reeled back. I fell on top of him.

Now the fight was about leverage and technique and

size. I had him beat right now in two of the three—
leverage and size. I was still dizzy from the initial attack
but the head butt had helped. I still had his leg. I gave it
a vicious twist. He rolled with it and that was when he
made the big mistake.

He turned his back to me, exposing it.

I let go and jumped on him, my legs snaking around
his waist, my right arm around his neck. He knew what
was coming. Panic made him start bucking. He dropped
his chin to block my elbow. I whacked him in the back of
the head with a palm strike. That weakened him just
enough. I quickly gripped his forehead and tugged back.
He tried to fight it, but I raised his chin just enough. My
elbow sneaked underneath the opening and reached his
throat. The choke hold was set.

I had him now. It was just a question of time.

And then I heard a noise, a voice actually, shouting in
a foreign language. I debated letting go to see who it
was, but I held on. That was my mistake. A second man
had entered the room. He hit me in the back of the neck,
probably with a knife hand, what you'd call a classic karate chop. A numbness swept through me as if my entire
body had just become my funny bone banged the wrong
way. My grip loosened.

I heard the man shout again, in the same foreign language. It confused me. The first man slipped out of my
grip, gasping for breath. He rolled away. There were two
of them now. I looked at the second man. He pointed a
gun at me.

I was finished.

"Don't move," the man said to me with a foreign accent.

My brain searched for an out, but I was too far away. The first man rose to his feet. He was still breathing hard. We looked at each other, our eyes met, and I saw something strange there. Not hatred. Respect maybe. I don't know.

I looked at the man with the gun again.

"Don't move," he said a second time. "And don't follow us."

Then they both ran away.

19

I stumbled to the elevator. I hoped that I could make it to my room without being seen, but the elevator stopped in the lobby. A family of six Americans looked at me, at my torn shirt and bleeding mouth and all the rest of it, and still got on and said, "Hi!" For the next few floors I heard the big sister picking on the brother and the mother begging them to stop and the father trying to ignore them and the other two siblings pinching each other when the parents weren't looking.

When I got to the room, Terese freaked out, but only briefly. She helped me in and called Win. Win arranged for a doctor. The doctor came quickly and declared nothing broken. I would be okay. My head hurt, probably from a concussion. I craved rest. The doctor gave me something and everything became a little fuzzy. The next thing I remember was sensing Win standing across the dark room. I opened one eye, then the other.

Win said, "You're an idiot."

"No, I'm fine, really. Don't start with all the concern."

"You should have waited for me."

"Nobody likes a Monday-morning quarterback." I struggled to sit up. My body was somewhat willing; my head shrieked in protest. I grabbed my skull with both hands, trying to keep it from splitting open.

"I think I learned something," I said.

"I'm listening."

The curtains were still open. Darkness had fallen. I looked at my watch. It was ten p.m. now, and I remembered something. "The graveyard," I said.

"What about it?"

"Are they exhuming the body?"

"You still want to go?"

I nodded and quickly got dressed. I didn't bother saying good-bye to Terese. We had discussed it earlier—she saw no reason to be there. Win had a limo pick us up at the front entrance, pull into a private lot, and then we changed cars.

"Here," Win said.

He handed me a minirevolver, the NAA Black Widow. I looked at it. "A twenty-two?"

Win usually favored larger weapons. Like, say, bazookas or rocket launchers.

"The UK has some pretty strict laws against carrying

a firearm." He handed me a nylon ankle holster. "Better to keep it concealed."

"Is that what you're carrying?"

"Heavens no. Do you want something bigger?"

I didn't. I strapped the gun onto my ankle. It reminded me of a brace I used when I played basketball.

When we arrived at the cemetery, I expected to be more ghouled out, if you will, but I wasn't. The two men were standing in the hole, almost done. They both wore matching aqua blue velour sweat suits from my aunt Sophie's Miami collection. The majority of the digging had been done earlier in the day by a small yellow excavator that sat to the right as if looking down at its handiwork. The two velour-clad gents just needed to scrape the coffin enough to open it and remove a few samples, some bone or something, and then they could close it back up and pour the dirt back over the contents.

Okay, maybe now I was feeling ghoulish.

A misty rain fell upon us. I stood and looked down. Win did too. It was dark, but our eyes had adjusted enough to see the shadows. The men were bent low now, almost out of sight.

"You said you learned something."

I nodded. "The men following me. They spoke Hebrew and knew Krav Maga."

Krav Maga is an Israeli martial art.

"And," Win added, "they were good."

"You see where I'm going with this?"

"A good tail, good fighter, got away without killing you, spoke Hebrew." Win nodded. "Mossad."

"Explains all the interest."

Below us, we heard one of the men curse.

"Is there a problem?" Win called down.

"They put a bleeding lock on these things," a voice said. He flicked on the flashlight. Now all we could see was the coffin. "For cripes' sake, why? My house doesn't have a lock this strong. We're trying different keys."

"Break it," Win said.

"You sure?"

"Who's going to know?"

The two men forced up a laugh the way, well, men digging up a grave might. "True, right that," one said.

Win turned his attention back to me. "So why would Rick Collins be involved with Mossad?"

"No clue."

"And why would a car accident from ten years ago reach a level where the Israeli secret service would show interest?"

"Again, no clue."

Win thought about it. "I will call Zorra. Maybe she can help."

Zorra, a very dangerous cross-dresser who had helped us out in the past, had worked for Mossad in the late eighties.

"That could work." I thought about it. "Suppose the guy I hit with the table was Mossad. That might explain a few things."

"Like why Interpol would freak out when we tried to get an ID," Win said.

I thought about that. "But if he was Mossad, so was the guy I shot."

Win thought about that. "We don't know enough yet. Let's contact Zorra and see what she can find out."

We heard exertion and scraping and pounding from below. Then a voice called up, "Got it!"

We looked down. The flashlight showed two sets of hands pulling up on the lid. The men grunted from the effort. The casket looked regulation size. That surprised me. I had expected something smaller for a seven-year-old girl. But maybe that was the point, right? Maybe that was what was saving me from feeling overly ghoulish—I didn't think we would find a seven-year-old's skeleton.

I really didn't want to watch anymore, so I stepped away. I was here just to observe, to make sure they actually took a sample from the grave. This was crazy enough without knowing that everything involving this test was rock solid. If it came back negative, I didn't want anyone saying, "But how do you know it was from the right grave?" or "Maybe they just said they dug but didn't." I wanted to eliminate as many variables as possible.

"Got the casket opened," one of the diggers called up.

I saw Win look down. Another voice floated up from the hole in a whisper: "Sweet Jesus."

Then silence.

"What?" I asked.

"A skeleton," Win said, still peering down. "Small. Probably a child's."

Everyone just stood there frozen.

"Get a sample," Win said.

One of the diggers said, "What kind of sample?"

"A bone. Some fabric if you find any. Seal it in those plastic bags."

A child was buried here. I guess that I really didn't expect that. I looked at Win. "Could we be all wrong about this?"

Win shrugged. "DNA doesn't lie."

"So if it's not Miriam Collins, whose skeleton is that?"

"There are," Win said, "other possibilities."

"Such as?"

"I had one of my people do a little investigating. Around the time of the car accident, a little girl from Brentwood went missing. People were sure the father did it, but no body was ever found. The father remains free to this day."

I thought about what Win had said before. "You're right. We're getting ahead of ourselves."

Win said nothing.

I looked back down into the hole. A dirty face from below handed up the plastic bag. "All yours, mate. Good luck to ya and go to hell."

Win and I left then, carrying a brittle bone of a child we had dug up from her quiet sleep in the middle of the night.

20

WE got back to Claridge's at two in the morning. Win immediately left for some "Mee Time." I took a long hot shower. When I checked the room's minibar, a small smile crossed my face. Stocked with chocolate Yoo-hoos. That Win.

I chugged down a cold one and waited for the sugar buzz. I put on the TV and continuously flipped stations because that's what real men do. American shows from last season. Terese's door was closed, but I doubted that she was sleeping. I sat by myself and took deep breaths.

The clock read two a.m. Eight p.m. back in New York. Five p.m. in Scottsdale, Arizona.

I looked down at my phone. I thought about Ali and Erin and Jack in Arizona. I didn't know much about Arizona. It was the desert, right? Who wants to live in the desert?

I dialed Ali's cell phone. It rang three times before she answered with a wary "Hello?"

"Hey," I said.

"Your number didn't pop up on the caller ID," Ali said.

"I have a different phone but it's the same number."

Silence.

Ali asked, "Where are you?"

"I'm in London."

"As in England?"

"Yep."

I heard a noise. Sounded like Jack. Ali said, "One second, honey. I'm on the phone." I noticed that she didn't say whom she was on the phone with. Normally she would have.

"I didn't realize you were overseas," Ali said.

"I got a call from a friend in trouble. She was—"

"She?"

I stopped. "Yes."

"Wow, that didn't take long."

I was about to say, *It's not like that*, but I stopped myself. "I've known her for ten years."

"I see. Just a sudden visit to London to see an old friend, then?"

Silence. Then I heard Jack's voice again, asking who was on the phone, the sound traveling from some desert across most of the continental United States and across the Atlantic Ocean and making me cringe.

"I have to go, Myron. Was there something you wanted?"

Good question. There probably was, but now was not the time. "I guess not," I said.

She hung up without another word. I looked at the phone, felt the weight, then thought, Wait a second—Ali had ended it, hadn't she? Hadn't she made it crystal clear just, what, two days ago? And what had I really wanted to accomplish with this damn phone call?

Why had I called?

Because I hate loose threads? Because I wanted to do the right thing here, whatever the heck that meant?

The pain from the fight was starting to come back. I rose, stretched, tried to keep my muscles loose. I looked at Terese's door. It was closed. I tiptoed over and peeked in her room. The light was out. I listened for her breathing. No sound. I started to close the door.

"Please don't go," Terese said.

I stopped and said, "Try to get some sleep."

"Please."

I have always treaded so carefully when it comes to matters of the heart. I did the right thing always. I never just acted. Except for that one time on an island ten years ago, I worried about feelings and repercussions and what came next.

"Don't go," she said one more time.

And I didn't.

When we kissed, there was a surge and then a release, a letting-go like I had never known before, a letting-go like you are staying very still and surrendering and your heart pounds against your rib cage and your pulse races and your knees grow weak and your toes curl and your ears pop and every part of you relaxes and happily gives in.

We smiled that night. We cried. I kissed that beautiful bare shoulder. And in the morning, she was gone again.

BUT only from the bed.

I found Terese having coffee in the sitting room. The curtain was open. To paraphrase an old song, the morning sun in her face showed her age—and I liked it. She wore the hotel's terry-cloth robe and it was opened just a little, just a hint at the bounty beneath. I don't think I had ever seen anything so damn beautiful.

Terese looked at me and smiled.

"Hi," I said.

"Stop with the smooth lines. You already got me in bed."

"Dang, I was up all night working on that one."

"Well, you were up all night anyway. Coffee?"

"Please."

She poured. I sat next to her oh so gingerly. The beating was taking effect now. I winced and thought about grabbing some of those painkillers the doctor had left for me. But not just yet. Right now I wanted to sit with this spectacular woman and drink our coffee in silence.

"Heaven," she said.

"Yes."

"I wish we could just stay here forever."

"I'm not sure I could afford the room."

She smiled. Her hand reached out and took mine. "Do you want to hear something awful?"

"Tell me."

"Part of me wants to forget all this and just run away with you."

I knew what she meant.

"I have dreamed so many times about this chance at redemption. And now that it may be here, I can't help but have the feeling it will destroy me."

She looked at me.

"What do you think?"

"I won't let it destroy you," I said.

Her smile was sad. "You think you have that power?"

She was right, but I make dumb declarations like that sometimes. "So what do you want to do?"

"Find out what really happened that night."

"Okay."

"You don't have to help," she said.

"Have to," I said, "especially since you put out last night."

"That's true."

"So what's our next step?" I asked.

"I just got off the phone with Karen. I told her it was time she came clean."

"How did she respond?"

"She didn't argue. We're going to meet in an hour."

"Do you want me to come?"

She shook her head. "This time it has to be just the two of us."

"Okay."

We sat there and had our coffee and didn't want to move or talk or do anything.

Terese broke the silence. "One of us should say, 'About last night.'"

"I will leave it to you."

"It was pretty frigging awesome."

I smiled. "Yeah. I knew I should leave it to you."

She rose. I watched her. She wore only the bathrobe. Ladies, save your frilly lace, your merry widows, your Victoria's Secret, your Frederick's of Hollywood, your G-strings, your thongs, your silk stockings, your petticoats and baby dolls. Give me a beautiful woman in a hotel-room terry-cloth robe any day of the week.

"I'm taking a shower," she said.

"Is that an invitation?"

"No."

"Oh."

"Not enough time."

"I can work fast."

"I know. But when you do, it's not your best work."

"Ouch."

She bent down and kissed me gently on the lips. "Thank you," she said.

I was about to crack wise—something like "tell all your friends" or "sigh, another satisfied customer"—but something in her tone made me pull up. Something in her tone overwhelmed me and made me ache. I squeezed her hand and stayed silent and then I watched her walk away.

21

WIN took one look at me and said, "You finally got some."

I was going to argue, but what would have been the point? "Yep."

"Details, please," he said.

"A gentleman doesn't kiss and tell."

He gave me crestfallen. "But you know I love details."

"And you know I never tell you any."

"You used to let me watch. When we were dating Emily in college, you used to let me look in the window."

"I didn't let you. You just did. And when I fixed the shade, you usually broke it again. You're a pig—you know that?"

"Some would call me an interested friend."

"But most would call you a pig."

Win shrugged. "Love me for all my faults."

"So where are we?" I asked.

"We're both getting some."

"Besides that."

"I had a thought," Win said.

"I'm listening."

"Maybe there's a simpler explanation for how the dead girl's blood got to the crime scene. This Save the Angels charity. One of the things it deals with is stem cell research, correct?"

"In some manner, I guess. They're against it, I think."

"And we know that Rick Collins may have discovered that he has Huntington's disease. Certainly his father had it."

"Okay."

"People save their children's umbilical cord blood nowadays—they freeze it or some such thing for future use. They're full of stem cells and the idea is that somewhere down the line those stem cells could save your child's life, or even your own. Perhaps Rick Collins saved his daughter's. When he found out he had Huntington's, he decided that he could use it."

"Stem cells can't cure Huntington's."

"Not yet, no."

"So you figure he had the frozen cord blood when he was murdered and it—what?—thawed out?"

Win shrugged. "Does that scenario make less sense than Miriam Collins being alive this whole time?"

"And the blond hair?"

"There are lots of blondes in this world. The young woman you saw might just be another."

I thought about it. "It still doesn't tell us who killed Rick Collins."

"True."

"I still think whatever this is, it started with the car accident ten years ago. We know that Nigel Manderson was lying."

"We do," Win agreed.

"And Karen Tower is holding something back."

"What about this Mario fellow?"

"What about him?"

"Is he holding something back?"

I thought about that. "Could be. I'm seeing him this morning to go over Rick's work files. I'll take another run at him then."

"Then we also have the Israelis—maybe Mossad—following you. I called Zorra. She'll check her sources."

"Good."

"And last, your Parisian confrontation and the mug shot that sent warning bells all the way up the Interpol hierarchy."

"Your visit with Interpol went well?"

"They asked their questions. I told them my story."

"One thing I don't get," I said. "Why haven't they brought me in yet?"

Win smiled. "You know why."

"They're tailing me."

"Correct answer."

"You see them?"

"Black car on right corner."

"Mossad is probably following me too."

"You're a very popular man."

"It's because I'm a good listener. People like a good listener."

"Indeed."

"I'm also fun at parties."

"And a snazzy dancer. What do you want to do about the tails?"

"I'd like to lose them for the day."

"No problem."

LOSING a tail is fairly easy. In this case, Win got us a car with tinted windows. We drove into an underground garage with several exits. The car left. Two others came along. I hopped in one, Win the other.

Terese was at Karen's now. I was on my way to see Mario Contuzzi.

Twenty minutes later, I rang the doorbell at the Contuzzi apartment. No answer. I checked my watch. I was about five minutes early. I thought about the case, about how Interpol had gone crazy over that mug shot.

So who was the guy who had pulled a gun on me in Paris?

I had tried all the cute 'n' fancy ways to find the man's identity. Maybe, while I had a free minute, I should try the most direct route.

I called Berleand's private line.

Two rings later, a voice answered and said something to me in French.

"I would like to speak to Captain Berleand, please."

"He is on holiday. May I help you?"

Holiday? I tried to picture Berleand enjoying some leisure time on the beach in Cannes, but the picture wouldn't hold. "I really need to reach him."

"May I ask who's calling?"

No point in not saying. "Myron Bolitar."

"I'm sorry. He's on holiday."

"Could you please contact him and ask him to call Myron Bolitar? It's urgent."

"Please hold."

I held.

A minute later, another voice—this one gruff and speaking perfect, uh, American—came on the line. "May I help you?"

"I don't think so. I wanted to talk to Captain Berleand."

"You can talk to me, Mr. Bolitar."

"But you don't sound like a very nice man," I said.

"I'm not. Cute how you slipped our tail, but this isn't very funny."

"Who are you?"

"You can call me Special Agent Jones."

"Can I call you *Super*special Agent Jones? Where is Captain Berleand?"

"Captain Berleand is on holiday."

"Since when?"

"Since he sent you that mug shot against protocol. He was the one who sent you that mug shot, wasn't he?"

I hesitated. Then I said, "No."

"Sure. Where are you, Bolitar?"

From inside the Contuzzi apartment I heard the phone ring. Once, twice, three times.

"Bolitar?"

It stopped after six rings.

"We know you're still in London. Where are you?"

I hung up and looked at Mario's door. The ringing phone—ringing like a phone used to, not like some ring-tone on a cell—had sounded very much like a landline. Hmm. I put my hand on the door. Thick and sturdy. I pressed my ear against the cool surface, hit Mario's cell phone number, watched the LCD display on my mobile. It took a moment or two before the connection went through.

When I heard the faint chime of Mario's cell phone through the door—the landline had been loud; this was not—dread flooded my chest. True, it may be nothing, but most people nowadays do not travel even the short-est of distances, including bathroom visits, without the ubiquitous cell phone clipped or carried upon their person. You can bemoan this fact, but the chances that a guy working in television news would leave his cell phone behind while heading to his office seemed remote.

"Mario?" I shouted.

I started pounding on the door.

"Mario?"

I didn't expect him to answer, of course. I pressed my

ear against the door again, listening for I'm not sure what—a groan maybe. A grunt. Calling out. Something.

No sound.

I wondered about my options. Not many. I reared back, lifted my heel, and kicked the door. It didn't budge.

"Steel-enforced, mate. You'll never kick it down."

I turned toward the voice. The man wore a black leather vest without any sort of shirt underneath, and sadly, he didn't have the build to pull it off. His physique, on too clear a display, managed to be both scrawny and soft. He had a cattle-ring piercing in his nose. He was balding but the little hair he had left was done up in what might be called a comb-over Mohawk. I placed his age at early fifties. It looked like he had gone out to a gay bar in 1979 and had just gotten home.

"Do you know the Contuzzis?" I asked.

The man smiled. I expected another dental nightmare, but while the rest of him might be in various stages of decay, his teeth were gleaming. "Ah," he said. "You're an American."

"Yes."

"Friends with Mario, are we?"

No reason to go into a long answer here: "Yes."

"Well, what can I tell you, mate? Normally they're a quiet couple, but you know what they say—when the wife's away, the mouse will play."

"What do you mean?"

"Had a girl in there, he did. Must have hired her out—you know what I'm saying? The music was loud too. And bloody awful. The Eagles. God, you Americans should be ashamed."

"Tell me about the girl."

"Why?"

I didn't have time for this. I took out my gun. I didn't point it at him. I just took it out. "I'm with the American police," I said. "I'm worried Mario may be in serious danger."

If my gun or pleas ruffled the Billy Idol wannabe, I couldn't see it. He shrugged his bony shoulders. "What can I tell you? Young, blond. I didn't get a good look. Came around last night as I was heading out."

Young, blond. My heart started thumping. "I need to get into that apartment."

"You can't kick it in, mate. You'll break your foot."

I aimed my gun at the lock.

"Whoa, hold up. You really think he's in danger?"

"I do."

He sighed. "There's a spare key above the door. On the ledge there."

I reached up and felt along the small edge of the doorframe. Sure enough, a key. I put it in the lock. Billy Idol moved next to me. The stench of cigarette smoke came off him as though he'd been used as an ashtray. I opened the door and started inside. Billy Idol was right behind me. We both took two steps in and froze.

"Oh, sweet Jesus . . ."

I said nothing. I stood and stared, unable to move. The first thing I saw was Mario's feet. They were strapped to the coffee table with duct tape. The baby booster and plush tot toys I had seen yesterday had been strewn to the side. I wondered if Mario had looked at them in his last moments.

His feet were bare. Next to them lay a power drill. There were small neat holes, perfect tiny circles of maroon red, through his toes and deep into his heel. The holes had come, I knew, from the drill. I found my legs and managed to move closer. There were other drill marks. Through the kneecaps. The rib cage. My eyes slowly traveled up toward his face. There were drill marks beneath the nose, through the cheekbone and into the mouth, another in the chin. Mario's thin face stared up at me, his eyes twisted. He had died in horrible pain.

Billy Idol again whispered: "Oh, sweet Jesus . . ."

"What time did you hear the loud music?"

"Huh?"

I didn't have the strength to say it again, but he caught on. "Five in the morning."

Tortured. The music had been used to cover the screams. I didn't want to touch anything, but the blood looked fresh enough. Off-white bone dust littered the floor. I looked back at the drill. The whirring screech, the sound of that, and the screams as it pierced through flesh and cartilage and penetrated bone.

Then I thought about Terese, just a few blocks away with Karen.

I started running for the door. "Call the police!" I shouted.

"Wait. Where are you going?"

No time to respond. I pocketed the gun and took out

my cell phone, still running. I dialed Terese's cell. One ring. Two rings. Three. My heart thumped in my chest. I pressed the button for the elevator repeatedly. I glanced at a window during the fourth ring and then I saw her, looking up at me.

The young blond girl from the van.

She saw me, turned, and ran. I didn't get a good look at her face. It could have been any blond girl, really. Except it wasn't. It was the same girl. I was sure.

What the hell was going on?

My head started twirling. I started looking for the stairway, but the elevator opened. I got in and pressed for the lobby.

The call to Terese went into her voice mail.

That shouldn't have happened. She should have been at Karen's. Karen's house got service—wasn't out of range. Even if they were in the middle of a serious conversation, Terese would have picked up. She'd know that I would call only if it was an emergency.

Damn. Now what?

I thought about the power drill. I thought about Terese. I thought about Mario Contuzzi's face. I thought about the blonde. Those images all swirled in my head as the elevator dinged and the door opened.

How far was I from Karen's?

Two blocks.

I sprinted outside, hitting the speed dial for Win. He answered on the first ring and before he even had a chance to utter "Articulate," I said, "Get to Karen's. Mario is dead. Terese is not answering her phone."

"Ten minutes away," Win said.

I hung up and immediately felt my phone vibrate. Still running, I put the phone up so I could see the caller ID. I stopped.

It was Terese.

I hit the ANSWER button and put it up to my ear. "Terese?"

No response.

"Terese?"

And then I heard the whirring, screeching sound of a power drill.

The adrenaline spike snatched my breath away. My eyes squeezed shut, but only for a second. No time to waste. My legs tingled, but I pumped them even harder.

The drilling sound stopped, and then a man's voice came on: "Payback is a bitch—don't you think?"

The refined English accent, that same cadence as when he said to me in Paris: *"Listen to me or I will shoot you dead. . . ."*

The man I hit with the table. The man in the mug shot.

The line went dead.

I grabbed my gun, running now with one hand holding the cell phone, one hand holding the weapon. Fear is a funny thing. It can make you do some miraculous things—you've read all the tales of people lifting cars off loved ones, for example—but it can also paralyze you, do crippling things to your body and mind, make it difficult to draw hard breath. Sprinting can suddenly feel heavy, like trudging dreamlike through deep snow.

I needed to calm myself even as the terror tore a hole in my chest.

Up ahead I could see Karen's house.

The young blonde stood by the front door.

When she saw me, she disappeared inside Karen's house. This was so obviously a trap, but really, what choice did I have here? The call from Terese's phone—the sound of the power drill—still rang in my ears. That had been the point, hadn't it? And what had Win said? Ten minutes. Probably down to six or maybe seven by now.

Should I wait? Could I?

I ducked down and moved closer to the houses. Hit my speed dial. Win said, "Five minutes." I hung up.

The blonde was in the house now. I didn't know who else was there or what the situation was. Five minutes. I could wait five minutes. They'd be the longest of my life, but I could do it, needed to do it, had to stay disciplined in the face of pure panic. I stayed low, crouched under a window, listened. Nothing. No screams. No power drill. I didn't know if that was a relief—or if I had gotten there too late.

I kept down, back against the brick. The window was above my head. I tried to picture the layout of the house. This window looked in on the living room. Okay, so? So nothing. I waited. The gun felt good in my hand, the weight a comfort. Guns of any size are substance. I was a good shot, not a great one. You had to practice a lot to be great. But I knew to aim at the center of the chest and I could usually come close enough.

So now what?

Stay calm. Wait for Win. He was good at this stuff.

"Payback is a bitch—don't you think?"

The refined accent, the calm tone. I flashed back to Mario and those damn holes, the unfathomable pain, while hearing that damn refined accent. How long had that gone on? How long had Mario had to endure the pain? Did he welcome death in the end or fight it?

Sirens crackled in the distance. The police heading to Mario's maybe.

I don't wear a watch anymore, so I checked the time on my cell phone. If Win was accurate—and he usually was—he was still three minutes from arriving. What to do here?

My gun.

I wondered if the blonde had seen it. I doubted it. As Win has pointed out, firearms are rare in the UK. Whoever was inside that house would probably figure I would be unarmed. Hard as it was, I put the gun away, back in my leg holster.

Three minutes.

My cell phone rang. The caller ID showed me that it was Terese's phone again. I said a tentative hello.

"We know you are outside," the refined voice said. "You have ten seconds to walk through that door with your hands up or I shoot one of these fine ladies in the head. One, two . . ."

"I'm coming."

"Three, four . . ."

No choice. I jumped up from my crouch and sprinted to the door.

"Five, six, seven . . ."

"Don't hurt them. I'm almost there."

Don't hurt them. Duh. But what else was there to say?

I turned the knob. It was unlocked. The door opened. I stepped inside.

The refined voice: "I said, hands up."

I put my hands high in the air. The man in the mug shot stood across the room from me. He had white tape across his face. His eyes were the black you get from a broken nose. I would have taken some satisfaction in that, but for one thing: He had a gun in his hand. For another, Terese and Karen were on their knees in front of him, hands behind their backs, facing me. They both looked relatively unharmed.

I glanced left and right. Two more men, both with guns trained on my head.

No sign of the blond girl.

I stayed perfectly still, hands up, trying to look as nonthreatening as possible. Win had to be close by now. Another minute or two. I needed to stall. I made eye contact with the man I'd fought with in Paris. I kept my tone even, controlled.

"Look, let's talk, okay? There's no reason—"

He put the gun against the back of Karen Tower's head, smiled at me, and pulled the trigger.

There was a deafening sound, a small spurt of red, absolute stillness; a moment of suspended animation followed, and then Karen's body dropped to the floor like a marionette with her strings cut. Terese screamed. Maybe I screamed too.

The man began to swing the gun toward Terese.

OhmyGodohmyGodohmyGod . . .

"No!"

Instinct took over and it was a mantra: Save Terese. I dived, literally as though I were in a pool, toward them. Bullets from the two guys on my left and right rang out, but they had made the common mistake of covering me by pointing their guns at my head. Their aim ended up being too high. Out of the corner of my eye, I saw Terese rolling away as he started training the gun on her.

Had to move faster.

I was trying to do several things at once: Keep low, avoid bullets, get across the room, pull the gun from my leg holster, and kill the bastard. I was closing the gap. Zigzagging would have been the preferred route here, but there was no time. The mantra kept ringing in my head: Save Terese. I had to get to him before he pulled the trigger again.

I screamed louder, not out of fear or pain, but to draw his attention, to make him at least hesitate or turn toward me—anything to divert, for even a half second, his goal of shooting Terese.

I was getting closer.

Time was doing the in-'n'-out thing. Probably a second, maybe two, had passed since Karen's execution. That was all. And now, with no time to think or plan, I was nearly on him.

But I was going to be too late. I could see that now. I reached out, as if I could cover the distance that way. I couldn't. I was still too far away.

He pulled the trigger again.

Another shot rang out. Terese went down.

My scream turned into a guttural cry of anguish. A hand reached into my chest and crushed my heart. I kept moving forward, even as he turned the gun toward me. Fear was gone—I moved on pure, instinctive hatred. The gun was almost pointed in my direction, almost on me, when I ducked low and slammed into his waist. He fired off another bullet, but it went wild.

I drove him hard toward the wall, sweeping him off his feet. He swung the butt of the gun down on my back. In some other world at some other time, it might have hurt, but right now, the blow had all the impact of a mosquito bite. I was beyond pain, beyond caring. We landed hard. I let him go, scooting away, trying to get a little distance so I could go for the weapon in my ankle holster.

That was a mistake.

I was so consumed with pulling out my gun, with killing the bastard, that I nearly forgot that there were two other armed adversaries in the room. The man who'd been on my right was running toward me, his weapon raised. I jumped back as he fired, but again it was too late.

The bullet hit me.

Hot pain. I could actually feel the hot metal rip into my body, stealing my breath, knocking me flat on my back. The man aimed again, but another shot rang out, striking the man in the neck with such force it nearly decapitated him. I looked past the fallen corpse, but I already knew.

Win had arrived.

The other man, the guy who'd been on my left, turned just in time to see Win spin and pull the trigger again. The big bullet hit him squarely in the face, and his head exploded. I looked over at Terese. She wasn't moving. The man in the mug shot—the man who had shot her—started running away, slipping into the drawing room. I heard more gunfire. I heard someone yell to freeze and stop. I ignored them. Somehow I crawled toward the drawing room. Blood poured off me. I couldn't tell exactly, but I figured the bullet had landed somewhere near my stomach.

I clawed through the opening, not even checking to see if it was safe. *Move forward,* I thought. *Grab the bastard and kill him.* He was by the window. I was in pain and maybe delirious, but I reached out and grabbed his leg. He tried to kick me off, but there was no way. I dragged him down to the ground.

We wrestled, but he was no match for my rage. I gouged his eye with my thumb, weakening him. I grabbed his windpipe and started to squeeze. He started to flail, hitting me in the face and neck. I held on.

"Freeze! Drop it!"

Voices in the distance. Commotion. I wasn't even sure they were real. More like something from the wind. Might be something I was hallucinating. The accent sounded American. Familiar even.

I still squeezed the windpipe.

"I said, freeze! Now! Let him go!"

Surrounded. Six, eight men, maybe more. Most with guns aimed at me.

My eyes met the killer's. There was something mocking in them. I felt my hold slacken. I don't know if it was the command to let him go or if the bullet wound was ebbing away my strength. My hand dropped off him. The killer coughed and sputtered and then he tried to take advantage.

He brought up his gun.

Just as I hoped.

I had pulled the small gun from my leg holster. I grabbed his wrist with my left hand.

The familiar American voice: "Don't!"

But I didn't really care if they shot me. Still holding his wrist, I took my gun, pushed it under his chin, and fired. I felt something wet and sticky hit my face. Then I dropped the gun and fell on top of his still body.

Men, a lot of them from the feel of it, tackled me. Now that I had done what I had to, my power and will to live drained away. I let them turn me and cuff me and do whatever, but there was no need for restraints. The fight was out of me. They flipped me onto my back. I swiveled my head and looked at Terese's still body. I felt a pain as enormous as any I had ever known consume me.

Her eyes were closed and soon, very soon, so were mine.

PART TWO

22

THIRSTY.

Sand in the throat. Eyes won't open. Or maybe they will.

Total darkness.

Engine roar. I sense someone standing over me.

"Terese . . ."

I think I say it out loud, but I'm not sure.

NEXT snippet of memory: voices.

They seem very far away. I don't understand any of the words. Sounds, that's all. Something angry. It gets closer. Louder. In my ear now.

My eyes open. I see white.

The voice keeps repeating the same thing over and over.

Sounds like "Al-sabr wal-sayf."

I don't understand. Gibberish maybe. Or a foreign language. I don't know.

"Al-sabr wal-sayf."

Someone is shouting in my ear. My eyes squeeze shut. I want it to stop.

"Al-sabr wal-sayf."

The voice is angry, incessant. I think I say I'm sorry.

"He doesn't understand," someone says.

Silence.

PAIN in my side.

"Terese . . . ," I say again.

No reply.

Where am I?

I hear a voice again, but I can't understand what it's saying.

Feel alone, isolated. I'm lying down. I think I'm shaking.

"LET me explain the situation to you."

I still can't move. I try to open my mouth, but I can't. Open my eyes. Blurry. Feels like my entire head is wrapped in thick, sticky cobwebs. I try to scrape the cobwebs away. They stay.

"You used to work for the government, didn't you?"

Is the voice talking to me? I nod but stay very still.

"Then you know places like this exist. That they've always existed. You heard the rumors, at the very least."

I never believed the rumors. Maybe after 9/11. But not before. I think I say no but that might just be in my head.

"Nobody knows where you are. Nobody will find you. We can keep you forever. We can kill you anytime we please. Or we can let you go."

Fingers around my biceps. More fingers around my wrist. Struggle but pointless. Feel a pinch in my arm. I can't move. Can't stop it. I remember when I was six my dad took me to the Kiwanis carnival on Northfield Avenue. Cheesy rides and attractions. The Madhouse. That was the name of one. Mirrors and giant clown heads and a horrible laugh track. Went in alone. I was a big boy, after all. Got lost and turned around and couldn't find my way out. One of those clown heads jumped out at me. I started to cry. I spun around. Another giant clown head was right there, mocking me.

That was what this felt like.

I cried and spun around again. I called for my dad. He shouted my name, ran inside, knocked through a thin wall, found me, and made it okay.

Dad, I think. *Dad will find me. Any second now.*

But no one comes.

"HOW do you know Rick Collins?"

I tell the truth. Again. So exhausted.

"And how do you know Mohammad Matar?"

"I don't know who that is."

"You tried to kill him in Paris. Then you killed him before we grabbed you in London. Who sent you to kill him?"

"Nobody. He attacked me."

I explain. Then something horrible happens to me, but I don't know what it is.

I am walking. My hands are tied behind my back. Can't see much, just small dots of light. A hand on either shoulder. They roughly pull me down.

Lying on my back.

Legs bound together. Belt tightened across my chest. Body lassoed to hard surface.

Can't move at all.

Suddenly the dots of light are gone. I think I scream. I may be upside down. I'm not sure.

A giant wet hand covers my face. Grabs my nose. Covers my mouth.

Can't breathe. Try to flail. Arms tied. Legs bound.

Can't move. Someone is holding my head. Can't even turn it. The hand presses down harder on my face. No air.

Panic. I'm being smothered.

Try to inhale. My mouth opens. Inhale. Must inhale. Can't. Water fills my throat and runs up my nose.

I choke. Lungs burning. About to burst. Muscles screaming. Must move. Can't. No escape.

No air.

Dying.

I hear someone weeping and realize the sound is coming from me.

Sudden searing pain.

My back arches. My eyes bulge. I scream, "Oh, God, please . . ."

The voice is my own, but I don't recognize it. So weak. I am so damn weak.

"WE have some questions for you."

"Please. I answered them."

"We have more."

"And then I can go?"

The voice is pleading.

"It's pretty much your only hope."

I startle awake to a bright light in my face.

I blink. Heart racing. Can't catch my breath. Don't know where I am. My mind travels back. What is the last thing I remember? Putting the gun under the bastard's chin and pulling the trigger.

Something else is there, in the corner of my brain, just out of reach. A dream maybe. You know the feeling—you wake up and the nightmare is so damn vivid but even as you try to recall, you can feel the memory dissipating, like rising smoke. That is what is happening with me now. I try to hold on to the images, but they're fading away.

"Myron?"

The voice is calm, modulated. I am afraid of the voice. I cringe. I feel horrible shame, though I'm not sure why.

My voice sounds meek in my own ears. "Yes?"

"You'll forget most of this anyway. That's for the best. No one will believe you—and even if they do, we can't be found. You don't know where we are. You don't know what we look like. And remember: We can do this again. We can grab you anytime we want. And not just you. Your family. Your mother and father down in Miami. Your brother in South America. Do you understand?"

"Yes."

"Just let it go. You'll be fine if you do, okay?"

I nod. My eyes roll back. I slip back into the dark.

23

I woke up scared.

That wasn't like me. My heart raced. Panic seized my chest, making it hard to breathe. All of this before I even opened my eyes.

When my eyes finally did blink open—when I looked across the room—I felt the heart rate slow and the panic ease. Esperanza sat in a chair, concentrating on her iPhone. Her fingers danced across the letters; she was working no doubt with one of our clients. I like our business, but she loves it.

I watched her for a moment because the familiar sight was so damn comforting. Esperanza wore a white blouse under her gray business suit, hoop earrings, her blue-black hair tucked behind her ear. The window shade behind her was open. I could see that it was night.

"What client are you dealing with?" I asked.

Her eyes widened at the sound of my voice. She dropped the iPhone onto the table and rushed to my side. "Oh, my God, Myron. Oh, my God . . ."

"What? Am I dying?"

"No, why?"

"The way you rushed over. You usually move much slower."

She started crying and kissed my cheek. Esperanza never cried.

"Oh, I must be dying."

"Don't be a jackass," she said, wiping the tears off her cheek. She hugged me. "Wait, no. Be a jackass. Be your wonderful jackass self."

I looked over her shoulder. I was in your basic standard-issue hospital room. "How long have you been sitting there?" I asked.

"Not long," Esperanza said, still holding me. "What do you remember?"

I thought about it. Karen and Terese being shot. The guy who killed them. Me killing him. I swallowed and braced myself. "How is Terese?"

Esperanza stood upright and released me. "I don't know."

Not the answer I was expecting. "How can you not know?"

"It's a little hard to explain. What's the last thing you remember?"

I concentrated. "My last clear memory," I said, "was

killing the bastard who shot Terese and Karen. Then a bunch of guys jumped on me."

She nodded.

"I was shot too, wasn't I?"

"Yes."

That explained the hospital.

Esperanza leaned back into my ear and whispered, "Okay, listen to me for a second. If that door opens, if a nurse comes in or anything, don't say anything in front of her. Do you understand?"

"No."

"Win's orders. Just do it, okay?"

"Okay." Then I said, "You flew to London to be with me?"

"No."

"What do you mean, no?"

"Trust me, okay? Just take your time. What else do you remember?"

"Nothing."

"Nothing between the time you got shot and now?"

"Where is Terese?"

"I already told you. I don't know."

"That makes no sense. How can you not know?"

"It's a long story."

"How about sharing it with me?"

Esperanza looked at me with her green eyes. I didn't like what I saw there.

I tried to sit up. "How long have I been unconscious?"

"I don't know that either."

"Again I repeat: How can you not know?"

"For one thing, you're not in London."

That made me pause. I looked around the hospital room as if that would give me the answer. It did. My blanket had a logo on it and the words: NEW YORK–PRESBYTERIAN MEDICAL CENTER.

This couldn't be.

"I'm in Manhattan?"

"Yes."

"I was flown back?"

She said nothing.

"Esperanza?"

"I don't know."

"Well, how long have I been in this hospital?"

"A few hours maybe, but I can't be sure."

"You're not making any sense."

"I don't quite get it either, okay? Two hours ago, I got a call that you were here."

My brain felt fuzzy—and her explanations weren't helping. "Two hours ago?"

"Yes."

"And before that?"

"Before that call," Esperanza said, "we didn't have any idea where you were."

"When you say 'we'—"

"Me, Win, your parents—"

"My parents?"

"Don't worry. We lied to them. Told them you were in an area of Africa with spotty phone service."

"None of you knew where I was?"

"That's right."

"For how long?" I asked.

She just looked at me.

"For how long, Esperanza?"

"Sixteen days."

I just lay there. Sixteen days. I had been out for sixteen days. When I tried to remember, my heart started racing. I felt panic.

"Just let it go . . ."

"Myron?"

"I remember getting arrested."

"Okay."

"Are you telling me that was sixteen days ago?"

"Yes."

"You contacted the British police?"

"They didn't know where you were either."

I had a million questions, but the door opened, interrupting us. Esperanza shot me a warning glance. I stayed silent. A nurse walked in, saying, "Well, well, you're awake."

Before the door could swing closed, someone else pushed it open.

My dad.

Something akin to relief washed over me at the sight of this admittedly old man. He was out of breath, no doubt from running to see his son. Mom came in behind him. My mother has this way of always rushing at me, even during the most routine visit, as if I were a recently released POW. She did it again this time, knocking the nurse out of the way. I used to roll my eyes when she did it, though I would be secretly pleased. I didn't roll my eyes this time.

"I'm okay, Mom. Really."

My father hung back for a moment, as was his way. His eyes were wet and red. I looked at his face. He knew. He hadn't bought the story about Africa with no phone service. He had probably helped peddle it to Mom. But he knew.

"You're so skinny," Mom said. "Didn't they feed you anything there?"

"Leave him alone," Dad said. "He looks fine."

"He doesn't look fine. He looks skinny. And pale. Why are you in a hospital bed?"

"I told you," Dad said. "Didn't you hear me, Ellen? Food poisoning. He's going to be fine—some kind of dysentery."

"Why were you in Sierra Madre, anyway?"

"Sierra Leone," Dad corrected.

"I thought it was Sierra Madre."

"You're thinking of the movie."

"I remember. With Humphrey Bogart and Katharine Hepburn."

"That was *The African Queen*."

"Ohhh," Mom said, now understanding the confusion.

Mom let go of me. Dad moved over, smoothed my hair off my forehead, kissed my cheek. The rough skin from his beard rubbed against me. The comforting smell of Old Spice lingered in the air.

"You okay?" he asked.

I nodded. He looked skeptical.

They both suddenly looked so old. That was how it was, wasn't it? When you don't see a child for even a little while, you marvel at how much they've grown. When you don't see an old person for even a little while, you marvel at how much they've aged. It happened every time. When did my robust parents cross that line? Mom had the shakes from Parkinson's. It was getting bad. Her mind, always a tad eccentric, was slipping somewhere more troubling. Dad was in relatively good health, a few minor heart scares, but they both looked so damn old.

"Your mother and father down in Miami . . ."

My chest started to hitch. I was having trouble breathing again.

Dad said, "Myron?"

"I'm fine."

The nurse pushed through now. My parents stepped to the side. She put a thermometer in my mouth, started checking my pulse. "It's after visiting hours," she said. "You'll all have to go now."

I didn't want them to go. I didn't want to be alone. Terror gripped me, and I felt great shame. I forced up a smile as she took out the thermometer and said with a little too much cheer, "Get some sleep, okay? I'll see you all in the morning."

I met my father's eye. Still skeptical. He whispered something to Esperanza. She nodded and escorted my mother from the room. My mother and Esperanza left. The nurse turned back at the door.

"Sir," she said to my father, "you'll have to leave."

"I want to be alone with my son for a minute."

She hesitated. Then: "You have two minutes."

We were alone now.

"What happened to you?" Dad asked.

"I don't know," I said.

He nodded. He pulled the chair close to the bed and held my hand.

"You didn't believe that I was in Africa?" I asked.

"No."

"And Mom?"

"I would tell her you called when she was out."

"She bought that?"

He shrugged. "I never lied to her before, so, yes, she bought it. Your mother isn't as sharp as she once was."

I said nothing. The nurse came in. "You have to leave now."

"No," my father said.

"Please don't make me call security."

I could feel the panic start up in my chest. "It's okay, Dad. I'm fine. Get some sleep."

He looked at me for a moment and turned to the nurse. "What's your name, sweetheart?"

"Regina."

"Regina what?"

"Regina Monte."

"My name is Al, Regina. Al Bolitar. Do you have any children?"

"Two daughters."

"This is my son, Regina. You can call security if you want. But I'm not leaving my son alone."

I wanted to protest, but then again I didn't. The nurse turned and left. She didn't call security. My father stayed all night in that chair next to my bed. He refilled my water cup and adjusted my blanket. When I cried out in my sleep, he shushed me and stroked my forehead and told me that everything would be okay—and for a few seconds, I believed him.

24

WIN called first thing in the morning.

"Go to work," Win said. "Ask no questions."

Then he hung up. Sometimes Win really pisses me off.

My father ran down to a bagel store across the street because the hospital breakfast resembled something monkeys fling at you in a zoo. The doctor stopped by while he was gone and gave me a clean bill of health. Yes, I had indeed been shot. The bullet had passed through my right side, above the hip. But it had been properly treated.

"Would it have required a sixteen-day hospital stay?" I asked.

The doctor looked at me funny, at the fact that I had just sort of shown up at the hospital unconscious, a gunshot-wound victim, now mumbling about sixteen days—and I'm sure he was sizing me up for a psych visit.

"Hypothetically speaking," I quickly added, remembering Win's warning. Then I stopped asking questions and started nodding a lot.

Dad stayed with me through checkout. Esperanza had left my suit in the closet. I put it on and felt physically pretty good. I wanted to hire a taxi, but Dad insisted on driving. He used to be a great driver. In my childhood he would have that easy way about him on the road, whistling softly with the radio, steering with his wrists. Now the radio stayed off. He squinted at the road and hit the brake a lot more.

When we got to the Lock-Horne Building on Park Avenue—again Win's full name is Windsor *Horne Lock-*wood III, so you do the math—Dad said, "You want me to just drop you off?"

Sometimes my father leaves me awestruck. Fatherhood is about balance, but how can one man do it so well, so effortlessly? Throughout my life he pushed me to excel without ever crossing the line. He reveled in my accomplishments yet never made them seem to be all that important. He loved without condition, yet he still made me want to please him. He knew, like now, when to be there, and when it was time to back off.

"I'll be okay."

He nodded. I kissed the rough skin on his cheek again, noticing the sag now, and got out of the car. The elevator opens up directly into my office. Big Cyndi was at her desk, wearing something that looked like it'd been ripped off Bette Davis after shooting the climactic beach scene in *Whatever Happened to Baby Jane?* There were pigtails in her hair. Big Cyndi is, well, big—as I said before, north of six five and three hundred pounds—everywhere. She has big hands and big feet and a big head. The furniture around her always looks like Toys "R" Us specials built for toddlers, an almost Alice-in-Wonderland effect, where the room and all its belongings seem to shrink around her.

She rose when she saw me, nearly toppling her own desk, and exclaimed, "Mr. Bolitar!"

"Hey, Big Cyndi."

She gets mad when I call her "Cyndi" or, uh, "Big." She insists on formalities. I am Mr. Bolitar. She is Big Cyndi, which, by the way, is her real name. She had it legally changed more than a decade ago.

Big Cyndi crossed the room with an agility that belied the bulk. She wrapped me in an embrace that made me feel as if I'd been mummified in wet attic insulation. In a good way.

"Oh, Mr. Bolitar!"

She started sniffling, a sound that brought images of moose mating on the Discovery Channel.

"I'm fine, Big Cyndi."

"But someone shot you!"

Her voice changed depending on her mood. When she first worked here, Big Cyndi didn't talk, preferring to growl. Clients complained, but not to her face and usually anonymously. Right now Big Cyndi's pitch was high and little-girlish, which frankly was a hell of a lot scarier than any growl.

"I shot him worse," I said.

She let go of me and giggled, covering her mouth with a hand the approximate size of a truck tire. The giggling echoed through the room, and all over the tristate area, small children were reaching up and grabbing their mommies' hands.

Esperanza came to the door. Back in the day, Esperanza and Big Cyndi had been tag-team wrestling partners for FLOW, the Fabulous Ladies of Wrestling. The federation had originally wanted to call themselves "Beautiful" instead of "Fabulous" but the network balked at the ensuing acronym.

Esperanza, with her dark skin and looks that could best be described—as they often were by the panting wrestling announcers—as "succulent," played Little Pocahontas, the lithe beauty who was winning on skill before the bad guys would cheat and take advantage of her. Big Cyndi was her partner, Big Chief Mama, who rescued her so that they could, together and with the roar of the crowd, vanquish the scantily clad and implant-enhanced evildoers.

Entertaining stuff.

"We got work," Esperanza said, "and lots of it."

Our space was fairly small. We had this foyer and two offices, one for me, one for Esperanza. Esperanza had started here as my assistant or secretary or whatever the politically correct term for Girl Friday is. She'd gone to law school at night and taken over as a full partner right around the time I freaked out and ran away with Terese to that island.

"What did you tell the clients?" I asked.

"You were in a car accident overseas."

I nodded. We headed into her office. The business was a bit in shambles after my most recent disappearance. There were calls to be made. I made them. We kept most of the clients, almost all, but there were a few who did not like the fact that they could not reach their agent for more than two weeks. I understood. This is a personal business. It involves a lot of hand-holding and ego stroking. Every client needs to feel as if he is the only one—part of the illusion. When you're not there, even if the reasons are justified, the illusion vanishes.

I wanted to ask about Terese and Win and a million things, but I remembered the call from this morning. I worked. I just worked and I confess that it was therapeutic. I felt jittery and anxious for reasons I can't quite explain. I even bit my nails—something I hadn't done since I was in the fourth grade—and searched my body for scabs I could pick. Work somehow helped.

When I had a break, I did some Web searches for "Terese Collins" and "Rick Collins" and "Karen Tower." First I did all three names. Nothing came up. Then I tried Terese alone. Very little, all of it old from her days at CNN. Someone still kept a Web site about "Terese the AnchorBabe," complete with images, mostly head shots and video grabs from news shows, but it hadn't been updated in three years.

Then I tried Google Newsing Rick and Karen.

I'd expected to find little, maybe an obituary, but that wasn't the case. There was plenty, albeit most of it from papers in the United Kingdom. The news somehow shocked me and yet it all made bizarre sense:

REPORTER AND WIFE MURDERED
BY TERRORISTS
Cell Broken Up, Killed in Wild Shoot-out

I started reading. Esperanza came to my door. "Myron?"

I held up a finger asking for a moment.

She came around my desk and saw what I was doing. She sighed and sat.

"You knew about this?" I asked.

"Of course."

According to the articles, "special forces working on international terrorism" engaged and "eliminated" legendary terrorist Mohammad Matar, aka "Dr. Death." Mohammad Matar had been born in Egypt but raised in the finest schools in Europe, including Spain (thus the name, combining the Islamic first name with a last name that meant "death" in Spanish), and was indeed a medical doctor who'd done his training in the United States. The special forces also killed at least three other men in his cell—two in London, one in Paris.

There was a photograph of Matar. It was the same mug shot that Berleand had sent me. I looked at the man I had, to use the journalistic term, eliminated.

The articles further noted that news producer Rick

Collins had gotten close to the cell, trying to infiltrate and expose it, when his identity was breached. Matar and his "henchmen" murdered Collins in Paris. Matar slipped through a French dragnet (though apparently one of his men was killed in it), made his way to London and tried to clean up all evidence of his cell and his "fiendish terrorist plot" by killing Rick Collins's longtime production partner, Mario Contuzzi, and Collins's wife, Karen Tower. It was there, in the home Collins and Tower shared, that Mohammad Matar and two members of his cell had met their demise.

I looked up at Esperanza. "Terrorists?"

She nodded.

"So that explains why Interpol freaked out when we showed them the picture."

"Yes."

"So where's Terese?"

"No one knows."

I sat back, tried to process that. "It says government agents killed the terrorists."

"Yep."

"Except they didn't."

"True. You did."

"And Win."

"Right."

"But they left our names out of it."

"Yes."

I thought about the sixteen days, about Terese, about the blood tests, about the blond girl. "What the hell is going on?"

"Don't know about the details," she said. "Didn't really care."

"Why not?"

Esperanza shook her head. "You can be such a dope sometimes."

I waited.

"You were shot. Win saw that. And for more than two weeks we had absolutely no idea where you were—if you were alive or dead or anything."

I couldn't help it. I grinned.

"Stop grinning like an idiot."

"You were worried about me."

"I was worried about my business interest."

"You like me."

"You're a pain in the ass."

"I still don't get it," I said, and the grin slid off my face. "How can I not remember where I was?"

"Just let it go. . . ."

My hands started shaking. I looked down at them, tried to make them stop. They wouldn't. Esperanza was looking too.

"You tell me," she said. "What do you remember?"

My leg started twitching. I felt something catch in my chest. Panic began to set in.

"You okay?"

"I could use some water," I said.

She hurried out and came back with a cup. I drank it slowly, almost afraid I would choke. I looked at my hands. The quake. I couldn't make it stop. What the hell was wrong with me?

"Myron?"

"I'm fine," I said. "So what now?"

"We have clients who need our help."

I looked at her.

She sighed. "We thought you might need time."

"For?"

"To recover."

"From what? I'm fine."

"Yeah, you look great. That shake is a terrific addition. And don't get me started on your new facial tic. *Très* sexy."

"I don't need time, Esperanza."

"Yeah, you do."

"Terese is missing."

"Or dead."

"You trying to shock me?"

She shrugged.

"And if she's dead, I still need to find her daughter."

"Not in your condition."

"Yeah, Esperanza, in my condition."

She said nothing.

"What is it?"

"I don't think you're ready."

"Not your call."

She thought about that. "I guess not."

"So?"

"So I have some stuff on the doctor Collins saw about Huntington's disease and that angel charity."

"Like?"

"It can wait. If you're really serious about this, if

you're really ready, you need to call this number on this phone."

She handed me a cell phone and left the room, closing the door behind her. I stared at the phone number. Unfamiliar, but I wouldn't have expected anything else. I put in the digits and pressed SEND.

Two rings later, I heard a familiar voice say, "Welcome back from the dead, my friend. Let's meet in person at a secret locale. We have much to discuss, I'm afraid."

It was Berleand.

25

BERLEAND'S "secret locale" was an address in the Bronx.

The street was a pit, the location a dive. I checked the address again, but there was no mistake. It was a strip joint called, according to the sign, UPSCALE PLEASURES, though to my eye the establishment appeared to be neither. A smaller sign written in neon script noted that it was a CLASSY GENTLEMEN'S LOUNGE. The term "classy" here is not so much an oxymoron as an irrelevance. "Classy strip club" is a bit like saying "good toupee." It might be good and it might be bad—but it's still a toupee.

The room was dark and windowless so that noontime, which was when I arrived, looked the same as midnight.

A large black man with a shaved head asked, "May I help you?"

"I'm looking for a Frenchman in his midfifties."

He folded his arms across his chest. "That's Tuesdays," he said.

"No, I mean—"

"I know what you mean." He stifled the smile and pointed a beefy arm tattooed with a green *D* toward the dance floor. I expected Berleand to be in a quiet shadowy corner, but no, there he was by the stage, front and center, eyes up and focused on the, uh, talent.

"Is that your Frenchman over there?"

"It is."

The bouncer turned back to me. His name tag said ANTHONY. I shrugged. He looked through me.

"Anything else I can do for you?" he asked.

"You can tell me I don't look like the type of guy who'd come to a place like this, especially during the daytime."

Anthony grinned. "You know what type of guy doesn't come to a place like this, especially during the daytime?"

I waited.

"Blind guys."

He walked away. I made my way toward Berleand and the bar. The sound track blasted Beyoncé singing to her boyfriend that he must not know about her, that she could have another man in a minute, that he was replaceable. This indignation was kind of silly. You're Beyoncé, for crying out loud. You're gorgeous, you're famous, you're rich, and you're buying your boyfriend expensive cars and clothes. Gee, yeah, it will be impossible for you to land another guy. Girl power.

The topless dancer onstage had moves that I would describe as "languid" if she dialed it up several notches. Her bored expression made me think she was watching C-SPAN 2, the pole not so much a tool of the dance trade as something that kept her upright. I don't want to sound prudish, but I don't quite get the appeal of topless places. They simply don't do it for me. It isn't that the women are unappealing—some are; some aren't. I discussed this once with Win, always a mistake when it comes to anything involving the opposite sex, and concluded that I can't quite buy into the fantasy. It may be a weakness in my character but I need to believe that the lady is really, truly into me. Win couldn't care less, of course. I do get the merely physical, but my ego doesn't like sexual encounters to be mixed with commerce, resentment, and class warfare.

Label me old-fashioned.

Berleand wore his shiny gray Members Only jacket. He kept pushing his dorky glasses up and smiling at the bored dancer. I sat next to him. He turned, did his hand-rub-wash thing, and studied me for a moment.

"You look terrible," he said.

"Yeah," I said, "but you look great. New moisturizer?"

He tossed back a few beer nuts.

"So this is your secret locale?"

He shrugged.

"Why here?" Then, thinking about it: "Wait. I get it. Because it's so off the radar, right?"

"That," Berleand agreed, "and I like looking at naked women."

He turned back to the dancer. I'd already had enough.

"Is Terese alive?" I asked.

"I don't know."

We sat there. I started chewing a fingernail.

"You warned me," I said. "You said it was more than I could handle."

He watched the dancer.

"I should have listened."

"It wouldn't have mattered. They would have killed Karen Tower and Mario Contuzzi, anyway."

"But not Terese."

"You, at least, put a stop to it. It was their screwup, not yours."

"Whose screwup?"

"Well, mine in part." Berleand took off the too-big glasses and rubbed his face. "We go by many names. Homeland Security is probably the most well-known. As you may have surmised, I am a French liaison working for what your government termed the 'war on terror.' The British equivalent should have been watching closer."

The busty waitress came over wearing a neckline that plunged to somewhere just above her knees. "Want some champagne?"

"That's not champagne," Berleand said to her.

"Huh?"

"It's from California."

"So?"

"Champagne can only be French. You see, Champagne is a place, not merely a beverage. That bottle in your hand is what those who lack taste buds dub 'sparkling wine.'"

She rolled her eyes. "Want some sparkling wine?"

"My dear, that stuff shouldn't be used as a gargle for a dog." He held up his empty glass. "Please get me another tremendously watered-down whiskey." He turned to me. "Myron?"

I didn't think they would have Yoo-hoo here. "Diet Coke." When she sauntered away, I said, "So what's going on?"

"As far as my people go, the case is over. Rick Collins stumbled across a terrorist plot. He was murdered in Paris by the terrorists. They killed two more people connected with Collins in London—before being killed themselves. By you, no less."

"I didn't see my name in any of the papers."

"Were you looking for credit?"

"Hardly. But I do wonder why they kept my name out."

"Think about it."

The waitress came back. "Korbel calls it champagne, Mr. Smarty Pants. And they're from California."

"Korbel should call it septic-tank droppings. That would be closer to the truth."

She put our drinks down and went away.

"Government forces aren't trying to hog the credit," he said. "There are two reasons to leave your name out. First off, your safety. From what I understand, Mohammad Matar made it personal with you. You took out one of his men in Paris. He wanted to make you watch Karen Tower and Terese Collins die—before killing you. If it somehow gets out that you killed Dr. Death, there are people who will seek retribution on you and your family." Berleand smiled at the dancer and held his palm out toward me. "Do you have any singles?"

I dug into my wallet. "And the second reason?"

"If you weren't there—if you weren't at the scene of the killings in London—then the government doesn't have to explain where you've been for the past two-plus weeks."

The antsy feeling came back. I shook my leg, looked around, wanted to get up. Berleand just watched me.

I said, "Do you know where I've been?"

"I have an idea, yes. So do you."

I shook my head. "I don't."

"You have absolutely no memory of the past two weeks?"

I said nothing. My chest tightened. I found it hard to catch my breath. I grabbed my Diet Coke and started taking little sips.

"You're shaking," he said.

"So?"

"Last night. Did you have bad dreams? Nightmares?"

"Of course. I was in a hospital. Why?"

"Do you know what twilight sleep is?"

I thought about it. "Doesn't it have something to do with pregnancy?"

"Childbirth, actually. It was quite popular in the fifties and sixties. The theory was, why should a mother have to suffer through the horrible pain of childbirth? So they would give the mother a combination of morphine and scopolamine. In some cases it would knock the mother out. Other times—the end goal—the morphine would lessen the pain while the combination would make it so she didn't remember. Medical amnesia—or twilight sleep. The practice was stopped because, one, the babies would often come out in something of a drug stupor, and two, there was the whole experience-the-moment movement. I don't get that second one exactly, but I'm not a woman."

"Is there a point?"

"There is. That was way back in the fifties or sixties. More than half a century ago. Now we have other drugs and we've had lots of time to fiddle with them. Imagine the tool if we could perfect what they were able to do more than fifty years ago. You could theoretically hold someone for an extended length of time and they'd never remember it."

He waited. I wasn't that slow a study.

"And this is what happened to me?"

"I don't know what happened to you. You've heard of CIA black sites."

"Sure."

"Do you think they exist?"

"Places where the CIA takes prisoners and doesn't tell anyone? Sure, I guess."

"Guess? Don't be naive. Bush admitted we had some. But they didn't start with nine-eleven and they didn't end when Congress held a few hearings. Think about what you could do there if you simply put prisoners into extended twilight sleep. It made women forget the pain of childbirth—the worst pain there is. They could interrogate you for hours, get you to say and do whatever, and then you'd forget it."

My leg started jackhammering in place. "Pretty diabolical."

"Is it? Let's say you captured a terrorist. You know the old debate about if you know another bomb is about to go off, is it right to torture him to save lives? Well, here you wipe the slate clean. He doesn't remember. Does that make the act more ethical? You, my dear friend, were probably interrogated harshly, maybe tortured. You don't remember it. So did it happen?"

"Like a tree falling in the woods when nobody's around," I said.

"Precisely."

"You French and your philosophizing."

"We're about more than Sartre's little death."

"Too bad." I shifted in my seat. "I'm having trouble believing this."

"I'm not sure I believe it either. But think about it. Think about people who suddenly vanish and never reappear. Think about people who are productive and healthy and suddenly they are suicidal or homeless or mentally ill. Think about the people—people who always seemed fine and normal—who suddenly claim alien abductions or start suffering post-traumatic stress syndrome."

"Let it go. . . ."

Breathing was a struggle again. I felt my chest hitch and get caught.

"Can't be that simple," I said.

"It isn't. Like I said, think about people who suddenly become psychotic or the rational people who suddenly claim religious rapture or alien hallucinations. And again the moral question—is trauma okay, for the greater good, if it is immediately forgotten? The men who run these places aren't evildoers. They feel they are making it more ethical."

I lifted my hand to my face. Tears were running down my cheeks. I didn't know why.

"Look at it from their viewpoint. The man you killed in Paris, the one working with Mohammad Matar. The government thought he was about to turn and provide us with inside information. There is a lot of infighting with these groups. Why were you in the middle of it? You killed Matar—yes, in self-defense, but maybe, just maybe, you were sent to kill him. Do you see? It was reasonable to conclude that you knew something that could save lives."

"So"—I stopped—"they tortured me?"

He pushed the glasses back up his nose, said nothing.

"Wouldn't someone remember, if this was really going on?" I asked. "Wouldn't someone tell?"

"Tell what? You may start remembering. What are you going to do about it? You don't know where you were. You don't know who held you. And you're terrified because you know in your heart of hearts they can grab you again."

"Your mom and dad . . ."

"So you'll stay quiet because you have no choice. And maybe, just maybe, what they are doing is saving lives. Don't you ever wonder how we break up so many terrorist plots before they hatch?"

"By torturing people and making them forget?"

Berleand gave me an elaborate shoulder shrug.

"If this is so effective," I said, "why didn't they use it on, say, Khalid Sheik Mohammad or some of the other al Qaeda terrorists?"

"Who says they haven't? To date, despite all the talk, the U.S. government has admitted waterboarding only three times and none since 2003. Do you really believe that to be the case? And in the case of Khalid, the world was watching. That was the mistake your government learned from Gitmo. You don't do it where everyone can see."

I took another sip of the Diet Coke. I looked around. The place wasn't packed, but it wasn't empty either. I saw business suits and guys in T-shirts and jeans. I saw white men, black men, Latino men. No blind men. Anthony the bouncer was right.

"So what now?" I said.

"The cell is broken up—and so too, most figure, is whatever plot they had planned."

"You don't think so."

"I don't."

"Why?"

"Because Rick Collins seemed to think he was onto something huge. Something long-term and far-reaching. The coalition I work with was upset I showed you the picture of Matar. Fair enough. That's why I'm on the outs."

"Sorry."

"Don't worry about it. They are searching for the next cell and plot. I'm not. I want to keep investigating this one. I have friends who want to help."

"What friends?"

"You met them."

I thought about it. "The Mossad."

He nodded. "Collins had enlisted their help too."

"That's why they were following me?"

"At first they thought maybe you murdered him. I assured them that you had not. Collins clearly knew something, but he wouldn't say exactly what. He played all sides against the middle—it's hard to say by the end where his loyalties lay. According to Mossad, he stopped contacting them and vanished a week before he died."

"Any idea why?"

"None." Berleand's eyes dropped to his glass. He stirred his drink with his finger.

"So why are you here now?" I asked.

"I flew over when they found you."

"Why?"

He took another deep swallow. "Enough questions for today."

"What are you talking about?"

He rose.

"Where are you going?"

"I explained to you the situation."

"Right, got it. We have work to do."

"We? You have no role in this anymore."

"You're kidding, right? I need to find Terese, for one."

He smiled down at me. "May I be blunt?"

"No, I'd rather you kept beating around the bush."

"I say that because I'm not good with delivering bad news."

"You seem pretty good at it so far."

"But not like this." Berleand kept his eyes off me and on the stage, but I don't think he was looking at the dancer anymore. "You Americans call it a reality check. So here it comes: Terese is either dead, in which case you can't help her. Or like you, she is being held at a black site, in which case you're helpless."

"I'm not helpless," I said in a voice that couldn't have sounded more feeble.

"Yes, my friend, you are. Even before I contacted him, Win knew to keep everyone quiet about your disappearance. Why? Because he knew that if anyone—your parents, whoever—made a stink, you'd maybe never come home. They'd stage a car accident and you'd be dead. Or a suicide. With Terese Collins, it is even easier. They could kill her and bury her and say she is back hiding in Angola. Or they can stage a suicide and say her daughter's death became too much for her. There is nothing you can do for her."

I sat back.

"You need to take care of yourself," he said.

"You want me to stay out of this?"

"Yes. And while I meant it when I said you're not to blame, I warned you once before. You chose not to listen."

He had a point.

"One last question," I said.

He waited.

"Why tell me all this?"

"About the black site?"

"Yes."

"Because despite what they think the medications will do, I don't believe you can totally forget. You need help, Myron. Please get it."

HERE was how I found out that maybe Berleand was right.

When I came back to the office, I called some clients. Esperanza ordered in sandwiches from Lenny's. We all ate at the desk. Esperanza talked about her baby boy, Hector. I realize that there are few bigger clichés than saying that motherhood changes a woman, but in the case of Esperanza, the changes seemed particularly startling and not all that appealing.

When we were done, I went back into my office and closed the door. I left the light off. I sat at my desk for a very long time. We all have our moments of contemplation and depression, but this was something different—something more profound and deeper and heavier. I could not move. My limbs felt heavy. I have gotten into my share of scrapes over the years, so I keep a weapon in my office.

A .38 Smith & Wesson to be more exact.

I opened the bottom drawer, took out the gun, and held it in my hand. Tears ran down my face.

I know how melodramatic this must sound. This image of poor, pitiful me, sitting alone at my desk, feeling depressed, a gun in my hand—it's laughable when you think about it. If there had been a photograph of Terese on my desk, I could have picked it up à la Mel Gibson in the first *Lethal Weapon* movie and jammed the barrel into my mouth.

I didn't do that.

But I had thoughts.

When the doorknob on my office door started to turn—no one knocks here, especially Esperanza—I moved fast, dropping the gun back into the drawer. Esperanza walked in and looked at me.

"What are you up to?" she asked.

"Nothing."

"What were you just doing?"

"Nothing."

She looked at me. "Were you pleasuring yourself under the desk?"

"Caught me."

"You still look terrible."

"That's the word on the street, yeah."

"I would tell you to go home, but you've missed enough days and I don't think wallowing around by yourself is going to do you much good."

"Agreed. Was there a reason you intruded?"

"Does there need to be?"

"Never been one in the past," I said. "By the way, what's up with Win?"

"That's why I intruded. He's on the Batphone." She gestured for me to turn around.

On the credenza behind my desk, there is a red phone that sits under what looks like a glass cake cover. If you saw the original *Batman* TV show, you know why. The red phone was blinking. Win. I picked it up and said, "Where are you?"

"Bangkok," Win said, his tone a tad too upbeat, "which is really an ironic name for this place when you stop and think about it."

"Since when?" I asked.

"Is that important?"

"Just seems like weird timing," I said. Then remembering: "What happened with that DNA sample we took from Miriam's grave?"

"Confiscated."

"By?"

"Men with shiny badges and shinier suits."

"How did they find out about it?"

Silence.

That wave of shame. Then I said, "Me?"

He did not bother replying. "Did you speak with Captain Berleand?"

"I did. What do you think?"

"I think," Win said, "that his hypothesis has merit."

"I don't get it. Why are you in Bangkok?"

"Where should I be?"

"Here, home, I don't know."

"That's probably not a very good idea right now."

I thought about it.

"Is this line safe?" I asked.

"Very. And your office was swept this morning."

"So what happened in London?"

"You saw me kill Tweedledee and Tweedledum?"

"Yes."

"You know the rest then. Officials crashed in. There was no way I could get you out, so I decided that it would be best for me to depart. I immediately headed out of the country. Why? Because I, as I just stated, believe Berleand's tale has merit. I thus did not think it would behoove either of us for me to be taken into custody too. Do you understand?"

"I do. So what's your plan now?"

"To stay hidden just a little while longer."

"Best way to make everyone safe is to get to the bottom of this."

"True dat, dawg," Win said.

I love it when he talks street.

"To that end, I'm putting out some feelers. I'm hoping to get someone to tell me the fate of Ms. Collins. To put it bluntly—and, yes, I know you have feelings for her—if Terese was killed, this is pretty much over for us. Our interests are gone."

"What about finding her daughter?"

"If Terese is dead, what would be the point?"

I thought about that. He made sense. I had wanted to

help Terese here. I had wanted to—man, it still sounded so crazy to think it—reunite her with her deceased daughter. What indeed would be the point, if Terese was dead?

I looked down and realized that again I was chewing on a fingernail.

"So what now?" I asked.

"Esperanza says you're a mess."

"You're going to patronize me too?"

Silence.

"Win?"

Win was the best at keeping his voice steady, but for maybe the second time since I've known him, I heard a crack. "The last sixteen days were difficult."

"I know, pal."

"I scorched the earth looking for you."

I said nothing.

"I did some things you would never approve of."

I waited.

"And I still couldn't find you."

I understood what he meant. Win has sources like no one else I know. Win has money and influence—and the truth is, he loves me. Not much scares him. But I knew that he'd had a tough sixteen days.

"I'm okay now," I said. "Come home when you think you can."

26

"HAVE another dumpling," Mom said to me.

"I've had enough, Mom. Thanks."

"One more. You're much too skinny. Try the pork one."

"I really don't like them."

"You what?" Mom gave me shocked. "But you used to love them at Fong's Garden."

"Mom, Fong's Garden closed when I was eight years old."

"I know. But still."

But still. The great Mom debate ender. One might understandably attribute her Fong's Garden recollection to an aging brain. One would be wrong. Mom had been making the same comment about my no longer liking dumplings since I was nine.

We sat in the kitchen of my childhood home in Livingston, New Jersey. Currently I split my nights between this abode and Win's lush apartment in the Dakota on West Seventy-second Street and Central Park West. When my parents moved down to Miami a few years back, I bought this house from them. You could rightly wonder about the psychology of buying the property—I had lived here with my parents well into my thirties and still, in fact, sleep in the basement bedroom I'd set up in high school—but in the end I rarely stayed here. Livingston is a town for families raising kids, not single men working in Manhattan. Win's place is far more conveniently located and only slightly smaller, square-footage-wise, than an average European principality.

But Mom and Dad were back in town, so here we were.

I came from the Blame Generation, where we all supposedly disliked our parents and found in their actions all the reasons why we ourselves are unhappy adults. I love my mother and father. I love being with them. I didn't live in that basement well into my adult years out of financial necessity. I did it because I liked it here, with them.

We finished dinner, threw away the take-out boxes, and rinsed off the utensils. We talked a little about my brother and sister. When Mom mentioned Brad's work in South America, I felt a small but sharp pang—something akin to déjà vu but far less pleasant. My stomach clenched. The nail-biting began again. My parents exchanged a glance.

Mom was tired. She gets that way a lot now. I kissed her cheek and watched her trudge up the stairs. She leaned on the banister. I flashed back to past days, of watching her take the steps with a hop and a bouncing ponytail, her hand nowhere near that damn banister. I looked back at Dad. He said nothing, but I think that he was flashing back too.

Dad and I moved to the den. He flipped on the TV. When I was little, Dad had a BarcaLounger recliner of hideous maroon. The vinyl-dressed-as-leather tore at the seams, and something metallic stuck out. My dad, not the handiest man in town, kept it together with duct tape. I know people criticize the hours Americans spend watching television, and with good reason, but some of my best memories were in this room, at night, him lounging on the duct-taped recliner, me on the couch. Anyone else remember that classic Saturday night prime-time CBS lineup? *All in the Family, M*A*S*H, The Mary Tyler Moore Show, The Bob Newhart Show,* and *The Carol Burnett Show.* My dad would laugh so hard at something Archie Bunker would say, and his laugh was so contagious, I would guffaw in kind, even though I didn't get a lot of the jokes.

Al Bolitar had worked hard in his factory in Newark. He wasn't a man who liked to play poker or hang with the boys or go to bars. Home was his solace. He liked relaxing with his family. He started very poor and was whip smart and probably had dreams beyond that Newark factory—great, grand dreams—but he never shared them with me. I was his son. You don't burden your child with stuff like that, not for anything.

On this night, he fell asleep during a *Seinfeld* repeat. I watched his chest rise and fall, his stubble coming in white. After a while I quietly rose, went down to the basement, climbed into bed, and stared at the ceiling.

My chest started hitching again. Panic swept through me. My eyes did not want to close. When they did, when I managed to start a nocturnal voyage of any kind, nightmares would jerk me back to consciousness. I could not recall the dreams, but the fear stayed behind. Sweat covered me. I sat in the dark, terrified, like a child.

At three in the morning, a bolt of memory flashed across my brain. Underwater. Not able to breathe. It lasted less than a second, this image, no more, and was quickly replaced with another, aural one.

"Al-sabr wal-sayf . . ."

My heart pounded as if it were trying to break free.

At three thirty a.m., I tiptoed up the stairs and sat in the kitchen. I tried to be as quiet as possible, but I knew. My father was the world's lightest sleeper. As a kid, I would try to sneak past his door late at night, just to make a quick bathroom trip, and he'd startle awake as though someone had dropped a Popsicle on his crotch. So now, as a full-grown middle-aged adult, a man who considered himself braver than most, I knew what would happen if I tiptoed into the kitchen.

"Myron?"

I turned as he made his way down the stairs. "I didn't mean to wake you, Dad."

"Oh, I was awake, anyway," he said. Dad wore boxers that had seen better days and a threadbare gray Duke

T-shirt two sizes too large. "You want me to make us some scrambled eggs?"

"Sure."

He did. We sat and talked about nothing. He tried not to look too concerned, which only made me feel even more cared for. More memories came back. My eyes would well up and then I would blink the tears away. Emotions swirled to the point where I couldn't really tell how I felt. I was in for a lot of bad nights. I could see that now. But I just knew one thing for certain: I couldn't stand still any longer.

When the morning came I called Esperanza and said, "Before I disappeared, you were looking up some stuff for me."

"Good morning to you too."

"Sorry."

"Don't worry about it. You were saying?"

"You were checking into Sam Collins's suicide and that opal code and the Save the Angels charity," I said.

"Right."

"I want to know what you found."

For a moment I expected an argument, but Esperanza must have heard something in my tone. "Okay, let's meet in an hour. I can show you what I got."

"SORRY I'm late," Esperanza said, "but Hector spit up on my blouse and I had to change it and then the baby-sitter started talking to me about a raise and Hector started clinging to me—"

"Don't worry about it," I said.

Esperanza's office still semireflected her colorful past. There were photographs of her in the skimpy suede costume of Little Pocahontas, the "Indian Princess" played by a Latina. Her Intercontinental Tag Team Championship Belt—a gaudy thing that if actually wrapped around Esperanza's waist would probably run from her rib cage to just above her knee, was framed behind her desk. The walls were painted periwinkle and some other shade of purple—I could never remember the name of it. The desk was ornate and serious oak, found in an antiques shop by Big Cyndi, and even though I was here when they delivered it, I still don't know how it fit through the doorway.

But now the dominant theme in this room, to quote the politician's handbook, was change. Photographs of Esperanza's infant son, Hector—poses so ordinary and obvious they bordered on the clichéd—lined the desk and credenza. There were the standard kid portraits— the swirling rainbow background à la Sears Portrait Studio—along with the on-Santa's-lap image and the colored-egg Easter Bunny. There was a photograph of Esperanza and her husband, Tom, holding a white-clad Hector at his baptism, and one with some Disney character I didn't recognize. The most prominent photograph featured Esperanza and Hector on some little kiddie ride, a miniature fire truck maybe, with Esperanza looking up at the camera with the widest, most dumb-struck smile I had ever seen on her.

Esperanza had been the freest of free spirits. She'd

been a promiscuous bisexual, proudly dating a man, then a woman, then another man, not caring what anyone thought. She had gone into wrestling because it was a fun buck, and when she got tired of that, she put herself through law school at night while working as my assistant during the day. This will sound awfully uncharitable, but motherhood had smothered some of that spirit. I had seen it before, of course, with other female friends. I get it a little. I didn't know about my own son until he was almost full grown, so I have never experienced that transforming moment when your baby is born and suddenly your entire world shrinks down to a six-pound, fifteen-ounce mass. That was what had happened with Esperanza. Was she happier now? I don't know. But our relationship had changed, as it was bound to, and because I am self-absorbed, I didn't like it.

"Here's the time line," Esperanza said. "Sam Collins, Rick's father, is diagnosed with Huntington's disease approximately four months ago. He commits suicide a few weeks later."

"Definitely a suicide?"

"According to the police report. Nothing suspicious."

"Okay, go on."

"After the suicide, Rick Collins visited Dr. Freida Schneider, his father's geneticist. There are several phone calls to her office too. I took the liberty of calling Dr. Schneider's office. She is rather busy, but she'll give us fifteen minutes during her lunch break today. Twelve thirty sharp."

"How did you wrangle that?"

"MB Reps is making a large donation to Terence Cardinal Cooke Health Care Center."

"Fair enough."

"It's coming out of your bonus."

"Fine. What else?"

"Rick Collins called the CryoHope Center near New York–Presbyterian. They do a lot with cord blood and embryonic storage and stem cells. Five doctors from a variety of specialties run it, so it's impossible to know which one he was dealing with. He also called the Save the Angels charity several times. So here is the chronology: First he speaks to Dr. Schneider, four times over the course of two weeks. Then he speaks to CryoHope. That somehow leads to Save the Angels."

"Okay," I said. "Can we get an appointment with CryoHope?"

"With whom?"

"One of the doctors."

"There's an ob-gyn," Esperanza said. "Should I tell him you need a pap smear?"

"I'm serious."

"I know you are, but I'm not sure who to try. I'm trying to figure out which doctor he called."

"Maybe Dr. Schneider can help."

"Could be."

"Oh, did you come up with anything on that opal to-do note?"

"No. I Googled all the letters. Opal of course had a million hits. When I Googled 'HHK,' the first thing that came up is a publicly traded health-care company. They deal with cancer investments."

"Cancer?"

"Yep."

"I don't see how that fits."

Esperanza frowned.

"What?"

"I don't see how any of this fits," she said. "This seems, in fact, like a colossal waste of time."

"How so?"

"What exactly do you hope to find here? The doctor treated an old man for Huntington's disease. What could it possibly have to do with terrorists murdering people in Paris and London?"

"I have no idea."

"Not a clue?"

"None."

"Probably no connection at all," she said.

"Probably."

"But we have nothing better to do?"

"This is what we do. We flail until something gives. This whole thing started with a car crash a decade ago. Then we have nothing until Rick Collins found out that his father has Huntington's. I don't know what the connection is, so the only thing I can think to do is go back and follow his path."

Esperanza crossed her legs, started twirling a free lock of hair. Esperanza had very dark hair, black-blue, that always had that just-mussed thing going on. When she twirled a hair, it meant something was bugging her.

"What?"

"I never called Ali while you were missing," she said.

I nodded. "And she never called me, right?"

"So you two are done?" Esperanza asked.

"Apparently."

"Did you use my favorite dumping line?"

"I forget it."

Esperanza sighed. "Welcome to Dumpsville. Population: you."

"Uh, no. Might be more apt to say, 'Population: me.'"

"Oh." We sat there. "Sorry."

"It's okay."

"Win said you did the sheet mambo with Terese."

I almost said, *Win did the sheet mambo with Mee*, but I worried that Esperanza might misinterpret.

"I don't see the relevance," I said.

"You wouldn't do the mambo-sheet thing, especially when you're ending with someone else, unless you really care about Terese. A lot."

I sat back. "So?"

"So we need to go full blast, if that will help. But we also need to understand the truth."

"Which is?"

"Terese is probably dead."

I said nothing.

"I've been there when you've lost loved ones," Esperanza said. "You don't take it well."

"Who does?"

"Good point. But you're also dealing with whatever else happened to you. It's a lot."

"I'll be fine. Anything else?"

"Yes," she said. "Those two guys you and Win beat up."

Coach Bobby and Assistant Coach Pat. "What about them?"

"The Kasselton police have been by a few times. You're supposed to call when you get back. You know that the guy Win popped belongs to the force, right?"

"Win told me."

"He had knee surgery and is recuperating. The other guy, the one who started it, used to own a small chain of appliance stores. He got knocked out of business by the big boys and now works as floor manager at Best Buy in Paramus."

I stood. "Okay."

"Okay, what?"

"We have time before we meet up with Dr. Schneider. Let's head out to Best Buy."

27

THE Best Buy employee blue polo shirt stretched across the beer belly of Coach Bobby. He was leaning on a TV, talking to an Asian couple. I looked for remnants of the beating and saw none.

Esperanza was with me. As we crossed the store a man wearing a logger flannel shirt ran over to her. "Excuse me," he said, his face alight like a child's on Christmas morn. "But, oh, my God, aren't you Little Pocahontas?"

I stifled a smile. It never fails to shock me how many people still remember her. She shot me a glare and turned to her fan.

"I am."

"Wow. Oh, I can't believe this. I mean, double wow. It's such a pleasure to meet you."

"Thanks."

"I used to have your poster in my bedroom. When I was, like, sixteen."

"I'm flattered—" she began.

"Got some stains on that poster too," he said with a wink, "if you know what I mean."

"—and nauseous." She finger-waved and walked away. "Bye now."

I followed her. "Stains," I said. "You have to be a little touched."

"Sadly, I kind of am," she said.

Forget what I said before about motherhood smothering her spirit. Esperanza was still the best.

We moved past Mr. Waaaay Too Much Information and toward Coach Bobby. I heard the Asian man ask what the difference was between a plasma TV and an LCD TV. Coach Bobby puffed out his chest and gave the pros and cons, none of which I understood. The man then asked about the DLP televisions. Coach Bobby liked DLPs. He started explaining why.

I waited.

Esperanza gestured with her head toward Coach Bobby. "Sounds like he deserved what he got."

"No," I said. "You don't fight people to teach them a lesson—you fight for survival or self-protection only."

Esperanza made a face.

"What?"

"Win is right. You can be such a little girl sometimes."

Coach Bobby smiled at the Asian couple and said,

"Take your time. I'll be right back and we can discuss free delivery."

He came over to me and held my gaze. "What do you want?"

"To say I'm sorry."

Coach Bobby didn't move. Three seconds of silence. Then: "There, you said it."

He spun around and headed back over to his customers.

Esperanza slapped me on the back. "Boy, that was cleansing."

DR. Freida Schneider was short and stocky with a big trusting smile. She was an Orthodox Jew, complete with modest dress and beret. I met her in the cafeteria at Terence Cardinal Cooke Health Care Center on Fifth Avenue by One Hundred Third Street. Esperanza was out front making some calls. Dr. Schneider asked me if I wanted anything to eat. I declined. She ordered a complicated sandwich. We sat down. She said a prayer to herself and began to devour said sandwich as though it had called her a bad name.

"I only have ten minutes," she said by way of explanation.

"I thought it was fifteen."

"I changed my mind. Thanks for the donation."

"I need to ask you some questions about Sam Collins."

Schneider swallowed the bite. "So your colleague

said. You know all about patient-client confidentiality, right? So I can skip that speech?"

"Please."

"He's dead, so maybe you should tell me your interest in him."

"I understand he committed suicide."

"You don't need me to tell you that."

"Is that common in patients with Huntington's?"

"Do you know what Huntington's disease is?"

"I know it's genetic."

"It's an inherited genetic neurological disorder." She said this between bites. "The disease does not kill you directly, but as the disorder progresses, it leads to a great deal of life-ending complications like pneumonia and heart failure and you don't want to know. HD messes with the physical, the psychological, the cognitive. It is not a pretty disorder. So, yes, suicide is not uncommon. Some studies show that one in four give it a try with about seven percent being successful, ironic as the term 'successful' is when discussing suicide."

"And that was the case with Sam Collins?"

"He had depression before being diagnosed. It's hard to say what came first. HD usually begins with a physical disorder, but there are plenty of times it starts with the psychiatric or cognitive. So his depression could have actually been the first signs of HD misdiagnosed. Doesn't really matter. Either way he is dead due to HD—suicide is just another life-ending complication."

"I understand that Huntington's has to be inherited."

"Yes."

"And that if one of the parents has it, the child has a fifty-fifty chance."

"To keep it simple, I will say, yes, that's accurate."

"And if the parent doesn't have it, the offspring won't either. That's it. The family line is clean."

"Go on."

"So that means one of Sam Collins's parents had it."

"That's correct. His mother lived to be in her eighties with no signs of Huntington's, so it probably came from his father, who died young and thus never had a chance to display any symptoms."

I leaned closer. "Did you test Sam Collins's children?"

"That's not really your concern."

"I'm speaking specifically of Rick Collins. Who is also dead. Murdered, in fact."

"At the hands of a terrorist, according to the news reports."

"Yes."

"Yet you think his father's diagnosis with Huntington's disease has something to do with his murder?"

"I do."

Freida Schneider took another bite and shook her head.

"Rick Collins has a son," I said.

"I'm aware of that."

"And he may have a daughter."

That stopped her midbite. "Excuse me?"

I wasn't sure how to play this. "Rick Collins may not have known she was alive."

"You want to elaborate?"

"Not really," I said. "We only have ten minutes."

"True."

"So?"

She sighed. "Rick Collins was tested, yes."

"And?"

"The blood test shows the number of CAG repeats in each of the HTT alleles."

I just looked at her.

"Right, never mind. In short, the results sadly were positive. We don't consider the blood test a diagnosis because it could be years, decades even, before the onset of symptoms. But Rick Collins was already exhibiting chorea—basically, jerky movements you can't really control. He asked us to keep it confidential. We of course agreed."

I thought about that. Rick had Huntington's. He had symptoms already—what would his last years have looked like? His father had asked himself that question and ended his life.

"Was Rick's son tested?"

"Yes, Rick insisted, which I confess is a bit unconventional. There is a lot of debate over testing, especially with a child. I mean, let's say you find out that a young boy will eventually contract this disorder—isn't that a terrible burden to live with? Or is it better to know now so you live life to the fullest? And if you're positive for HD, should you have children yourself who will have a fifty-fifty chance of contracting the illness—and even if you know that, isn't it still a life worth leading? The ethics are fairly mind-boggling."

"But Rick tested his son?"

"Yes. Rick was a reporter through and through. He didn't believe in not knowing. The son, thankfully, was negative."

"That must have been a relief to him."

"Yes."

"Do you know the CryoHope Center?"

She thought about it. "They do research and storage, I think. Mostly stem cell banking and the like, right?"

"After Rick Collins came to see you, he visited them. Any clue why?"

"No."

"How about the Save the Angels charity? Have you heard of it?"

Schneider shook her head.

"There is no cure for HD, correct?" I said.

"Correct."

"How about through stem cell research?"

"Wait, Mr. Bolitar. Let's back up. You said Rick Collins may have a daughter."

"Yes."

"Do you mind explaining that to me?"

"Did he tell you that he had a daughter who died ten years ago in a car crash?"

"No. Why would he?"

I mulled that over. "When Rick's body was found in Paris, there was blood at the scene. The DNA test showed it belonged to a daughter."

"But you just said his daughter is dead. I'm not following."

"Neither am I yet. But tell me about stem cell research."

She shrugged. "Highly speculative at this stage. You
could theoretically replace damaged neurons in the brain
by transplanting stem cells from cord blood. We've seen
some encouraging signs in animals, but it hasn't been
subject to human clinical trials."

"Still. If you're dying and desperate . . ."

A woman came into the cafeteria. "Dr. Schneider?"

The doctor held up a finger, downed the last bite of
sandwich, rose. "For the dying and desperate, yes, anything is possible. Everything from miracle cures to, well,
suicide. That's your ten minutes, Mr. Bolitar. Come back
sometime and I'll give you a tour of the facility. You'll be
surprised by the strength and good work. Thank you for
the donation, and good luck with whatever you're trying
to do."

28

THE CryoHope Center gleamed like, well, the ideal blend of a cutting-edge medical facility and an upscale bank. The reception desk was high and made of dark wood. I sidled up to it, Esperanza by my side. I noticed that the receptionist, a corn-fed cutie, was not wearing a wedding band. I debated changing plans. A single woman. I could turn on the charm, and she would fall under my spell and answer all my questions. Esperanza knew what I was thinking and just gave me the look. I shrugged. The receptionist probably didn't know anything, anyway.

"My wife is expecting," I said, nodding toward Esperanza. "We would like to see someone about storing our baby's umbilical cord blood."

The corn-fed receptionist gave me a practiced smile.

She handed us a bunch of four-color brochures on thick-stock paper and ushered us into a room with plush seating. There were large artistic photographs of children on the wall, and one of those diagrams of the human body that makes you think of ninth-grade biology class. We filled out a form on a CryoHope clipboard. They asked for my name. I was tempted to go with either I. P. Daily or Wink Martindale, but I stuck with Mark Kadison because he was a friend of mine, and if they called, he'd just laugh.

"Well, hello!"

A man stepped in wearing a white lab coat, a tie, and the same dark-framed glasses actors use when they want to look smart. He shook both our hands and sat in the other plush chair.

"So," he said, "how far along are you?"

I looked at Esperanza.

"Three months," she said with a frown.

"Congratulations. Is this your first?"

"Yes."

"Well, I'm glad you're doing the mature thing by looking into storing your baby's umbilical cord blood."

"Can you tell us the fee?" I asked.

"One thousand dollars for processing and shipping. Then there are yearly storage fees. I know that may sound expensive, but this is a onetime opportunity. Cord blood contains stem cells that save lives. Simple as that. They can treat anemias and leukemias. They can fight infection and help with certain kinds of cancer. We are on the edge of research that may lead to treatments for heart disease, Parkinson's, diabetes. No, we can't cure them yet. But who knows what will happen in a few years' time? Are you familiar with bone marrow transplants?"

"Somewhat," I said.

"Cord blood transplants work better and are, of course, safer—no surgical procedure to harvest it. You need an eighty-three percent HLA match to work with bone marrow. You only need a sixty-seven percent match with cord blood. That's now—right now. We are saving lives today with those stem cell transplants. Are you following me?"

We both nodded.

"Because here's the key fact: The only opportunity to store cord blood is right after your baby is born. That's it. You can't decide to do it when the child is three years old or, maybe, God forbid, when a sibling gets sick down the line."

"So how does it work exactly?" I asked.

"It is painless and easy. When you have your baby, the blood is collected from the umbilical cord. We separate out the stem cells and deep-freeze them."

"Where are the stem cells kept?"

He spread his arms. "Right here, in a safe, secure environment. We have guards and backup generators and a safe room. Like you'd find in any bank. The option we work with mostly—and what I would highly recommend for you—is called family banking. In short, you store your baby's stem cells for your use. Your baby might need it. A sibling. Even one of you or maybe an uncle or aunt. Whatever."

"How do you know the cord blood will be a match?"

"There are no guarantees. You should know that. But, of course, the odds are greatly improved you'll find a match. Plus—well, it looks like you are a couple of mixed heritage. It's harder to find matches, so this issue may be particularly important for you. Oh, and let me point out that the stem cells we are talking about are from cord blood—they have nothing to do with the controversies you've read about involving embryonic stem cells."

"You don't store embryos?"

"Oh, we do, but that's something totally separate from what you're interested in. That's for infertility issues and the like. No embryos are harmed in cord-blood stem cell research or storage. I just wanted to make that clear." He had a wide smile.

"Are you a doctor?" I asked.

The smile faltered just a wee bit. "No, but we have five on staff."

"What kinds of doctors?"

"CryoHope has leaders in all the fields." He handed me a brochure and pointed to the list of five doctors. "We have a geneticist who works with inherited diseases. We have a hematologist who works on the transplant side of things. We have an obstetrician-gynecologist who is a pioneer in the area of infertility. We have a pediatric oncologist who is doing research with stem cells to find cancer treatments for children."

"So," I said, "let me ask you a hypothetical."

He leaned forward.

"I store my baby's cord blood. Years pass. Now I get sick with something. Maybe you don't have a cure yet, but I want to try something experimental. Could I use the cord blood?"

"It's yours, Mr. Kadison. You can do with it what you want."

I had no idea where to go with this. I looked at Esperanza. She offered up nothing.

"May I talk to one of your doctors?" I asked.

"Are there any questions I haven't been able to answer?"

I tried to think of another avenue. "Do you have a client named Rick Collins?"

"I'm sorry?"

"Rick Collins. He's a friend of mine, recommended you. I wanted to make sure he's a client."

"That information would be confidential. I'm sure you understand. If someone was to ask about you, I would say the same thing."

Nowhere.

"Have you ever heard of a charity named Save the Angels?" I asked.

His face shut down.

"Have you?"

"What is this?" he asked.

"I just asked a question."

"I explained to you the process," he said, rising. "I suggest you read the literature. We hope that you choose CryoHope. Best of luck to you both."

OUT on the curb I said, "The bum's rush."

"Yep."

"Win had a theory early on that maybe the blood they found at the murder scene was cord blood."

"It would explain a lot," Esperanza said.

"Except I don't see how. Let's say Rick Collins did store his daughter's blood. So then what? He comes here, has it—what?—unfrozen, brings it to Paris, and it gets spilled on the floor when he's murdered?"

"No," she said.

"Then what?"

"We're missing something obviously. A step or a few steps. Maybe he had the frozen sample sent to Paris. Maybe he was working with some doctors in an experimental program, human testing, that our government wouldn't approve of. I don't know, but again—does it make more sense that the girl survived this car accident and has been hiding for ten years?"

"Did you see his face when we mentioned Save the Angels?"

"Hardly surprising. They're a group that protests abortions and embryonic stem cell research. Did you notice how his rehearsed spiel stressed that cord blood has nothing to do with the stem cell controversy?"

I mulled that over. "Either way, we need to look into Save the Angels."

"No one answers their phones," she said.

"Do you have an address for them?"

"They're in New Jersey," she said. "But . . ."

"But what?"

"We're running in circles here. We've learned nothing. And reality check: Our clients deserve better than this. We gave them our word we would work hard for them. And we're not."

I stood there.

"You are the best agent ever," she said. "I'm good at what I do. I'm very good. I'm a better negotiator than you'll ever be, and I know how to find more money-making venues for our clients than you do. But we get clients because they trust you. Because what they really want is for their agent to care about them—and you're good at that." She shrugged, waited.

"I get what you're saying," I said. "Most of the time I get us into these messes to protect a client. But this time it's bigger. Much bigger. You guys want me to stay focused on our personal interests. I get that. But I need to see this through."

"You have a hero complex," she said.

"Duh. That's hardly a news flash."

"It makes you fly blind sometimes. You do the most good when you know where you're going."

"Right now," I said, "I'm going to New Jersey. You go back to the office."

"I can take a ride with you."

"I don't need a babysitter."

"Too bad, you got one. We go to Save the Angels. If that's a dead end, we go back to the office and work all night. Deal?"

"Deal," I said.

29

A major dead end. Literally.

We followed the car's GPS to the office building located in Ho-Ho-Kus, New Jersey, at the end of a dead-end street. There was Ed's Body Shop, a karate studio called Eagle's Talon, and a supercheesy storefront photo studio called the Official Photography of Albin Laramie. I pointed at the stenciled-glass lettering as we walked past.

"Official," I said, "because, really, you wouldn't want Albin Laramie's unofficial photographs."

There were wedding shots using a lens so blurry it was hard to tell where groom began and bride ended. There were provocative model poses, mostly of women in bikinis. There were the most garish baby photographs in brown sepia tones that were faux Victorian. The babies were dressed in flowing gowns and looked creepy. Whenever I see a real Victorian baby picture I can't help thinking, "Whoever is in this picture is now dead and buried." Maybe I am more morose than most, but who wants such overly affected pictures?

We entered the ground floor and checked the directory. Save the Angels was supposed to be in suite 3B, but the door was locked. We could see the discoloration on the door where a nameplate had once been.

The closest office was for a CPA named Bruno and Associates. We asked about the charity next door.

"Oh, they've been gone for months," the receptionist told us. Her nameplate read "Minerva." I didn't know if that was her first name or last. "They moved out right after the break-in."

I arched an eyebrow and leaned closer. "Break-in?" I said.

I'm good with the probing interrogatories.

"Yep. They got cleaned out. Must have been—" She scrunched up her face. "Hey, Bob, when was that break-in next door?"

"Three months ago."

That was pretty much all Minerva and Bob could tell us. On TV, the detectives always ask if the inhabitant left a "forwarding address." I have never seen a person in real life do that. We went back and stared at the Save the Angels door another second. The door had nothing to say.

"You ready to go back to work?" Esperanza asked.

I nodded. We headed back outside. I blinked into the sunlight and heard Esperanza say, "Well, hello."

"What?"

She pointed at a car across the street. "Look at the decal on the back bumper."

You've seen them. They are white ovals with black lettering in them to show where you've been. It started, I think, with European cities. A tourist would return from a trip to Italy and put ROM on the back of his car. Now every town seems to have their own, a way to show civic pride or something.

This decal read: "HHK."

"Ho-Ho-Kus," I said.

"Yep."

I thought back to that code. "Opal in Ho-Ho-Kus. Maybe the four-seven-one-four is a house number."

"Opal could be a person's name."

We turned toward where we had parked, and another surprise greeted us. A black Cadillac Escalade was parked behind ours, blocking us in. I saw a heavy-set man in a brown vice principal's suit start toward us. He had a buzz cut and a big, angular face, and he looked like a Green Bay Packer offensive lineman from 1953.

"Mr. Bolitar?"

I recognized the voice. I had heard it twice before. Once on the phone when I called Berleand—and once in London, seconds before I passed out.

Esperanza stepped in front of me, as if to offer protection. I put a gentle hand on her shoulder to let her know that I was fine.

"Special Agent Jones," I said.

Two men—other agents I figured—got out of the Escalade. They stood with the door open and leaned against the side. Both men wore sunglasses.

"I'm going to need you to come with me," he said.

"Am I under arrest?" I asked.

"Not yet. But you really should come with me."

"Let's wait for the arrest warrant," I said. "I'll bring my attorney too. Keep it all on the up-and-up."

Jones moved a step closer. "I would rather not bring formal charges. But I know for a fact that you've committed crimes."

"You're a witness, no?"

Jones shrugged.

"Where did you take me after I passed out?" I asked.

He faked a sigh. "I'm sure I have no idea what you're talking about. But neither of us has time for this. Let's go for a ride, okay?"

As he reached out for my arm, Esperanza said, "Special Agent Jones?"

He looked at her.

"I have a call for you," she said.

Esperanza handed him her cell phone. He frowned but took it from her. I frowned too and looked at her. Her face gave me nothing.

"Hello?" Jones said.

The phone was set loud enough so that I could hear the voice on the other end clearly. The voice said:

"Chrome, military style, with the Gucci logo engraved on the lower left-hand corner."

It was Win.

Jones said, "Huh?"

"I can see your belt buckle through my rifle scope, though I'm aiming three inches lower," Win said. "Perhaps two inches would be more apropos in your case."

My eyes dropped toward the guy's buckle. Sure enough. I had no idea what military-style chrome meant, but there was a Gucci logo engraved on the lower left-hand corner.

Win said, "Gucci on a government salary? It has to be a knockoff."

Jones kept the phone against his ear, started looking around. "I assume this is Mr. Windsor Horne Lockwood."

"I'm sure I have no idea what you're talking about."

"What do you want?"

"Simple. Mr. Bolitar is not going with you."

"You're threatening a federal officer. That's a capital offense."

"I'm commenting on your fashion sense," Win said. "And since your belt is black and your shoes are brown, the only one committing a crime here is you."

Jones's eyes lifted and met mine. There was a strange calm in them for a guy with a rifle aimed at his groin. I glanced at Esperanza. She didn't meet my gaze. I realized something rather obvious: Win was not in Bangkok. He had lied to me.

"I don't want a scene," Jones said. He raised both hands. "So, okay, no one is forcing anything here. Have a good day."

He turned and began to walk back to his car.

"Jones?" I called out.

He looked back at me, shielding his eyes from the sun.

"Do you know what happened to Terese Collins?"

"Yes."

"Tell me."

"If you come with me," he said.

I looked at Esperanza. She handed the cell phone back to Jones.

Win said, "Just so we're clear. You won't be able to hide. Your family won't be able to hide. If something happens to him, it is total destruction. Everything you love or care about. And, no, that's not a threat."

The phone went dead.

Jones looked at me. "Sweet guy."

"You have no idea."

"You ready to go?"

I followed him to the Escalade and got in.

30

WE drove over the George Washington Bridge and back into Manhattan. Jones introduced me to the two agents in the front seat, but I didn't remember their names. The Escalade exited at West Seventy-ninth Street. A few minutes later it stopped by Central Park West. Jones opened the door, grabbed his briefcase, and said, "Let's take a walk."

I slid out. The sun was still bright.

"What happened to Terese?" I asked.

"You need to know the rest first."

I really didn't, but there was no point in pushing too much. He would tell me in his own time. Jones took off his brown suit jacket and laid it on the backseat. I waited for the other two agents to park and get out, but Jones slapped the top of the car and it took off.

"Just us?" I said.

"Just us."

His briefcase was from another era, perfectly rectangular with number locks on both bolts. My dad used to have one like it, carrying his contracts and bills and pens and a tiny tape recorder to and from his office in that Newark factory.

Jones started into the park on West Sixty-seventh Street. We passed Tavern on the Green, the lights on the trees dim. I caught up to him and said, "This seems a little cloak 'n' dagger."

"It's a precaution. Probably unnecessary. But when you deal with what I do, you sometimes like to see why."

I found this a tad melodramatic, but again I didn't want to push it. Jones was suddenly somber and reflective, and I didn't have a clue why. He watched the joggers, the Rollerbladers, the bike riders, the moms with designer-name strollers.

"I know it's corny," he said, "but they skate and run and work and love and laugh and throw Frisbees and they don't have a clue as to how fragile it all is."

I made a face. "But let me guess—you, Special Agent Jones, are the silent sentinel who protects them—the one who sacrifices his own humanity so the citizenry can sleep well at night. That about it?"

He smiled. "Guess I deserved that."

"What happened to Terese?"

Jones kept walking.

I said, "When we were in London, you took me into custody."

"Yes."

"And then?"

He shrugged. "It's compartmentalized. I don't know. I hand you over to someone from another department. My part is over."

"Morally convenient," I said.

He winced but kept walking.

"What do you know about Mohammad Matar?" he asked.

"Just what I read in the paper," I said. "He was, I assume, a serious bad guy."

"The baddest of the bad. A highly educated radical extremist who made other radical terrorists wet their beds in fear. Matar loved torture. He believed that the only way to kill the infidels was to infiltrate and live among them. He started up a terrorist organization called Green Death. Their motto is: *'Al-sabr wal-sayf sawf yudammir al-kafirun.'*"

A spasm ripped through me: *"Al-sabr wal-sayf."*

"What does that mean?" I asked.

" 'Patience and the sword will destroy the sinners.' "

I shook my head, trying to clear it.

"Mohammad Matar spent almost his entire life in the West. He grew up in Spain mostly, but spent some time in France and England, as well. And Dr. Death is more than a nickname—he went to medical school at Georgetown and did his residency right here in New York City. Spent twelve years in the United States under various assumed names. Guess what day he left the United States."

"I'm not really in the mood for guessing."

"September tenth, 2001."

We both stopped talking for a moment, almost sub-consciously turning south. No, we wouldn't be able to see those towers, even if they still stood. But respect had to be paid. Always and hopefully forever.

"Are you saying he was involved in that?"

"Involved? Hard to say. But Mohammad knew about it. His departure wasn't a coincidence. We have a witness who places him at the Pink Pony earlier that month. That name ring a bell?"

"Isn't that the strip club the terrorists went to before September eleventh?"

Jones nodded. A class trip crossed in front of us. The children—they looked about ten or eleven years old—all wore matching bright green shirts with the school name emblazoned on the front. One adult took the front, another the rear.

"You killed a major terrorist leader," Jones said. "Do you have any idea what his followers would do to you if they found out the truth?"

"And that's why you took credit for killing him?"

"That's why we kept your name out of it."

"I'm really grateful."

"Is that sarcasm?"

I wasn't really sure myself.

"If you keep stumbling around, the truth is going to come out. You'll kick a beehive and a bunch of jihadists will be there."

"Suppose I'm not afraid of them."

"Then you're demented."

"What happened to Terese?"

We stopped at a bench. Still standing, he put one knee on the seat and used it to balance his briefcase. He fumbled through it. "The night before you killed Mohammad Matar, you dug up the remains of Miriam Collins's grave for the purposes of a DNA test."

"Are you hoping for a confession?"

Jones shook his head. "You don't get it."

"Don't get what?"

"We confiscated the remains. You probably knew that."

I waited.

Jones pulled a manila folder out of the briefcase. "Here are the DNA test results you wanted."

I reached out. Jones played coy for a moment, as if debating whether he should let me see it. But we both knew. This was why I was here. He handed me the manila folder. I opened it. On top was a photograph of the bone sample Win and I had collected that night. I turned the page, but Jones was already walking.

"The tests were conclusive. The bones you dug up belong to Miriam Collins. The DNA matches Rick Collins as the father and Terese Collins as the mother. Furthermore, the bones matched the approximate size and development for a seven-year-old girl."

I read the report. Jones kept walking.

"This could be faked," I said.

"It could," Jones agreed.

"How do you explain the blood found at the murder scene in Paris?"

"You just raised an interesting possibility," he said.

"That being?"

"Maybe those results were faked."

I stopped.

"You just said that maybe I faked a DNA blood test. But wouldn't it be more rational to assume that the French did?"

"Berleand?"

He shrugged.

"Why would he do that?"

"Why would I? But don't take my word for it. In this briefcase, I have your original bone sample. When we are done, I will give it to you. You can test it for yourself, if you wish."

My head swam. He kept walking. This made sense. If Berleand lied, everything else fell into place. Removing emotion and want from the equation, which seemed more likely—that Miriam Collins had actually survived the crash and ended up in her murdered father's room, or that Berleand was lying about the test results?

"You got involved in this because you wanted to find Miriam Collins," Jones said. "Now you have. The rest you should leave to us. Whatever else is going on here, you now know for certain that Miriam Collins is dead. This bone sample will give you all the proof you need."

I shook my head. "There's too much smoke for there to be no fire."

"Like what? The terrorists? Almost all of your so-called smoke can be attributed to Rick Collins's attempt to infiltrate the cell."

"The blond girl."

"What about her?"

"Did you capture her in London?"

"No. She was gone by the time we arrived. We know you saw her. We have a witness from Mario Contuzzi's apartment, a neighbor, who says he saw you chase her."

"So who was she?"

"A member of the cell."

I arched an eyebrow. "A blond teen jihadist?"

"Sure. The cells are always a mix. Disenfranchised immigrants, Arab nationals, and, yes, a few crazy Westerners. We know that the terror cells are stepping up the effort to recruit Caucasian Westerners, especially women. The reason is pretty obvious—a cute blonde can go places an Arab man can't. Most of the time the girl has serious daddy issues. You know the deal—some girls turn to porn; some sleep with radicals."

I wasn't sure I bought that.

A small grin played on his lips. "Why don't you tell me what else is bothering you?"

"A lot of things," I said.

He shook his head. "Not really, Myron. It's pretty much down to one thing now, isn't it? You're wondering about the car accident."

"The official version is a lie," I said. "I talked to Karen Tower before she was murdered. I talked to Nigel Manderson. The accident didn't happen the way they said."

"That's your smoke?"

"It is."

"So if I clear that smoke, you will drop this?"

"They were covering something up that night."

"And if I clear that smoke, you will drop this?" Jones said again.

"I guess," I said.

"Okay, so let's discuss alternate theories." Jones kept walking. "The car accident ten years ago. You think what really happened is . . ." He stopped and turned to me. "Well, no, you tell me. What do you think they were covering up?"

I said nothing.

"The car crashed—I guess that you buy that part. Terese was rushed to the hospital. I guess you buy that part too. So where does it go wrong for you? You think— help me here, Myron—that a cabal involving Terese Collins's best friend and at least one or two cops hid her seven-year-old daughter for some odd reason, raised her in hiding all these years. . . . And then?"

I still said nothing.

"And this conspiracy of yours assumes that I'm lying about the DNA test, which you can now learn independently I'm not."

"They were covering up something," I said.

"Yes," he said, "they were."

I waited. We headed down past the park's carousel.

"The crash happened pretty much as you were told. A truck bounded down A-Forty. Ms. Collins spun her steering wheel, and, well, that was that. Disaster. You know the backstory too. She was home. She got a call to come in so that she could anchor prime time. She hadn't planned on going out that night, so I guess in some ways it's understandable."

"What is?"

"There is a Greek expression: The humpback never sees the hump in his own back."

"What does that have to do with anything?"

"Maybe nothing. That expression is talking about flaws. We are quick to find flaws in others. We aren't so good with ourselves. We are also poor judges of our own abilities, especially when there is a nice carrot in front of us."

"You're not making any sense."

"Sure I am. You want to know what was covered up— but it's so obvious. With her daughter dead, hadn't Terese Collins been punished enough? I don't know if they were worried so much about the legal ramifications or just the guilt a mother would load on herself. But Terese Collins was drunk that night. Could she have avoided the accident if she had been sober? Who knows? The truck driver was at fault but maybe if her reaction time had been a little faster . . ."

I tried to take this in. "Terese was drunk?"

"Her blood test showed she was over the legal limit, yes."

"And that was the cover-up?"

"It was."

Lies have a certain smell. So does truth.

"Who knew?" I asked.

"Her husband. So did Karen Tower. They covered it up because they feared the truth would destroy her."

The truth might have done that anyway, I thought. A weight filled my chest as I realized yet another truth: Terese probably knew. On some level, she knew about her culpability. Any mother would have been devastated by a tragedy like that, but here it was, ten years later, and Terese was still trying to make amends.

How had Terese put it to me when she called from Paris? She didn't want to rebuild.

She knew. Maybe subconsciously. But she knew.

I stopped walking.

"What happened to Terese?"

"Does that clear the smoke, Myron?"

"What happened to her?" I asked again.

Jones turned and faced me full. "I need you to let this go, okay? I'm not much of an ends-justify-means sort of guy. I know all the arguments against torture and I agree with them. But the issue is murky. Let's say you catch a terrorist who has already killed thousands—and right now he has a bomb hidden that will kill millions of children. Would you punch him in the face to get the answer and save those children? Of course you would. Would you punch him twice? Suppose it was only a thousand children or a hundred or ten? Anyone who doesn't get it at all . . . Well, I would be wary of such a person. That's an extremist too."

"What's your point?"

"I want you to have your life back." Jones's voice was soft now, almost a plea. "I know you don't buy that. But I don't like what happened to you. That's why I'm telling you this. I'm protected. Jones isn't even my real name,

and we are here in this park because I don't have an office. Even your friend Win would have trouble locating
me. I know everything about you now. I know your past.
I know how you destroyed your knee and how you tried
to move past it. You don't get many second chances. I'm
giving you one right now."

Jones looked off into the distance. "You need to let
this go and move on with your life. For your sake." He
gestured with his chin. "And hers."

For a moment I was afraid to look. I followed his
gaze, my eyes sweeping left to right, when I suddenly
froze. My hand fluttered toward my mouth. I tried to
take the blow standing, felt something blow across my
chest.

Standing across the expanse of green, staring back at
me with tears in her eyes but looking as achingly beautiful as ever, was Terese.

31

DURING the attack in London, Terese had been shot in the neck.

I was back at that lovely shoulder, kissing it gently, when I saw the scar. No, she had not been drugged or taken to a black site. She had been kept in a hospital outside of London and then flown to New York. Her injuries had been more severe than mine. She had lost blood. She was still in a great deal of pain and moved gingerly.

We were back at Win's Dakota apartment, in my bedroom, holding each other and looking up at the ceiling. She rested her head on my chest. I could feel my heart beating against her.

"Do you believe what Jones said?" I asked her.

"Yes."

I ran my hand down the curve of her back and pulled

her closer. I felt her shake a little. I didn't want her out of my sight.

"Part of me always knew that I was deceiving myself," she said. "I wanted it so badly. This chance at redemption, you know? Like my long-lost child was out there and I had a chance to rescue her."

I understood the feeling.

"So what do we do now?" I asked.

"I want to lie here with you and just be. Can we do that?"

"We can." I kept my eyes on the ceiling's wainscoting. Then, because I can never leave well enough alone: "When Miriam was born, did you and Rick store her cord blood?"

"No."

Dead end.

I asked, "Do you still want us to run the DNA test to be sure?"

"What do you think?"

"I think we should," I said.

"Then let's do that."

"You'll have to give a DNA sample," I said. "So we have something to compare it with. We don't have Rick's DNA, but if we confirm the child was yours, well, I assume you only gave birth that one time?"

Silence.

"Terese?"

"I only gave birth that one time," she said.

More silence.

"Myron?"

"Yes?"

"I can't have any more children."

I said nothing.

"It was a miracle that Miriam was born. But right after I gave birth, they had to do an emergency hysterectomy because I had fibroids. I can't have more children."

I closed my eyes. I wanted to say something comforting, but it all sounded so patronizing or superfluous. So I pulled her in a little closer. I didn't want to look ahead. I wanted to just lie there and hold her.

The Yiddish expression came back to me yet again: Man plans. God laughs.

I could feel her start to move away from me. I pulled her back to me.

"Too early for this talk?" she said.

I thought about it. "Probably too late."

"Meaning?"

"Right now," I said, "I want to lie here with you and just be."

TERESE was asleep when I heard the key in the front door. I glanced at the bedroom clock. One a.m.

I threw on a robe as Win and Mee entered. Mee gave me a little wave and said, "Hi, Myron."

"Hi, Mee."

She headed into the next room. When she was gone, Win said, "When it comes to sex, I like to take a 'Mee first' approach."

I just looked at him.

"And the great thing is, it really doesn't take much to keep Mee satisfied."

"Please stop," I said.

Win stepped forward and hugged me hard, "Are you okay?" he asked.

"I'm fine."

"Do you want to know something weird?"

"What?" I said.

"This is the longest we've been apart since our days at Duke."

I nodded, waited for the hug to subside, pulled back. "You lied about Bangkok," I said.

"No, I didn't. I do think the name is rather ironic. Bang. Cock. All the sex clubs."

I shook my head. We headed into a Louis-the-Something-type room with heavy woods and ornate sculptures and busts of guys with long hair. We sat in leather club chairs in front of the marble fireplace. Win tossed me a Yoo-hoo and poured himself an expensive scotch out of a decanter.

"I was going to have coffee," Win said, "but that keeps Mee up all night."

I nodded. "Almost out of Mee jokes?"

"God, I hope so."

"Why did you lie about Bangkok?"

"Why do you think?" he asked.

But the answer was obvious. I felt the wave of shame crash over me again. "I gave you up, didn't I?"

"Yes."

I felt the tears, the fear, the now-familiar shortness

of breath. My right leg started doing the restless shake.

"You were afraid they might grab me again," I said. "And if they did, if they broke me again, I would give them wrong information."

"Yes."

"I'm sorry," I said.

"You have nothing to be sorry about."

"I thought . . . I guess I figured I'd be stronger."

Win took a sip of his drink. "You are the strongest man I have ever known."

I waited a beat and then, because I couldn't help myself, I said, "Stronger than Mee?"

"Stronger. But not nearly as flexible."

We sat in the comfortable silence.

"Are you remembering at all?" he asked.

"It's vague."

"You'll need help with it."

"I know."

"You have the bone sample for the purposes of DNA?"

I nodded.

"And if it confirms what this Jones fellow told you, will this be over?"

"Jones answered most of my questions."

"I hear a 'but.'"

"There are several 'but's, actually."

"I'm listening."

"I called that number Berleand gave me," I said. "No answer."

"That's hardly a 'but.'"

"You know about his theory on Mohammad Matar's plot?"

"That it lives on after him? Yes."

"If that's true, that plot is a danger to everyone. We have a responsibility to help."

Win tilted his head back and forth and said, "Eh."

"Jones thinks if Matar's followers find out what I did, they'll come after me. I don't feel like waiting around or living in fear."

Win liked that reasoning better. "You'd rather take a proactive stance?"

"I think I would."

Win nodded. "What else?"

I took another deep swig. "I saw that blond girl. I saw her walk. I saw her face."

"Ah," Win said. "And as you stated before, you noticed similarities, perhaps genetic, between her and the delectable Ms. Collins?"

I drank the Yoo-hoo.

Win said, "Do you remember the optical illusion games we used to play when we were children? You'd look at a picture and you could see either an old witch or a pretty young girl? Or there was one that could be either a rabbit or a duck."

"That's not what happened here."

"Ask yourself this: Suppose Terese hadn't called you in Paris. Suppose you were walking on the street to your office and that blond girl walked past you. Would you have stopped and thought, 'Gee, that girl has to be Terese's daughter'?"

"No."

"So it's situational. Do you see that?"

"I do."

We sat in silence a little while longer.

"Of course," Win said, "just because something is situational, doesn't mean it isn't true."

"There's that."

"And it might be fun to bag a major terrorist."

"Are you with me?"

"Not yet," he said. "But after I finish this drink and go into my bedroom, I will be."

3²

THE mind can be pretty goofy and ornery.

Logic is never linear. It dashes to and fro and bounces off walls and makes hairpin turns and gets lost during detours. Anything can be a catalyst, usually something unrelated to the task at hand, ricocheting your thoughts into an unexpected direction—a direction that inevitably leads to a solution linear thinking could never have approached.

That was what happened to me. That was how I started to put this all together.

Terese stirred when I returned to the bedroom. I didn't tell her my thoughts on the blond girl, situational or otherwise. I didn't want to keep anything from her, but there was no reason to tell her yet. She was trying to heal. Why rip out those sutures until I knew more?

She drifted back to sleep. I held her and closed my eyes. I realized how little I had slept since returning from my sixteen-day hiatus. I slipped into nightmare world and woke up with a start at about three in the morning. My heart pounded. There were tears in my eyes. I only remembered the sensation of something pressing down hard on me, pinning me down, something so heavy I couldn't breathe. I got out of bed. Terese was still asleep. I bent down and kissed her gently.

There was a laptop in the room off the bedroom. I signed on to the Internet and searched for Save the Angels. The Web site came up. On the top was a banner that read SAVE THE ANGELS and, in smaller print, CHRISTIAN SOLUTIONS. The language spoke of life and love and God. It talked about replacing the word "choice" with the word "solutions." There were testimonials from women who had gone with the "adoption solution" rather than "murder." There were couples who'd had infertility issues talking about how the government wanted to "cruelly experiment" on their "preborns" while Save the Angels could help a frozen embryo "realize its ultimate purpose—life" through the Christian solution of helping another infertile couple.

I had heard such arguments before, remembered Mario Contuzzi briefly addressing them. He said that the group seemed somewhat right-wing but not extreme. I tended to agree. I kept surfing. There was a mission statement about sharing God's love and saving "preborn children." There was a statement of faith that began with a belief in the Bible—that it is "the complete, inspired word of God without error"—and moved into the sanctity of life. There were buttons to click on adoption care, on rights, on upcoming events, on resources for birth mothers.

I clicked the FAQ section, seeing how they answered the hows and whys, supporting unwed mothers, matching infertile couples to frozen embryos, forms to fill out, costs, how you can donate, how you can join the Save the Angels team. It was all pretty impressive. The Picture Gallery was next. I clicked on page one. There were pictures of two rather glorious mansions that were used for unwed mothers. One looked like something you'd see on a Georgian plantation, all white with marble columns and enormous weeping willow trees surrounding it. The other home looked like the perfect bed-and-breakfast—a picturesque, almost overly done Victorian home with turrets, towers, stained-glass windows, a lemonade porch, and a blue-gray mansard roof. The captions stressed the confidentiality of both the location and the inhabitants no names, no address—while the postcardlike photographs almost made you long to be knocked up.

I clicked on Gallery page two—and that was when I had my goofy-ornery-nonlinear-catalyst moment.

There were photographs of babies. The images were beautiful and adorable and heartbreaking, the sort of pictures designed to elicit wonder and awe in anyone with a pulse.

My ornery mind likes to play the contrast game. You watch a terrible stand-up comic, you think of how great

Chris Rock is. You watch a movie that tries to scare you with excessive Technicolor gore, you think of how Hitchcock kept you riveted, even in black and white. Right now, as I stared at the "saved angels," I thought about how perfect these images were compared with those creepy Victorian photographs I had seen in that cheesy storefront earlier in the day. That reminded me of what else I had learned there, the HHK, the possibility of that meaning Ho-Ho-Kus, and how Esperanza had come up with that.

Again the human brain—billions of random synapses cracking, popping, mixing, twisting, and sparking. You can't really get a grip on it, but here was how it must have gone inside my head: Official Photography, HHK, Esperanza, how we first met, her wrestling days, FLOW, the acronym for the Fabulous Ladies of Wrestling.

Suddenly it all came together. Well, maybe not all of it. But some. Enough so that I knew where I would be headed the next morning: to that cheesy storefront in Ho-Ho-Kus. To the Official Photography of Albin Laramie, or, as it might be known if you were jotting down an acronym, OPAL.

THE man behind the counter at the Official Photography of Albin Laramie had to be Albin. He wore a cape. A shiny cape. Like he was Batman or Zorro. The facial hair looked Etch-A-Sketched, his hair was a tangled yet calculated mess, and his whole persona screamed that he was not merely an artist, but an "artiste"! He was talking on the phone and scowling when I entered.

I started toward him. He signaled me to wait with a finger. "He doesn't get it, Leopold. What can I tell you? The man doesn't get angles or texture or coloring. He has no eye."

He held up his finger again for me to wait another minute. I did. When he hung up the phone, he sighed theatrically. "May I help you?"

"Hi," I said. "My name is Bernie Worley."

"And I," he said, hand to heart, "am Albin Lara-mie."

He made this pronouncement with great pride and flair. It reminded me of Mandy Patinkin in *The Princess Bride*; I half expected him to tell me that I had killed his father, prepare to die.

I gave him the world-weary smile. "My wife asked me to pick up some photographs."

"Do you have your claim stub?"

"I lost it."

Albin frowned.

"But I have the order number, if that will help."

"It may." He pulled over a keyboard, got his fingers ready, turned back to me. "Well?"

"Four-seven-one-four."

He looked at me as though I were the dumbest thing on God's green earth. "That's not an order number."

"Oh. Are you sure?"

"That's a session number."

"A session number?"

He pushed the cape back with both hands like a bird might before spreading its wings. "As in photo session."

The phone rang and he turned away as though dismissing me. I was losing him. I took a step back and did my own theatrics. I blinked and made my mouth into a perfect O. Myron Bolitar, Awestruck Ingénue. He was watching me with curiosity now. I circled the store and kept the awestruck look on my face.

"Is there a problem?" he asked me.

"Your work," I said. "It's breathtaking."

He preened. You don't often see an adult man preen in real life. For the next ten minutes or so, I snowed him with a bit more about his work, asking him about inspiration and letting him prattle on about hue and tone and style and lighting and other stuff.

"Marge and I have a baby," I said, shaking my head in admiration at the hideous Victorian monstrosity that made an otherwise cute baby look like my uncle Morty with a case of shingles. "We should set up a time to bring her in."

Albin continued to preen in his cape. Preening, I thought, was meant for a man in a cape. We discussed price, which was absolutely ridiculous and would require a second mortgage. I played along. Finally, I said, "Look, that's the number my wife gave me. The session number. She said that if I saw those photographs, it would simply blow me away. Do you think I could see the shots from session four-seven-one-four?"

If it struck him as odd that I had originally come in claiming to pick up photographs and now wanted to look at pictures from a session, the note hadn't sounded over the din of true genius.

"Yes, of course, it's on the computer here. I must tell you. I don't like digital photography. For your little girl, I want to use a classic box camera. There is such a texture to the work."

"That'd be super."

"Still, I use the digital for Web storage." He began typing and hit RETURN. "Well, these aren't baby pictures—that's for sure. Here you are."

Albin turned the monitor toward me. A bunch of thumbnails loaded onto the screen. I felt my chest tighten even before he clicked on one, making the image large enough to fill the entire monitor. No doubt about it.

It was the blond girl.

I tried to play it cool. "I'll need a copy of that."

"What size?"

"Whatever, eight-by-ten would be great."

"It will be ready a week from Tuesday."

"I need it now."

"Impossible."

"Your computer is hooked up into the color printer over there," I said.

"Yes, but that hardly produces photo quality."

No time to explain. I took out my wallet. "I'll give you two hundred dollars for a computer printout of that picture."

His eyes narrowed, but only for a second. It was finally dawning on him that something was up, but he was a photographer, not a lawyer or doctor. There was no confidentiality agreement here. I handed him the two hundred dollars. He started for the printer. I noticed a link that said Personal Info. I clicked it as he pulled the photograph from the printer.

"Pardon me?" Albin said.

I backed off, but I had seen enough. The girl's name was only listed as a first: Carrie. Her address?

Right next door. Care of the Save the Angels Foundation.

ALBIN did not know Carrie's last name. When I pressed him, he let me know he took pictures for Save the Angels—that was all. They gave him first names only. I took the printout and went next door. Save the Angels was still locked up. No surprise. I found Minerva, my favorite receptionist, at Bruno and Associates and showed her the picture of the blond Carrie.

"Do you know her?"

Minerva looked up at me.

"She's missing," I said. "I'm trying to find her."

"Are you like a private eye?"

"I am." It was easier than explaining.

"Cool."

"Yeah. Her first name is Carrie. Do you recognize her?"

"She worked there."

"At Save the Angels?"

"Well, not worked. She was one of the interns. Was here for a few weeks last summer."

"Can you tell me anything about her?"

"She's beautiful, isn't she?"

I said nothing.

"I never knew her name. She wasn't very nice. None of their interns were, truthfully. Plenty of love for God, I guess, but not real people. Anyway, our offices share a bathroom down the hall. I would say hi. She would look through me. You know what I mean?"

I thanked Minerva and headed back to suite 3B. I stood in front of it and stared at the door for Save the Angels. Again: the mind. I started letting the pieces tumble through ye olde brain cavity like socks in a dryer. I thought about the Web site I had surfed through last night, about the very name of this organization. I looked down at the photograph in my hand. The blond hair. The beautiful face. The blue eyes with that gold ring around each pupil, and yet I saw exactly what Minerva meant.

No mistake.

Sometimes you see strong genetic similarities in a face, like the gold ring around the pupil—and sometimes you also see something more like an echo. That was what I saw on this girl's face. An echo.

An echo, I was certain, of her mother.

I looked again at the door. I looked again at the photograph. And as the realization sank in, I felt the coldness seep into my bones.

Berleand hadn't lied.

My cell phone rang. It was Win.

"The DNA test on those bones has been completed."

"Don't tell me," I said. "It's a match for Terese as mother. Jones was telling the truth."

"Yes."

I stared at the picture some more.

"Myron?"

"I think I get it now," I said. "I think I know what's going on."

33

I drove back to New York City—more specifically, to the offices of CryoHope.

This can't be.

That was the thought that kept rambling through my mind. I didn't know if I hoped that I was right or wrong—but like I said, truth has a certain smell to it. And as far as the "can't be" aspect, I again bring up the Sherlock Holmes axiom: When you eliminate the impossible, whatever remains, no matter how improbable, must be the truth.

I was tempted to call Special Agent Jones. I had the girl's picture now. This Carrie was probably a terrorist or a sympathizer or maybe—best-case scenario—she was being held against her will. But it was too early for that.

I could talk to Terese, run this possibility by her, but that, too, felt premature.

I needed to know for sure before I got Terese's hopes up—or down.

CryoHope had valet parking. I gave the keys to the man and started inside. Immediately after Rick Collins found out that he had Huntington's disease, he had come here. It made sense on the surface. CryoHope was a leader in cutting-edge research with stem cells. It was natural to think that he had visited here in hopes of finding that something might save him from his genetic fate.

But that hadn't been it.

I remembered the name of the doctor from the brochure. "I want to see Dr. Sloan," I said to the receptionist.

"Your name?"

"Myron Bolitar. Tell him it's about Rick Collins. And a girl named Carrie."

WHEN I came back out, Win was waiting by the front door, leaning against the wall with the ease of Dino at the Sands. His limo was outside, but he stayed with me.

"So?" he said.

I told him everything. He listened without interrupting or asking any follow-up questions. When I was done, he said, "Next step?"

"I tell Terese."

"Any thoughts on how she'll react?"

"None."

"You could wait. Do more research."

"On what?"

He picked up the photograph. "The girl."

"We will. But I need to tell Terese now."

My cell phone chirped. The caller ID showed me Unknown Number. I flipped on the speakerphone setting and said, "Hello?"

"Miss me?" It was Berleand.

"You didn't call me back," I said.

"You were supposed to stay out of it. Calling you back might have encouraged you to rejoin the investigation."

"So why are you calling now?"

"Because you have a very big problem," he said.

"I'm listening."

"Am I on speakerphone?"

"Yes."

"Is Win there with you?"

Win said, "I am."

"So what's the problem?" I asked.

"We've been picking up some dangerous chatter coming out of Paterson, New Jersey. Terese's name was mentioned."

"Terese's," I said, "but not mine?"

"It may have been alluded to. This is chatter. It isn't always clear."

"But you think they know about us?"

"It seems likely, yes."

"Any idea how?"

"None. The agents involved with Jones, the ones who

took you into custody, are the best. None of them would have talked."

"One must have," I said.

"Are you sure about that?"

I ran it through my head. I thought about who else had been there that day in London, who might have told other jihadists that I had killed their leader, Mohammad Matar. I glanced at Win. He held up the photograph of Carrie and arched an eyebrow.

When you eliminate the impossible . . .

Win said, "Call your parents. We'll move them to the Lockwood compound in Palm Beach. We'll add the best security for Esperanza—maybe Zorra is available or that Carl guy from Philadelphia. Is your brother still on a dig in Peru?"

I nodded.

"He should be safe then."

I knew that Win would stay with Terese and me. Win started making calls. I picked up the phone, taking it off speaker. "Berleand?"

"Yes."

"Jones implied that you might have been lying about that DNA test in Paris."

Berleand said nothing.

"I know you were telling the truth," I said.

"How?"

But I had already said too much. "I have some calls to make. I'll call you back."

I hung up and called my parents. I was hoping my father would answer, so naturally my mother picked up.

"Mom, it's me."

"Hello, darling." Mom sounded tired. "I'm just back from the doctor."

"Are you okay?"

"You can read about it on my blog tonight," Mom said.

"Hold up. You just got back from the doctor, right?"

Mom sighed. "I just said that, didn't I?"

"Right, so I'm asking about your health."

"That's going to be my blog topic. If you want to know more, read it."

"You won't tell me?"

"Don't take it personally, sweetie. This way I don't have to repeat myself when someone else asks."

"So you blog about it instead?"

"It increases traffic to my site. See, now you're interested. Am I right? So I'll get more hits."

My mother, ladies and gentlemen.

"I didn't even know you had a blog."

"Oh, sure, I'm very now, very today, very hip. I'm on MyFace too."

I heard my father in the background shout out, "It's MySpace, Ellen."

"What?"

"It's called MySpace."

"I thought it was MyFace."

"That's Facebook. You have one of those too. And MySpace."

"Are you sure?"

"Yes, I'm sure."

"Listen to Mr. Billy Gates back there. Knows everything about the Internet all of a sudden."

"And your mother is fine," Dad yelled out.

"Don't tell him," she whined. "Now he won't click my blog."

"Mom, this is important. Can I talk to Dad for a minute?"

Dad came on. I explained quickly and with as little detail as possible. Again Dad got it. He didn't question or argue. I had just finished explaining about how we'd get someone to pick them up and take them to the compound when my call-waiting beeped in another call. It was Terese.

I finished up with my father and switched over.

"I'm about two minutes from you," I said to Terese. "Stay inside until I get there."

Silence.

"Terese?"

"She called."

I heard the sob in her voice.

"Who called?"

"Miriam. I just got off the phone with her."

34

I met her at the door.

"Tell me what happened."

Her whole body shook. She moved close to me and I held her and closed my eyes. This conversation, I knew, would be devastating. I got it now. I got why Rick Collins told her to be prepared. I got why he had warned that what he would say would change her entire life.

"My phone rang. I picked it up and a girl on the other end said, 'Mommy?'"

I tried to imagine the moment, hearing that word from your own child, believing that it was someone you loved more than anything else in the world and that you had a hand in killing.

"What else did she say?"

"They were holding her hostage."

"Who?"

"Terrorists. She said not to tell anyone."

I said nothing.

"A man with a thick accent took the phone away from her then. He said he'd call back with demands."

I just held her.

"Myron?"

We managed to find our way to the couch. She looked at me with hope and—I know how this will sound—love. My heart was cracking in my chest as I handed her the photograph.

"This is the blond girl I saw in Paris and London," I said.

She studied the picture for a full minute without speaking. Then: "I don't understand."

I wasn't sure what to say here. I wondered if she saw the resemblance, if maybe some of the pieces were coming together for her too.

"Myron?"

"That's the girl I saw," I said again.

She shook her head.

I knew the answer, but I asked the question anyway: "What's wrong?"

"That's not Miriam," she said.

She looked down again, wiped her eyes. "Maybe—I don't know—maybe if Miriam had had some facial surgery and it's been a lot of years. Looks change, right? She was seven the last time I saw her. . . ."

Her eyes jumped back to my face, hoping to find some

reassurance. I offered her none. I realized that the time had come, dived in headfirst.

"Miriam is dead," I said.

The blood slowly drained from her face. My heart shattered anew. I wanted to reach out to her, but I knew that it would be the wrong move. She swam through it, tried to stay rational, knew how important this all was. "But that phone call . . . ?"

"Your name has come up in some chatter. My guess is, they're trying to draw you out."

She looked back down at the picture. "So it was all a hoax?"

"No."

"But you just said . . ." Terese was trying so hard to stay with me. I tried to think of the best way to say this and realized that there was none. I would have to let her see it the way I had.

"Let's go back a few months," I said, "when Rick found out he had Huntington's disease."

She just looked at me.

"What would he have done first?" I asked.

"Have his son tested."

"Right."

"So?"

"So he also went to CryoHope. I kept thinking that he went there to find a cure."

"He didn't?"

"No," I said. "Do you know a Dr. Everett Sloan?"

"No. Wait. I saw the name on the brochure. He works for CryoHope."

"Right," I said. "He also took over the practice of Dr. Aaron Cox."

She said nothing.

"I just found out his name," I said. "But Cox was your ob-gyn. When you and Rick had Miriam."

Terese just stared at me.

"You and Rick had serious fertility issues. You told me about how difficult it was until, well, what you called a medical miracle, though it's rather common. In vitro fertilization."

She still wouldn't or couldn't talk.

"In vitro, by definition, is where eggs are fertilized by sperm outside the womb and then the embryo is transferred into the woman's uterus. You mentioned taking Pergonal to up your egg count. This happens in almost every instance. And then there are the extra embryos. For the past twenty-plus years, the embryos have been frozen. Sometimes they were thawed for use in stem cell research. Sometimes they were used when the couple wanted to try again. Sometimes, when one spouse died, the other would use it, or if you've just found out you have cancer and still want a kid. You know all this. There are complex legal issues involving divorce and custody, and many embryos are simply destroyed or stay frozen while a couple decides."

I swallowed because by now she had to see where I was going with this. "What happened to your extra embryos?"

"It was our fourth try," Terese said. "None of the embryos had taken. You can't imagine how crushing that was. And when it finally worked, it was such a wonderful, happy surprise. . . ." Her voice drifted off. "We only had two more embryos. We were going to save them in case we wanted to try again, but then my fibroids came up, and, well, there was no way I could get pregnant again. Dr. Cox told me that the embryos hadn't survived the freezing process anyway."

"He lied," I said.

She looked back at the picture of the blond girl.

"There is a charity called Save the Angels. They are against any sort of embryonic stem cell research or destruction of embryos in any way, shape, or form. For nearly two decades they've lobbied for the embryos to be adopted, if you will. It makes sense. There are hundreds of thousands of stored embryos, and there are couples who could conceive with those embryos and give them a life. The legal issues are complicated. Most states don't allow embryo adoptions because, in a sense, the birth mother is no more than a surrogate. Save the Angels wants the stored embryos implanted in infertile women."

She saw it now. "Oh my God . . ."

"I don't know all the details. One of Dr. Cox's residents was a big supporter of Save the Angels, I guess. Do you remember a Dr. Jiménez?"

Terese shook her head.

"Save the Angels pressured Cox just as he was starting up CryoHope. I don't know if he didn't want the press or if there was a payoff or if he was sympathetic to the Save the Angels cause. Cox probably realized that there were embryos that had no chance of being used, so, well, why not? Why let them stay frozen or be destroyed? So he gave them up for adoption."

"So this girl"—her eyes stayed on the picture—"this is my daughter?"

"Biologically speaking, yes."

She just stared at the face, not moving.

"When Dr. Sloan took over six years ago, he found out what had been done. He was in a tough spot. For a while he debated just keeping quiet but felt that was both illegal and medically unethical. So he took something of an in-between route. He contacted Rick and asked permission to allow the embryos to be adopted. I don't know what must have gone through Rick's mind, but I guess when the choice was having embryos destroyed or giving them a chance at life, he chose life."

"Wouldn't they have to contact me too?"

"You had already given that permission way back when. Rick hadn't. And no one knew where you were. So Rick signed off on it. I don't know if it was legal or not. But the deed had already been done, anyway. Dr. Sloan was just trying to clean up the mess now, in case there was something out there that screening might help with. And in this case, there was. When Rick found out he had Huntington's disease, he wanted to make sure the family who'd adopted the embryos knew about his medical condition. So he went to CryoHope. Dr. Sloan told him the truth—that the actual embryos had been implanted years ago via Save the Angels. He didn't know who the adoptive parents were, so he told Rick that he would make a request to get the information with Save the Angels. My guess is, Rick didn't want to wait."

"You think he broke into their offices?"

"It adds up," I said.

She finally wrested her eyes off the photograph. "So where is she now?"

"I don't know."

"She's my daughter."

"Biologically."

Something crossed her face. "Don't hand me that. You found out about Jeremy when he was fourteen. You still consider him your son."

I wanted to say that my situation was different, but she had a point. Jeremy was biologically my son, but he had never known me as his father. I had found out about him too late to make a significant difference in his up-bringing—but I was now still a part of his life. Was this situation any different?

"What's her name?" Terese asked. "Who raised her? Where does she live?"

"Her first name might be Carrie, but I can't say for sure. The rest of it I don't know yet."

She lowered the photograph onto her lap.

"We need to tell Jones about this," I said.

"No."

"If your daughter was kidnapped—"

"You don't believe that, do you?"

"I don't know."

"Come on, be honest with me. You think that she's

involved with these monsters—that she's one of those girls Jones talked about, with daddy issues."

"I don't know. But if she is innocent—"

"She's innocent either way. She can't be more than seventeen. If she somehow got caught up in this because she was young and impressionable, Jones and his pals at Homeland Security will never understand. Her life will be over. You saw what they did to you."

I said nothing.

"I don't know why she's with them," Terese said. "Maybe it's Stockholm syndrome. Maybe she had terrible parents or is a rebellious teenager— Hell, I know I was. Doesn't matter. She's just a kid. And she's my daughter, Myron. Do you get that? It's not Miriam, but I have a second chance here. I can't turn my back on her. Please."

I still said nothing.

"I can help her. It's like . . . it's like it was meant to be. Rick died trying to save her. Now it's my turn. The call said not to tell anyone but you. Please, Myron. I'm begging you. Please help me rescue my daughter."

35

WITH Terese still beside me, I called Berleand back.

"Jones implied that you somehow lied or doctored the DNA test," I said.

"I know."

"You do?"

"He wanted you off the case. I did too. That was why I didn't return your call."

"But you called before."

"To warn you. That's all. You should still stay out of it."

"I can't."

Berleand sighed. I thought about that first meeting, at the airport, the tired hair, the glasses with the over-size frames, the way he took me out on that roof at 36 quai des Orfèvres and how much I liked him.

"Myron?"

"Yes."

"Before, you said you knew that I didn't lie about the DNA test."

"Right," I said.

"Is this something you deduced because I have a trustworthy face and almost supernatural charisma?"

"That would be a no."

"Then please enlighten me."

I looked over at Terese. "I need you to promise me something."

"Uh-oh."

"I have information you'll find valuable. You probably have information I will find valuable."

"And you'd like to make an exchange."

"For starters."

"Starters," he repeated. "Then before I agree, why don't you fill me in on the main course?"

"We team up. We work on this together. We keep Jones and the rest of the task force out of it."

"What about my Mossad contacts?"

"Just us."

"I see. Oh, wait, No, I don't see."

Terese moved closer so she could hear what he was saying.

"If Matar's plot is ongoing," I said, "I want us to bring it down. Not them."

"Because?"

"Because I want to keep the blond girl out of it."

There was a pause. Then Berleand said, "Jones told

you that he tested the bone samples from Miriam Collins's grave."

"He did."

"And that it's a match for Miriam Collins."

"I know."

"So forgive me but I'm confused. Why, then, would you be interested in protecting this probably hardened terrorist?"

"I can't tell you unless you agree to work with me."

"And keep Jones out of it?"

"Yes."

"Because you want to protect the blond girl who probably had a role in the murders of Karen Tower and Mario Contuzzi?"

"As you said, probably."

"That's why we have courts."

"I don't want her to see the inside of one. You'll understand why after I tell you what I know."

Berleand went quiet again.

"Do we have a deal?" I asked.

"Up to a point."

"Meaning?"

"Meaning that once again you are thinking small-time. You are worried about one person. I understand that. I assume that you will tell me why she is important to you in a moment. But what we are dealing with could involve thousands of lives. Thousands of fathers, mothers, sons, and daughters. The chatter I heard suggests something huge is in play, not just one strike, but a variety of attacks over the course of many months. I don't really care about one girl—not against the thousands who might be slaughtered."

"So what exactly are you promising?"

"You didn't let me finish. My not caring about the girl cuts both ways. I don't care if she gets caught—and I don't care if she escapes prosecution. So, yes, I am with you. We will try to solve this ourselves—something I've been doing pretty much, anyway. But if we are out-manned or outgunned, I reserve the right to call in Jones. I will keep my word and help you protect the girl. But the priority here has to be stopping the jihadists from carrying out their mission. One life is not worth thousands."

I wondered about that. "Do you have any children, Berleand?"

"No. But please don't play that paternal-bond card with me. It is insulting." Then: "Wait. Are you telling me that the blond girl is Terese Collins's daughter?"

"In a manner of speaking."

"Explain."

"We have a deal?" I said.

"Yes. With the caveats I just laid out. Tell me what you know."

I ran him through it, my visits to Save the Angels, to the Official Photography of Albin Laramie, to the discovery of the embryo adoptions, to the "Mommy" phone call that Terese had just received. He interrupted several times with questions. I answered them as best as I could. When I finished he dived in.

"First, we need to find the identity of the girl. We'll

make copies of the picture. I'll e-mail one over to Lefeb-vre. If she's American, maybe she was in Paris on some kind of exchange program. He can show it around."

"Okay," I said.

"You said the call came in on Terese's cell phone?"

"Yes."

"I assume the incoming number was blocked?"

I hadn't even thought to ask. I looked at Terese. She nodded. I said, "Yes."

"What time exactly?"

I looked at Terese. She checked her phone log and told me the time.

"I will call you back in five minutes," Berleand said. He hung up.

Win came in and said, "All well?"

"Peachy."

"Your parents are taken care of. Same with Esperanza and the office."

I nodded. The phone rang again. It was Berleand.

"I may have something," he said.

"Go ahead."

"The call to Terese came from a throwaway phone purchased with cash in Danbury, Connecticut."

"That's a pretty big city."

"Maybe I can shrink it down then. I told you we heard chatter coming from a possible cell in Paterson, New Jersey."

"Right."

"Most of the communications went or came from overseas, but we have seen some that stayed here in the

United States. You know that criminal elements often communicate via e-mail?"

"I guess it makes sense."

"Because it's somewhat anonymous. They set up an account with a free provider and use that. What many people don't know is that we can now tell where the e-mail account was created. It doesn't help much. Most of the time it's created on a public computer, at the library or an Internet café, something like that."

"And in this case?"

"The chatter involved an e-mail address created eight months ago at the Mark Twain Library in Redding, Connecticut, less than ten miles from Danbury."

I thought about it. "It's a link."

"Yes. More than that, the library is used by the local coed prep school, Carver Academy. We could get lucky. Your 'Carrie' could be a student there."

"You can check?"

"I have a call in now. In the meantime, Redding is only about an hour and a half from here. We could take a ride up and show the picture around."

"Want me to drive?"

Berleand said, "I think that would be best."

36

I persuaded Terese to stay behind, no easy task, in case we needed something in the city. I promised her that we would call the moment we knew something. She grudgingly agreed. We didn't need all of us up there spreading our resources. Win would stay nearby, mostly for Terese's protection, but the two of them could try to investigate other avenues too. The key was probably Save the Angels. If we could locate their records, we could find Carrie's full name and address, track down her adoptive or surrogate or whatever-you-call-them parents, and see if we could locate her that way.

On the drive up, Berleand asked, "Have you ever been married?"

"Nope. You?"

He smiled. "Four times."

"Wow."

"All ended in divorce. I don't regret a single one."

"Would your ex-wives say the same?"

"I doubt it. But we're friends now. I'm not good with keeping women, just getting them."

I smiled. "Wouldn't expect you to be the type."

"Because I'm not handsome?"

I shrugged.

"Looks are overrated," he said. "Do you know what I do have?"

"Don't tell me. A great sense of humor, right? According to women's magazines, a sense of humor is the most important quality in a man."

"Sure, of course, and the check is in the mail," Berleand said.

"So that's not it."

"I am a very funny man," he said. "But that's not it."

"What then?" I asked.

"I told you before."

"Tell me again."

"Charisma," Berleand said. "I have charisma on an almost supernatural level."

I smiled. "Hard to argue with that."

Redding was more rural than I'd expected, a sleepy, unassuming town of New England–Puritan architecture, postmodern suburban McMansions, roadside antiques shops, aging farmland. Above the green door of the modest library, a plaque read MARK TWAIN LIBRARY, and then in slightly smaller print, GIFT OF SAMUEL L. CLEMENS.

I found that curious, but now was hardly the time. We headed to the librarian's desk.

Since Berleand had the official badge, even if we were way out of his district, I let him take the lead. "Hello," he said to the librarian. Her nameplate read "Paige Wesson." She looked up with jaded eyes, as if Berleand were returning an overdue book and offering up a lame excuse she had heard a million times before. "We are looking for this missing girl. Have you seen her?"

He held out his badge in one hand, the blonde's picture in the other. The librarian looked at the badge first.

"You're from Paris," she said.

"Yes."

"Does this look like Paris?"

"Not even close," Berleand agreed. "But the case has international implications. The girl was last seen under duress in my jurisdiction. We believe that she may have used the computers at this library."

She picked up the picture. "I don't think I've seen her."

"Are you sure?"

"No, I'm not sure. Look around you." We did. There were teens at nearly every table. "Tons of kids come in here every day. I'm not saying she has never been in here. I'm just saying I don't know her."

"Could you check in your computers, see if you have a card registered to anyone with the first name Carrie?"

"Do you have a court order?" Paige asked.

"Could we look at your computer sign-up logs from eight months ago?"

"Same question."

Berleand smiled at her. "Have a pleasant day."

"You too."

We moved away from Paige Wesson and started for the door. My phone buzzed. It was Esperanza.

"I was able to get through to someone at Carver Academy," Esperanza said. "They have no student registered with the first name Carrie."

"Bummer," I said. I thanked her, hung up, filled in Berleand.

Berleand said, "Any suggestions?"

"We split up and show her picture to the students in here," I said.

I scanned the room and saw a table with three teenage boys in the corner. Two wore varsity jackets, the kind with the name stenciled on the front and the pleather sleeves—the same kind I'd worn when I was at Livingston High. The third was pure prep boy—the set jaw, the fine bone structure, the collared polo shirt, the expensive khaki pants. I decided to start with them.

I showed them the picture.

"Do you know her?"

Prep Boy did the talking. "I think her name is Carrie."

Pay dirt.

"Do you know her last name?"

Three head shakes.

"Does she go to your school?"

"No," Prep Boy said. "She's a townie, I assume. We've seen her around."

Varsity Jacket One said, "She's hot."

Prep Boy with the set jaw nodded his agreement. "And she has a terrific ass."

I frowned. *Meet Mini-Win,* I thought.

Berleand looked over at me. I signaled that I might have something. He joined us.

"Do you know where she lives?" I asked.

"No. But Kenbo had her."

"Who?"

"Ken Borman. He had her."

Berleand said, "Had her?"

I looked at him. Berleand said, "Oh. Had her."

"Where can we find Kenbo?" I asked.

"He's in the weight room on campus."

They gave us directions and we were on our way.

37

I expected Kenbo to be bigger.

When you hear a nickname like Kenbo, and you hear he's had the hot blonde and that he's in the weight room, a certain image of a muscle-headed pretty boy sort of rises to the surface. That wasn't the case here. Kenbo had hair so dark and straight it had to be colored and ironed. It hung over one eye like a heavy black curtain. His complexion was pale, his arms reedy, his fingernails polished black. We called this look "Goth" way back in my day.

When I handed him the photograph, I saw his eye—I could see only one because the other was covered by the hair—widen. He looked up at us and I could see fear on his face.

"You know her," I said.

Kenbo stood up, backed up a few steps, turned, and

then suddenly sprinted away. I looked at Berleand. He said, "You don't expect me to chase him, do you?"

I took off after him. Kenbo was outside now, dashing across the rather spacious Carver Academy campus. The gunshot wound ached but not enough to slow me down. There were very few students out and about, and no teachers that I could see, but someone was bound to call the authorities. This couldn't be good.

"Wait!" I shouted.

He didn't. He spun left and disappeared behind a brick building. He wore his pants fashionably loose, too loose, and that helped. He had to keep hitching them up. I followed, closing the gap. I felt an ache in my knee—a reminder of my old injury—and leapt a wire-mesh fence. He ran across a sports field made of artificial turf. I didn't bother calling out again. That would only waste strength and time. He was heading to the outskirts of campus, away from witnesses, and I took this as a positive thing.

When he reached an opening near the woods, I dived for his feet, wrapped my arms around his leg in a manner that would have made any NFL defensive back envious, and drove him to the ground. He fell harder than I would have liked, spinning away from me, trying to kick me off.

"I'm not going to hurt you," I shouted.

"Just leave me alone."

I actually straddled his chest and pinned his arms, as if I were his big brother. "Calm down."

"Get off me!"

"I'm just trying to find this girl."

"I don't know anything."

"Ken—"

"Get off me!"

"Promise you won't run?"

"Get off. Please!"

I was pinning down a helpless, terrified high school kid. What would I do for an encore? Drown a kitten? I rolled off him.

"I'm trying to help this girl," I said.

He sat up. There were tears on his face. He wiped them away and hid his face in his arm.

"Ken?"

"What?"

"This girl is missing and probably in serious danger."

He looked up at me.

"I'm trying to find her."

"You don't know her?"

I shook my head. Berleand was finally in view.

"Are you cops?"

"He is. I'm working on this for a personal reason."

"What reason?"

"I'm trying to help—" I didn't see any other way to say it. "I'm trying to help her birth mother locate her. Carrie is missing, and she may be in serious trouble."

"I don't understand. Why come to me?"

"Your friends told us you dated her."

He lowered his head again.

"In fact, they said you did more than just date her."

He shrugged. "So?"

"So what's her full name?"

"You don't know that either?"

"She's in trouble, Ken."

Berleand had caught up to us. He was breathing heavily. He reached into his pocket—I thought for a pencil—and pulled out a cigarette. Yeah, that should help.

"Carrie Steward," Ken said.

I looked at Berleand. He nodded, wheezed, managed to say: "I'll call it in."

He grabbed his phone and started walking, phone in the air, searching for service.

"I don't understand why you ran," I said.

"I lied," he said. "To my friends, okay? I never slept with her. I just said that."

I waited.

"We met at the library, actually. I mean, she was so beautiful, you know? And she was surrounded by these two other blondes, all staring off like something out of *Children of the Corn*. It was spooky. Anyway I'm watching her for, like, three days and she finally goes off by herself and I walk up and say hi. She totally ignores me at first. I mean, I've been given the cold shoulder but this chick is giving me chills. But I figure, what have I got to lose? So I keep talking and I have my iPod, right, so I ask her what music she likes and she says she doesn't like music. I couldn't believe it, so I play her something from Blue October. I can see her face change. The power of music, right?"

He stopped. I looked over. Berleand was on the phone. I texted the name "Carrie Steward" to both Esperanza and Terese. Let them start digging into her too.

I kept waiting for someone from the school to start over toward us, but so far, no one had. We both sat on the grass now, facing back toward the campus. The sun was beginning to dip down, painting the sky burnt orange.

"So what happened?" I asked.

"We started talking. She told me her name was Carrie. She wanted to hear other songs. But she kept looking around, like she was afraid her friends would see her hanging out with me. Made me feel like a loser, but maybe it was a townie-versus-preppy thing, I don't know. That's what I thought anyway. At first. We met a few more times after that. She would be at the library with her friends and then we'd sneak out in the back and just talk and listen to music. One day I told her about a band that was playing in Norwalk. I asked her if she wanted to go. Her face turned white. She looked so scared. I said no big deal, but Carrie said maybe we could try. I said I could pick her up at her house. She freaked. I mean, really freaked."

The air was getting cool. Berleand finished on the phone. He looked back at me, saw our faces, knew it was best to stay away.

"So what happened next?"

"So she tells me to park at the end of Duck Run Road. She said she'd meet me there at nine o'clock. So I park there a few minutes before nine. It's dark out. I'm just sitting there. There's no light on the road or anything. I'm waiting. It's nine fifteen now. I hear a noise and then suddenly my car door opens and I'm being pulled out."

Ken stopped. There were more tears on his face. He wiped them away.

"Someone punches me straight in the mouth. Knocks out two teeth." He showed me. "They drag me out of the car. I don't know how many of them. Four, maybe five, and they're kicking me. I just cover up, you know, put my hands over my head, and I think I'm going to die. Then I'm rolled onto my back. And held down. I still can't see any faces—and, man, I don't want to. One of them puts a knife right in front of me. He says, 'She doesn't want you to talk to her again. If you say a word about this, we kill your family.'"

Ken and I sat there and said nothing for a few moments. I looked over at Berleand. He shook his head. Nothing on Carrie Steward.

"That's it," he said. "I never saw her again. Or any of those kids she hung out with. It's like they disappeared."

"Did you tell anyone?"

He shook his head.

"How did you explain your injuries?"

"I said I got jumped outside the concert. You won't tell anyone, will you?"

"I won't tell anyone," I said. "But we need to find her, Ken. Do you have any clue where Carrie might be?"

He said nothing.

"Ken?"

"I asked her where she lived. She wouldn't tell me."

I waited.

"But one day"—he stopped, took a deep breath—"I followed her after she left the library."

Ken looked away and blinked.

"So you know where she lives?"

He shrugged. "Maybe. I don't know. I don't think so."

"Can you show me where you followed her to?"

Ken shook his head. "I can give you directions," he said. "But I don't want to go with you, okay? Right now I just want to go home."

38

THE chain that blocked our way had a sign on it that read: PRIVATE ROAD.

We pulled ahead and parked around the corner. There was nothing in view but crop fields and woods. So far, our various sources had come up with nothing on any Carric Steward. The name might have been a pseudonym, but everyone was still searching. Esperanza called me and said, "I have something that might interest you."

"Go ahead."

"You mentioned a Dr. Jiménez, a young resident who worked with Dr. Cox when he was starting up Cryo-Hope?"

"Right."

"Jiménez is also connected to Save the Angels. He attended a retreat that they sponsored sixteen years ago.

I'm going to run a search on him, see if he can give us some information on the embryo adoption."

"Okay, good."

"Is Carrie short for anything?" she asked.

"I don't know. Maybe Caroline?"

"I'll check and get back to you when I know something."

"One more thing." I gave her the closest intersection. "Can you Google the address and see what you come up with?"

"Nothing coming up under the address in terms of who lives there. Looks like you're on farmland or something. No idea who owns it. Want me to look into it?"

"Please."

"Back to you as soon as I can."

I hung up. Berleand said, "Take a look."

He pointed at a tree near the front of the road. A security camera was aimed at the entrance.

"Strict security," he said, "for a farm."

"Ken told us about the private road. He said Carrie walked up it."

"If we do that, we will most certainly be seen."

"If the camera is even in use. It could be just a prop."

"No," Berleand said. "A prop would be more in plain sight."

He had a point.

"We could simply walk up the road anyway," I said.

"Trespassing," Berleand added.

"Big deal. We need to do something here, right?

There must be a farmhouse or something up the drive."
Then I thought about something. "Wait a second."

I called Esperanza back.

"You're in front of the computer, right?"

"Right," she said.

"Google-map the location I just gave you."

Quick typing. "Okay, got it."

"Now click the Satellite Photo option and zoom in."

"Hold on. . . . Okay, it's up."

"What's up that small road on the right side of the road?"

"Lots of green and what looks like a pretty big house from the top. Maybe two hundred yards from where you are, no more. It's all alone up there."

"Thanks."

I hung up. "There's a big house."

Berleand took off his glasses, cleaned them, held them up to the light, cleaned them some more. "What do we think is going on here exactly?"

"Truth?"

"Preferably."

"I don't have a clue."

"Do you think Carrie Steward is in that big house?" he asked.

"Only one way to find out," I said.

WITH the chain blocking the driveway, we decided to take it on foot. I called Win and filled him in on everything that was going on in case something went very wrong. He decided to come up after he checked on Terese one more time. Berleand and I debated and concluded that we might as well try just going up to the door and ringing the bell.

There was still light, but the sun was in its death throes. We stepped over the chain, started up the middle of the road, past the security camera. There were trees on either side of us. It seemed at least half of them had NO TRESPASSING signs stapled to them. The road wasn't paved but it seemed to be in pretty good shape. In some spots there was gravel, but for the most part it was loose dirt. Berleand made a face and walked on tiptoes. He kept wiping his hands against the sides of his legs and licking his lips.

"I don't like this," he said.

"Don't like what?"

"Dirt, the woods, bugs. It all feels so unclean."

"Right," I said, "but that strip joint, Upscale Pleasures, that was sanitary."

"Hey, that was a classy gentlemen's club. Didn't you read the sign?"

Up ahead, I saw a line of shrubs, and over that, a little bit in the distance, I could make out a gray-blue mansard roof.

A little ding sounded in my head. I picked up my pace.

"Myron?"

Behind us I heard the chain drop to the ground and a car come up. I moved faster, wanting to get a better look. I glanced behind me as a county police car pulled up. Berleand stopped. I didn't.

"Sir? You're trespassing on private property."

I rounded the corner. There was a fence surrounding the property. More security. But now, from this vantage point, I could see the mansion straight on.

"Stop right there. That's far enough."

I did stop. I looked ahead at the mansion. The sight confirmed what I'd suspected the moment I had seen the mansard roof. The house looked like the perfect bed-and-breakfast—a picturesque, almost overdone Victorian home with turrets, towers, stained-glass windows, a lemonade porch, and, yep, a blue-gray mansard roof.

I had seen the house on the Save the Angels Web site.

It was one of their homes for unwed mothers.

TWO police officers got out of the car.

They were young and muscle-bloated and had the cocky cop stride. They also wore Mountie hats. Mountie hats, I thought, looked silly and seemed counterproductive to law-enforcement activities, but I kept that to myself.

"Something we can do for you gentlemen?" one of the officers said.

He was the taller of the two, his shirtsleeves cutting into his biceps like two tourniquets. His name tag read "Taylor."

Berleand took out the photograph. "We are looking for this girl."

The officer took the photograph, glanced at it, handed it to his partner with the name tag "Erickson." Taylor said, "And you are?"

"Captain Berleand from the Brigade Criminelle in Paris."

Berleand handed Taylor his badge and identification. Taylor took it with two fingers as though Berleand had handed him a paper bag full of steaming dog poo. He studied the ID for a moment and then gestured toward me with his chin. "And who's your friend here?"

I waved. "Myron Bolitar," I said. "Nice to meet you."

"How are you involved in this, Mr. Bolitar?"

I was going to say, Long story, but thought that maybe it wasn't really that complicated: "The girl we're looking for may be the daughter of my girlfriend."

"May be?" Taylor turned back to Berleand. "Okay, Inspector Clouseau, you want to tell me what you're doing here?"

"'Inspector Clouseau,'" Berleand repeated. "That's very funny. Because I'm French, right?"

Taylor just stared at him.

"I'm working on a case involving international terrorism," Berleand said.

"That a fact?"

"Yes. This girl's name has come up. We believe she lives here."

"Do you have a warrant?"

"Time is of the essence."

"I will take that as a no." Taylor sighed, glanced at his partner, Erickson. Erickson chewed gum, showed nothing. Taylor looked over at me. "This true, Mr. Bolitar?"

"It is."

"So your girlfriend's maybe daughter is somehow mixed up with an international terrorist investigation?"

"Yes," I said.

He scratched an itch on his baby-faced cheek. I tried to guess their ages. Probably still in their twenties, though they could pass for high schoolers. When did cops start looking so damn young?

"Do you know what this place is?" Taylor asked.

Berleand started shaking his head, even as I said, "It's a home for unwed mothers."

Taylor pointed at me, nodded. "That's supposed to be confidential."

"I know," I said.

"But you're exactly right. So you can see how they might be touchy about their privacy."

"We do," I said.

"If a place like this isn't a safe haven, well, what is? They come here to escape prying eyes."

"I get that."

"And you're sure your girlfriend's maybe daughter isn't just here because she's pregnant?"

Now that I thought about it, that was a fair question. "That's irrelevant. Captain Berleand can tell you. This is about a terror plot. If she's pregnant or not, it makes no difference."

"The people who run this place—they've never caused any trouble."

"I understand that."

"And this is still the United States of America. If they don't want you on their property, you have no right to be here without a warrant."

"I understand that too," I said. Looking at the mansion, I asked, "Were they the ones who called you?"

Taylor squinted at me then, and I figured he was about to tell me that was none of my business. Instead he too looked toward the house and said, "Strangely enough, no. Normally they do. When kids trespass, whatever. We found out about you from Paige Wesson at the library and then someone else saw you chasing a kid over at Carver Academy."

Taylor kept looking at the house as if it had just materialized.

Berleand said, "Please listen to me. This case is very important."

"This is still America," Taylor said again. "If they don't want to speak to you, you have to honor that. That said . . ." Taylor looked back at Erickson. "You see any reason not to knock on the door and show them this picture?"

Erickson thought about it a moment. Then he shook his head.

"Both of you stay here."

They sauntered past us, opened the gate, headed toward the front door. I heard an engine in the background. I turned. Nothing. Might have been a car passing from the main road. The sun was gone now, the sky darkening. I looked at the house. It was still. I hadn't seen any movement at all, not once since we arrived.

I heard another car engine, this time coming from the general direction of the house. Again I saw nothing. Berleand moved closer to me.

"Do you have a bad feeling here?" he asked.

"I don't have a good one."

"I think we should call Jones."

My cell phone buzzed just as Taylor and Erickson reached the porch steps. It was Esperanza.

"I have something you need to see."

"Oh?"

"Remember I told you Dr. Jiménez attended a Save the Angels retreat?"

"Yes."

"I found some other people who did too. I visited their Facebook pages. One of them has a whole gallery up on the retreat. I'm sending one of the photos to you now. It's a group shot, but Dr. Jiménez is standing on the far right."

"Okay, let me get off the line."

I hung up, and the BlackBerry began to hum. I opened the e-mail from Esperanza and clicked the attachment. The picture loaded slowly. Berleand looked over my shoulder.

Taylor and Erickson reached the front door. Taylor rang the bell. A blond teenage boy answered the door. I wasn't close enough to hear. Taylor said something. The boy said something back.

The picture loaded on my BlackBerry. The screen was so small, and so too were the faces. I clicked the ZOOM option, moved the cursor to the right, hit ZOOM again. The picture came in closer, but now it was blurry. I hit ENHANCE. An hourglass appeared as the picture started to focus.

I glanced back at the front door of the Victorian home. Taylor stepped forward, as if he wanted to go in. The blond boy held up his hand. Taylor looked at Erickson. I could see surprise on his face. Now I heard Erickson. He sounded angry. The teenage boy looked scared. Still waiting for the photo enhancement to take effect, I stepped closer.

The picture came into focus. I looked down, saw the face of Dr. Jiménez, and nearly dropped my phone. It was a shock, and yet, remembering what Jones had told me, things were starting to click in a horrible, horrible way.

Dr. Jiménez—clever to use a Spanish name and probably identity for a dark-skinned man—was Mohammad Matar.

Before I could process what it all meant, the teenage boy shouted, "You can't come in!"

Erickson: "Son, step aside."

"No!"

Erickson didn't like that answer. He put his arms up as though preparing to push this blond teenager to the side. The teenager suddenly had a knife in his hand. Before anyone could move, he raised it overhead and jammed it deep into Erickson's chest.

Oh no . . .

I stuck my phone into my pocket as I started running toward the door. A sudden burst of noise made me stop cold.

Gunfire.

Erickson was hit. He spun around with the knife still in his chest and then dropped to the ground. Taylor started reaching for his gun, but he had no chance. More gunfire shattered the night. Taylor's body jerked once, then twice, then collapsed in a heap.

I heard the engines again now, a car roaring up the drive, another coming from behind the house. I looked for Berleand. He was sprinting toward me.

"Run to the woods!" I shouted.

Tires shrieking to a stop. Another burst of gunfire.

I ran toward the trees and dark, away from both the house and the private road. *The woods,* I thought. If we could make it to the woods, we could hide. A car sped across the grounds, its headlights searching for us. There were random barrages of bullets. I didn't look back to see where they were coming from. I found a rock and ducked behind it. I turned and saw Berleand still in view.

More gunfire. And Berleand went down.

I rose from behind the rock, but Berleand was too far away from me. Two men were on him. Three others jumped out of a Jeep, all armed. They ran toward Berleand, firing blindly into the woods. One bullet smacked the tree behind me. I ducked back down as another volley went past in a wave.

For a moment there was nothing. Then: "Come out now!"

The man's voice had a heavy Middle Eastern accent. Staying low, I glanced out. It was dark, night making more of its claim with each passing moment, but I could make out that at least two of the men had dark hair and dark skin and full beards. Several wore green bandannas around their necks, the kind you could pull up to cover your face. They shouted at one another in a language I didn't understand but figured had to be Arabic.

What the hell was going on?

"Show yourself or we will hurt your friend."

The man saying that appeared to be the leader. He barked out orders and pointed right and left. Two men started circling toward me. One man got back into the car and used his headlights to sweep the woods. I stayed low, my cheek against the ground. My heart pounded in my chest.

I hadn't brought a weapon. Stupid. So goddamn stupid.

I dug into my pocket and tried to get my phone.

The leader called out: "Last chance! I will begin by shooting his knees."

Berleand shouted, "Don't listen to him!"

My fingers found the phone just as a single bullet blast exploded through the night air.

Berleand screamed.

The leader: "Come out now!"

I fumbled with the phone and hit Win's number on speed dial. Berleand was whimpering now. I closed my eyes, tried to wish it away, needed to think.

Then Berleand's voice fighting through tears: "Don't listen to him!"

"The other knee!"

Another gunshot.

Berleand screamed in obvious agony. The sound ripped at me, shredded my insides. I knew that I couldn't give up. If I showed myself, we would both be dead. Win would have heard what was going on by now. He'd call Jones and law enforcement. It wouldn't be long.

I could hear Berleand crying.

Then one more time, weaker this time, Berleand's voice: "Don't . . . listen . . . to . . . him!"

I heard men in the woods, not far from me. No choice. Had to make a move. I looked at the Victorian mansion on my right. My fingers wrapped themselves around a large rock as something close to a plan started running through my head.

The leader: "I have a knife. I'm going to cut out his eyes now."

There was movement in the house now. I could see it through the window. Not much time. I got up, my knees bent, ready to spring into action.

I heaved the rock as hard as I could in the direction opposite the house. The rock landed against a tree with a thud.

The leader's head turned toward the sound. The men

moving through the woods started in that direction too, firing their weapons. The Jeep veered away from me and toward where the rock had landed.

At least, that was what I hoped was happening.

I didn't wait and watch. As soon as the rock left my hand, I dashed through the trees toward the side of the house. I was moving farther away from Berleand's cries and the men who were trying to kill me. It was darker now, almost impossible to see, but I didn't let that stop me. Branches whipped my face. I didn't care. I knew I had only seconds. Time was everything now, but it seemed to be taking me too long to get close to the house.

Without breaking stride, I picked up another rock.

The leader: "I'm taking out an eye now!"

I heard Berleand shout, "No!"—and then he began to shriek.

Time was up.

Still running, I used my momentum to hurl the rock toward the house. I gave the throw everything I had, nearly dislocating my shoulder. Through the darkness I saw the rock move in an upward arc. On the right side of the house—the side I was on—there was a beautiful picture window. I followed the rock's trajectory, thinking it was going to land short.

It didn't.

The rock crashed through the window, shattering it into small shards of glass. Panic erupted. It was what I had counted on. I doubled back into the woods as the armed men ran toward the house. I saw two blond teenagers—one male, one female—come toward the broken window from the inside. Part of me wondered if the girl was Carrie, but there was no time to take a second look. The men shouted something in Arabic. I didn't see what happened next. I was circling back, moving as fast as I could, using the diversion to get behind the leader.

I saw the man in the Jeep stop and get out. He ran toward the smashed window too. That was their main job here: protect the house. I had broken through their perimeter. They were scattering and trying to regroup. Confusion set in.

Staying out of sight and not wasting any time, I had managed to move back down, past my original hiding place. The leader had his back to me now, facing the house. I was maybe sixty, seventy yards away from him.

How long until help came?

Too long.

The leader was shouting out orders. Berleand was on the ground by his feet. Motionless. And worse, Berleand was silent. No more cries. No more whimpers.

Had to get to him.

I wasn't sure how. Once I stepped out from behind this tree, I would be in the open and ridiculously vulnerable. But there was no choice now.

I started sprinting toward the leader.

I had moved maybe three steps when I heard someone shout out a warning. The leader turned toward me. I was still forty yards away. My legs pumped fast, but everything else slowed down. The leader too wore a green bandanna around his neck, like an outlaw in an old

Western. His beard was thick. He was taller than the others, maybe six two, and stocky. There was a knife in one hand, a gun in the other. He raised the gun toward me. I debated dropping to the ground or veering to the side, anything to avoid the shot, but my mind quickly sized up the situation and I realized that a sudden shift wouldn't work here. Yes, he might miss with the first bullet, but then I would be totally exposed. The second shot would certainly not miss. Plus my diversion was over. The other men were already coming back toward us. They would fire too.

I had to hope that he'd panic and miss me.

He aimed the gun. I met his eyes and saw the calm that simple moral certainty brings a man. I had no chance. I could see that now. He would not miss. And then, right before he pulled the trigger, I heard him howl in pain and saw him look down.

Berleand was biting his calf, holding on with his teeth like an angry Rottweiler.

The leader's gun hand dropped to his side, aiming at the top of Berleand's head. With a surge of adrenaline, I launched myself at the leader, arms in front of me. But before I could get there, I heard the blast and saw the gun recoil. Berleand's body jerked as I reached the leader. I wrapped my arms around the son of a bitch, kept my momentum going. As we toppled toward the ground, I positioned my forearm against the leader's nose. We landed hard, my full body weight behind the forearm. His nose exploded like a water balloon. Blood smacked me in the face. It felt warm against my skin. He cried out, but he still had a lot of fight in him. So did I. I dodged a head butt. He tried to get me in a bear hug. A fatal move. I let his arms encircle me. When he started to squeeze, I quickly snaked my arms free. Now the leader was totally vulnerable. I did not hesitate. I thought about Berleand, about how this man had made my friend suffer.

Time to end this.

The fingers of my right hand formed a claw. I didn't go for the eyes or the nose or any other soft target to disable or maim. At the base of the throat, right above the thoracic cage, sits a hollowed area where the trachea isn't protected. With two fingers and my thumb, I dug full force into the opening and grabbed his throat in a talonlike grip. I was crying as I jerked his windpipe toward me, screaming like an animal while a man died by my hand.

I plucked the gun from his still hand.

The men were running back toward us. They hadn't yet shot for fear of hitting their leader. I rolled toward the body on my right.

"Berleand?"

But he was dead. I could see that now. His dorky glasses with those oversize frames were askew on that soft, malleable face. I wanted to cry. I wanted just to give up and hold him and cry.

The men were getting closer. I looked up. They were having trouble seeing me, but the lights from the house behind them made them perfect silhouettes. I raised the gun and fired. One man went down. I turned the gun to the left. I fired again. Another man went down. Now they started firing back. I rolled back toward the leader and used his body as a shield. I fired again. Another man went down.

Sirens.

I kept low and sprinted toward the house. Cop cars came rushing up. I heard a helicopter, maybe more than one, above us. More gunfire. I would let them handle it. I wanted to get into that house now.

I ran past Taylor. Dead. The door was still open. Erickson's body was on the front porch next to it, the knife still deep in his chest. I stepped over him and dived into the foyer.

Silence.

I didn't like that.

I still had the leader's gun in my hand. I pushed my back against the wall. The place was in total disrepair. The wallpaper was peeling. The light was on. Out of the corner of my eye, I saw someone sprint by, heard footsteps going down the stairs. Had to be a lower level. A basement.

Outside I could hear gunfire. I could hear someone calling through a bullhorn for surrender. Might have been Jones. I should wait now. There was no chance I was going to get Carrie out of here, anyway. I should sit tight, cover the door, not let anyone in or out. That was the smart play here. Wait it out.

I might have done that. I might have just stayed right there and never gone into that basement if the blond boy hadn't come racing down the stairs.

I called him a boy. That wasn't fair. He looked to be about seventeen, maybe eighteen, not much younger than the dark-haired men I had just shot without hesitation. But when this teenager with the blond hair and khaki pants and dress shirt came tearing down the stairs—a gun in his hand—I didn't shoot right away.

"Freeze!" I shouted. "Drop the gun."

The boy's face twisted into some kind of hideous death mask. His gun hand rose toward me, and he took aim. I jumped, rolled to the left, and came up firing. I didn't go for the death shot, as opposed to what I had been like outside. I went for his legs. I fired low. The teen screamed and fell. He still held the gun, though, still had the twisted death-mask expression. He aimed for me again.

I jumped out of the foyer and into the hallway—where I came face-to-face with the basement door.

The blond teen had been hit in the leg. There was no way he could follow me down. I caught my breath, grabbed the knob with my free hand, and opened the door.

Total darkness.

I kept my gun against my chest. Pressed myself against the wall to make myself a smaller target. I slowly started down the stairs, feeling my way with my front foot. One hand held the gun; the other searched for a light switch. I couldn't find one. With my body still turned to the side, I took the steps slowly, left foot down a step, right foot met up with it. I wondered about ammunition. How many bullets did I have left? No idea.

I heard whispers below.

No doubt about it. The lights might have been off, but someone was down in the darkness. Probably more than one someone. Again I debated doing the wise thing—just stopping, staying still, moving back to the top of the stairs, waiting for reinforcements. The gunfire outside had stopped. Jones and his men, I was sure, had secured the premises.

But I didn't do that.

My left foot reached the bottom step. I heard a scuffling sound that made the hairs on the back of my neck stand up. My free hand felt along the wall until I found the light switch. Or to be more precise, switches. Three in a row. I put my hand underneath them, got my gun ready, took one deep breath, and then I flipped up all three at the same time.

Later I would remember the other details: the Arabic graffiti spray-painted on the walls, the green flags with the blood-soaked crescent moon, the posters of martyrs in battle fatigues carrying assault weapons. Later I would remember the portraits of Mohammad Matar during many different stages of his life, including the time when he worked as a medical resident named Jiménez.

But right now, all of that was little more than backdrop.

Because there, in the far corner of the basement, I saw something that made my heart stop. I blinked my eyes, looked again, couldn't believe it, and yet maybe it made perfect sense after all.

A group of blond teenagers and children were huddled against a pregnant woman in a black burqa. Their eyes were ice blue, and they all stared at me with hatred. They began to make a noise, a snarl maybe, as one, and then I realized that it wasn't a snarl. These were words, repeated over and over. . . .

"Al-sabr wal-sayf."

I backed away from them, shaking my head.

"Al-sabr wal-sayf."

The brain started doing the synapse thing again: the blond hair. The blue eyes. CryoHope. Dr. Jiménez being Mohammad Matar. Patience. The sword.

Patience.

I bit back a scream as the truth rained down on me: Save the Angels hadn't used the embryos to help infertile couples. They had used them to create the ultimate weapon of terror, to infiltrate, to get ready for global jihad.

Patience and the sword will defeat the sinners.

The blondes started coming toward me, even though I was the one with the gun. Some kept chanting. Some just shrieked. Some dived back behind the burqa-clad pregnant woman, looking terrified. I moved faster, heading up the stairs. From above, I heard a familiar voice call my name.

"Bolitar? Bolitar?"

I turned my back on the ice blue, hell-spawned monstrosity below me, scrambled to the top of the stairs, dived through the basement door, slammed it closed behind me. Like that might help. Like that might make it all go away.

Jones was there. So were his men in bulletproof vests. Jones saw the look on my face.

"What is it?" he asked me. "What's down there?"

But I couldn't even speak, couldn't make out words. I ran outside, toward Berleand. I collapsed next to his still body. I was hoping for a reprieve, hoping that maybe in the confusion, I had made a mistake. I hadn't. Berleand, the poor, beautiful bastard, was dead. I held him for just a second, maybe two. No more than that.

The job wasn't over. Berleand would have been the first to tell me that.

I still needed to find Carrie.

As I ran back to the house, I called Terese. No answer.

I quickly joined the house search. Jones and his men were in the basement already. The blondes were brought upstairs. I looked at them, at their hate-filled eyes. None was Carrie. We found two more women dressed in face-covering, traditional black burqas. Both were pregnant. As his men started bringing the captives outside, Jones looked at me in horror and disbelief. I looked back and nodded. These women weren't mothers. They were incubators—embryo carriers.

We searched some more, opened up all the closets,

found training manuals and film clips, laptops, horror upon horror. But no Carrie.

I took out my phone and tried Terese again. Still no answer. Not on her cell. Not at the apartment at the Dakota.

I staggered outside. Win had arrived. He stood on the porch, waiting for me. Our eyes met.

"Terese?" I ask.

Win shook his head. "She's gone."

Again.

39

39

WE have been driving in this pickup truck for more than eight hours now through the craziest terrain. I haven't seen a person or even a building in more than six. I have been to remote areas before, but this takes remote to the tenth power.

When we reach the hut, the driver pulls over and turns off the engine. He opens the door for me and hands me a backpack. He shows me the walking path. There is a phone in the hut, he tells me. When I want to return, I should call him on it. He will come and get me. I thank him and start down the path.

Four miles later, I see the clearing.

Terese is there. Her back is to me. When I returned to the Dakota that night, she was, as Win had said, gone. She had left a simple note behind: *"I love you so very much."*

That was it.

Terese's hair is dyed black now. The better to keep her hidden, I assume. Blondes would stand out, even here. I like her hair this way. I watch her walking away from me, and I can't help but smile. Her head held high, her shoulders back, the perfect posture. I flash back to that surveillance tape, the way I could see that Carrie had that same perfect posture, that same confident walk.

Terese is surrounded by three black women in colorful garb. I start toward them. One of the women spots me and whispers something. Terese turns, curious. When her eyes land on me, her entire face lights up. So, I guess, does mine. She drops the basket in her hand and sprints in my direction. There is no hesitation at all. I run to meet her. She wraps her arms around me and pulls me close.

"God, I missed you," she says.

I hug her back. That's all. I don't want to say anything. Not yet. I want to melt into this hug. I want to disappear into it and stay in her arms forever. I know deep in my soul that this is where I belong, holding her, and for just a few moments, I want and need that peace.

Finally I ask, "Where is Carrie?"

She takes my hand and walks me to the corner of the opening. She points up the field, to another small clearing. A hundred yards away, Carrie sits with two black girls about her age. They are all working on something. I can't tell what it is. Peeling or picking. The black girls are laughing. Carrie is not.

Carrie's hair is black too.

I turn back to Terese. I look at her eyes of blue with the gold ring around the pupils. Her daughter has the same gold ring. I saw it in that picture. The confident walk, the gold ring. The unmistakable genetic echo.

What else, I wonder, was passed down?

"Please understand why I had to run," Terese says. "She's my daughter."

"I know."

"I had to save her."

I nod. "She gave you her phone number the first time she called."

"Yes."

"You could have told me."

"I know. But I heard Berleand. She isn't worth thousands of lives to anyone but me."

The mention of Berleand causes a sharp pang. I wonder what to say next. I shade my eyes and look back toward Carrie. "Do you understand what her life has been like?"

Terese does not look, does not blink. "She was raised by terrorists."

"It's worse than that. Mohammad Matar did his medical residency at Columbia-Presbyterian, right when in vitro fertilization and embryonic storage were becoming big. He saw an opportunity for a crushing blow—

patience and the sword. Save the Angels was a radical terrorist group disguising itself as right-wing Christians. He used coercion and lies to get embryos. He didn't give them to infertile couples. He used Muslim women sympathetic to his cause as surrogates—like a storage facility until the embryos were born. Then he and his followers raised the offspring to be terrorists from day one. Nothing else. Carrie wasn't allowed to bond with anyone. She never knew love, not even as an infant. Never knew tenderness. No one held her. No one comforted her when she cried in her sleep. She and the others were indoctrinated every day of their lives to kill infidels. That was it. Nothing else. They were raised to be the ultimate weapons, to fit in as one of us and be ready for the ultimate holy war. Imagine. Matar sought out embryos from parents who were blond and blue-eyed. His weapons could go anywhere because who would suspect them?"

I wait for Terese to react, to wince. She does not. "Did you capture them all?"

"Not me. I broke up the main group in Connecticut. Jones found more information inside that house—and, I assume, some of the surviving terrorists were interrogated." I don't want to think about how—or maybe I do. I don't know anymore. "Green Death had another camp outside of Paris. It was raided within hours. Mossad and the Israelis air-raided a larger training compound on the Syrian-Iraqi border."

"What happened to the children?"

"Some were killed. Others are in custody."

She begins to walk back down the hill. "You think

because Carrie never knew love before that she should never know love now?"

"That's not what I'm saying."

"Sounds like it."

"I'm telling you the reality."

"You have friends who raised children, don't you?" she asks.

"Of course."

"What is the first thing they'll tell you? That their children come out a certain way. Hardwired. Nature over nurture. Parents can steer them and try to keep them on the right road, but in the end, they are little more than caregivers. Some children will end up being sweet no matter what. Others will end up psychotic. You know friends who have raised their kids identically. One kid is outgoing, one is quiet, one is miserable, and one is generous. Parents quickly learn that their influence is limited."

"She's never known any love at all, Terese."

"And now she will."

"You don't know what she's capable of."

"I don't know what anyone is capable of."

"That's not an answer," I say.

"What else do you expect me to do? She's my daughter. I will watch her. Because that's what a parent does. I will also protect her. And you're wrong. You met Ken Borman, right? The prep school kid?"

I nod.

"Carrie was drawn to him. Despite the unspeakable hell she lived with every single day, she somehow still felt a connection. She tried to break away. That's why she was with Matar in Paris. To be retrained."

"Was she there when Rick was murdered?"

"Yes."

"Her blood was on the scene."

"She said she tried to defend him."

"Do you believe that?"

Terese smiles at me. "I lost a daughter. I would do anything, anything, to get her back. Do you get that? You could tell me, for example, that Miriam had survived and was now a horrible monster. It wouldn't change that."

"Carrie is not Miriam."

"But she's still my daughter. I'm not giving up on her."

Behind Terese, her daughter rises and starts down the hill. She stops and looks toward us. Terese smiles and waves. Carrie waves back. She might be smiling too, but I can't say for sure. And I can't say for sure that Terese is wrong here. But I wonder. I wonder about that blond teenager coming down the stairs to shoot me, about why I hesitated. Nature versus nurture. If the girl up on that hill had been genetically Matar's, if a child conceived and then raised by crazy extremists becomes a crazy extremist, we will kill him or her without thought. Is it different because of genetics? Because of blond hair and blue eyes?

I don't know. I'm too damn tired to think about it.

Carrie had never known any love. Now she would. Suppose you and I had been raised like Carrie. Would it be best if we were simply destroyed like so much damaged goods? Or would some of that basic humanity win out in the end?

"Myron?"

I look at Terese's beautiful face.

"I wouldn't give up on your child. Please don't give up on mine."

I say nothing. I take her beautiful face in my hands, pull her to me, kiss her forehead, hold my lips there, close my eyes. I feel her arms around me.

"Take care of yourself," I say.

I pull back. There are tears in her eyes. I start back toward the path.

"I didn't have to come back to Angola," she says.

I stop and turn toward her.

"I could have gotten to Myanmar or Laos or someplace where you would have never found me."

"So why did you choose here?"

"Because I wanted you to find me."

Now the tears are in my eyes too.

"Please don't leave," she says.

I am so very tired. I don't sleep anymore. The faces of the dead are there when I close my eyes. The ice blue eyes stare at me. Nightmares haunt my dreams, and when I wake up, I am alone.

Terese walks toward me. "Please stay with me. Just for tonight, okay?"

I want to say something, but I can't. The tears come faster now. She pulls me to her, and I try so very hard not to break down. My head falls onto her shoulder. She strokes my hair and shushes me.

"It's okay," Terese whispers. "It's over now."

And as long as she holds me in her arms, I believe it.

BUT on this same day, somewhere in the United States, a chartered bus pulls up to a crowded national monument. The bus is carrying a group of sixteen-year-olds on a cross-country teen tour. Today is day three of their journey. The sun is shining. The skies are clear.

The bus door swings open. The giggling, gum-chewing teens spill out.

The last teen to get off the bus is a boy with blond hair.

He has blue eyes with a gold ring around each pupil.

And though he wears a heavy backpack, he walks into the crowd with his head held high, his shoulders back, and his posture perfect.

Acknowledgments

Okay, let's start the thanks with the officials from 36 quai des Orfèvres because they are in law enforcement and I don't want any of them angry with me: Monsieur le Directeur de la Police Judiciaire, Christian Flaesch; Monsieur Jean-Jacques Herlem, Directeur-Adjoint chargé des Brigades Centrales; Madame Nicole Tricart, Inspectrice Générale, conseiller auprès du Directeur Général de la Police Nationale; Monsieur Loïc Garnier, Commissaire Divisionnaire, Chef de la Brigade Criminelle; Mademoiselle Frédérique Conri, Commissaire Principal, Chef-Adjoint de la Brigade Criminelle.

In no particular order but with tons of gratitude: Marie-Anne Cantin, Eliane Benisti, Lisa Erbach Vance, Ben Sevier, Melissa Miller, Françoise Triffaux, Jon Wood, Malcolm Edwards, Susan Lamb, Angela McMahon, Ali Nasseri, David Gold, Bob Hadden, Aaron Priest, Craig Coben, Charlotte Coben, Anne Armstrong-Coben, Brian Tart, Mona Zaki, and Dany Cheij.

Certain characters in this book came out of something akin to various prisms. Years ago I created them, others cast them in a different light, and then still others interpreted them—and then I re-created them as entirely different beings here. That's why I also need to thank Guillaume Canet, Philippe Lefebvre (twice), and François Berleand.

New York Times bestselling author
Harlan Coben
is back with a brand-new thriller.
Read on for a preview from

CAUGHT

Available in hardcover from Dutton

I KNEW opening that red door would destroy my life.

Yes, that sounds melodramatic and full of foreboding, and I'm not big on either, and true, there was nothing menacing about the red door. In fact, the door was beyond ordinary, wood and four paneled—the kind of door you see standing guard in front of three out of every four suburban homes, with faded paint and a knocker no one ever used at chest level and a faux-brass knob.

But as I walked toward it, a distant streetlight barely illuminating my way, the dark opening yawning like a mouth ready to gobble me whole, the feeling of doom was unshakable. Each step forward took great effort as if I were walking not along a somewhat cracked walk but through still-wet cement. My body displayed all the classic symptoms of impending menace: chill down my spine? Check. Hairs standing up on my arms? Yep.

Prickle at the base of the neck? Present. Tingle in the scalp? Right there.

The house was dark, not a single light on. Chynna warned me that would be the case. The dwelling somehow seemed a little too cookie-cutter, a little too nondescript. That bothered me for some reason. This house was also isolated at the tippy end of the cul-de-sac, hunkering down in the darkness as though fending off intruders.

I didn't like it.

I didn't like anything about this, but this is what I do. When Chynna called I had just finished coaching the inner-city fourth-grade Newark Biddy basketball team. My team—all kids who, like me, were products of foster care (we call ourselves the NoRents, which is short for No Parents—gallows humor)—had managed to blow a six-point lead with two minutes left. On the court as in life, the NoRents aren't great under pressure.

Chynna called as I was gathering my young hoopsters for my postgame pep talk, which usually consisted of giving my charges some life-altering insight like "Good effort," "We'll get them next time," or "Don't forget we have a game next Thursday," always ending with "Hands in" and then we yell, "Defense," choosing to chant that word, I suppose, because we play none.

"Dan?"

"Who is this?"

"It's Chynna. Please come."

Her voice trembled, so I dismissed my team, jumped

in my car, and now I was here. I hadn't even had time to shower. The smell of gym sweat mixed now with the smell of fear sweat. I slowed my pace.

What was wrong with me?

I probably should have showered, for one thing. I'm not good without a shower. Never have been. But Chynna had been adamant. Now, she had begged. Before anyone got home. So here I was, my gray T-shirt darkened with perspiration and clinging to my chest, heading to that door.

Like most youngsters I work with, Chynna was seriously troubled, and maybe that was what was setting off the warning bells. I hadn't liked her voice on the phone, hadn't really warmed to this whole setup. Taking a deep breath, I glanced behind me. In the distance, I could see some signs of life on this suburban night—house lights, a flickering television or maybe computer monitor, an open garage door—but in this cul-de-sac, there was nothing, not a sound or movement, just a hush in the dark.

My cell phone vibrated, nearly making me jump out of my skin. I figured that it was Chynna, but no, it was Jenna, my ex-wife. I hit ANSWER and said, "Hey."

"Can I ask a favor?" she asked.

"I'm a little busy right now."

"I just need someone to babysit tomorrow night. You can bring Shelly if you want."

"Shelly and I are, uh, having trouble," I said.

"Again? But she's great for you."

"I have trouble holding on to great women."

"Don't I know it."

Jenna, my lovely ex, has been remarried for eight years. Her new husband is a well-respected surgeon named Noel Wheeler. Noel does volunteer work for me at the teen center. I like Noel and he likes me. He had a daughter by a previous marriage, and he and Jenna have a six-year-old girl named Kari. I'm Kari's godfather, and both kids call me Uncle Dan. I'm the family go-to babysitter.

I know this all sounds very civilized and Pollyanna, and I suppose it is. In my case, it could be simply a matter of necessity. I have no one else—no parents, no siblings—ergo, the closest thing I have to family is my ex-wife. The kids I work with—the ones I advocate for and try to help and defend—are my life, and in the end I'm not sure I do the slightest bit of good.

Jenna said, "Earth to Dan?"

"I'll be there," I said to her.

"Six-thirty. You're the best."

Jenna made a smooching noise into the mouthpiece and hung up. I looked at the phone for a moment, remembered our own wedding day. It had been a mistake for me to get married. It is a mistake for me to get too close to people, and yet I can't help it. Someone cue the violins so I can wax philosophical about how it is better to have loved and lost than never to have loved at all. I don't think that applies to me. It is in humans' DNA to repeat the same mistakes, even after we know better. So here I am, the poor orphan who scraped his way up to the top of his class at an elite Ivy League school but never really scraped off who he was. Corny, but I want someone in my life. Alas, that is not destiny. I am a loner who isn't meant to be alone.

"We are evolution's refuse, Dan. . . ."

My favorite foster "dad" taught me that. He was a college professor who loved to get into philosophical debates.

"Think about it, Dan. Throughout mankind, the strongest and brightest did what? They fought in wars. That only stopped this past century. Before that, we sent our absolute best to fight on the frontlines. So who stayed home and reproduced while our finest died on distant battlefields? The lame, the sick, the weak, the crooked, the cowardly—in short, the least of us. That's what we are the genetic by-product of, Dan—millennia of weeding out the premium and keeping the flotsam. That's why we are all garbage—the worst leftovers from centuries of bad breeding."

I forwent the knocker, and rapped on the door lightly with my knuckles. The door creaked open a crack. I hadn't realized that it was ajar.

I didn't like that either. A lot I didn't like here.

As a kid, I watched a lot of horror movies, which was strange because I hated them. I hated things jumping out at me. And I really couldn't stand movie gore. But I would still watch them and revel in the predictably moronic behavior of the heroines, and right now those scenes were replaying in my head, the ones where said moronic heroine knocks on a door and it opens a little and you scream, "Run, you scantily clad bimbo!" and she wouldn't, and you couldn't understand it, and two minutes later, the killer would be scooping out her skull and munching on her brain.

I should go right now.

In fact, I will. But then I flashed back to Chynna's call, to the words she'd said, the trembling in her voice. I sighed, leaned my face toward the opening, peered into the foyer.

Darkness.

Enough with the cloak and dagger.

"Chynna?"

My voice echoed. I expected silence. That would be the next step, right? No reply. I slip the door open a little, take a tentative step forward. . . .

"Dan? I'm in the back. Come in."

The voice was muffled, distant. Again I didn't like this, but there was no way I was backing out now. Backing out had cost me too much throughout my life. My hesitation was gone. I knew what had to be done now.

I opened the door, stepped inside, and closed the door behind me.

Others in my position would have brought a gun or some kind of weapon. I had thought about it. But that just doesn't work for me. No time to worry about that now. No one was home. Chynna had told me that. And if they were, well, I would handle that when the moment came.

"Chynna?"

"Go to the den. I'll be there in a second."

The voice sounded . . . off. I saw a light at the end of the hall and moved toward it. There was a noise now. I stopped and listened. Sounded like water running. A shower maybe.

"Chynna?"

"Just changing. Out in a second."

I moved into the low-lit den. I saw one of those dimmer-switch knobs and debated turning it up, but in the end I chose to leave it alone. My eyes adjusted pretty quickly. The room had cheesy wood paneling that looked as if it were made from something far closer to vinyl than anything in the timber family. There were two portraits of sad clowns with huge flowers on their lapels, the kind of paintings you might pick up at a particularly tacky motel's garage sale. There was a giant open bottle of no-name vodka on the bar.

I thought I heard somebody whisper.

"Chynna?" I called out.

No answer. I stood, listened for more whispering. Nothing.

I started toward the back, toward where I heard the shower running.

"I'll be right out," I heard the voice say. I pulled up, felt a chill. Because now I was closer to the voice, I could hear it better. And here was the thing I found particularly strange about it.

It didn't sound at all like Chynna.

Three things tugged at me. One, panic. This wasn't

Chynna. Get out of the house. Two, curiosity. If it wasn't Chynna, who the hell was it and what was going on? Three, panic again. It had been Chynna on the phone—so what had happened to her?

I couldn't just run out now.

I took one step toward where I'd come in, and that was when it all happened. A spotlight snapped on in my face, blinding me. I stumbled back, hand coming up to my face.

"Dan Mercer?"

I blinked. Female voice. Professional. Deep tone. Sounded oddly familiar.

"Who's there?"

Suddenly there were other people in the room. A man with a camera. Another with what look liked a boom mike. And the female with the familiar voice, a stunning woman with chestnut brown hair and a business suit.

"Wendy Tynes, Eyewitness News. Why are you here, Dan?"

I opened my mouth, nothing came out. I recognized the woman from that TV newsmagazine . . .

"Why have you been conversing online in a sexual manner with a twelve-year-old girl, Dan? We have your communications with her."

. . . the one that sets up and catches pedophiles on camera for all the world to see.

"Are you here to have sex with a twelve-year-old girl?"

The truth of what was going on here hits me, freezing my bones. Other people flooded the room. Producers maybe. Another cameraman. Two cops. The cameras come in closer. The lights get brighter. Beads of sweat pop up on my brow. I start to stammer, start to deny.

But it's over.

Two days later, the show airs. The world sees.

And the life of Dan Mercer, just as I somehow knew when I approached that door, is destroyed.

WHEN Marcia McWaid first saw her daughter's empty bed, panic did not set in. That would come later.

She had woken up at six a.m., early for Saturday morning, feeling pretty terrific. Ted, her husband of twenty years, slept in the bed next to her. He lay on his stomach, his arm around her waist. Ted liked to sleep with a shirt on and no pants. None. Nude from the waist down. "Gives my man down there room to roam," he would say with a smirk. And Marcia, imitating her daughter's teenage singsong tone, would say, "T-M-I"—Too Much Information.

Marcia slipped out of his grip and padded down to the kitchen. She made herself a cup of coffee with the new Keurig pod machine. Ted loved gadgets—boys and their toys—but this one actually got some use. You take the pod, you stick it in the machine—presto, coffee. No video screens, no touchpad, no wireless connectivity. Marcia loved it.

They'd recently finished an addition on the house—one extra bedroom, one bathroom, the kitchen knocked out a bit with a glassed-in nook. The kitchen nook offered oodles of morning sun and had thus become Marcia's favorite spot in the house. She took her coffee and the newspaper and set herself on the duvet, folding her feet beneath her.

A small slice of heaven.

She let herself read the paper and sip her coffee. In a few minutes she would have to check the schedule. Ryan, her third grader, had the early Hoops Basketball game at eight a.m. Ted coached. His team was winless for the second straight season.

"Why do your teams never win?" Marcia had asked him.

"I draft the kids based on two criteria."

"That being?"

"How nice the father—and how hot the mom."

She had slapped at him playfully and maybe Marcia would have been somewhat concerned if she hadn't seen the moms on the sideline and knew, for certain, that he had to be joking. Ted was actually a great coach, not in terms of strategy but in terms of handling the boys. They all loved him and his lack of competiveness so that even the untalented players—the ones who were usually discouraged and quit during the season—showed up every week. Ted even took the Bon Jovi song and turned it around, "You give losing a good name." The kids would laugh and cheer every basket, and when you're in third grade, that's how it should be.

Marcia's fourteen-year-old daughter, Patricia, had rehearsal for the freshman play, an abridged version of the musical *Les Misérables*. She had several small parts, but that didn't seem to affect the workload. And her oldest child, Haley, the high school senior, was running a "captain's practice" for the girls' lacrosse team. Captain's practices were unofficial, a way to sneak in early practices under the guidelines issued by high school sports. In short, no coaches, nothing official, just a casual gathering, glorified pickup games if you will, run by the captains.

Like most suburban parents, Marcia had a love-hate relationship with sports. She knew the relative long-term irrelevancy and yet still managed to get caught up in it.

A half hour of peace to start the day. That was all she needed.

She finished the first cup, pod-made herself a second, picked up the "Styles" section of the paper. The house remained silent. She padded upstairs and looked over her charges. Ryan slept on his side, his face conveniently facing the door so that his mother could notice the echo of his father.

Patricia's room was next. She too was still sleeping.

"Honey?"

Patricia stirred, might have made a noise. Her room, like Ryan's, looked as if someone had strategically placed sticks of dynamite in the drawers, blowing them open. Some clothes sprawled dead on the floor; others lay wounded midway, clinging to the armoire like the fallen on a barricade before the French Revolution.

"Patricia? You have rehearsal in an hour."

"I'm up," she groaned in a voice that indicated she was anything but. Marcia moved to the next room, Haley's, and took a quick peek.

The bed was empty.

It was also made, but that was no surprise. Unlike her siblings' abodes, this one was neat, clean, anally organized. It could be a showroom in a furniture store. There were no clothes on this floor, every drawer fully closed. The trophies—and there were many—were perfectly aligned on four shelves. Ted had put in the fourth shelf just recently, after Haley's team had won the holiday tournament in Franklin Lakes. Haley had painstakingly divided the trophies among the four shelves, not wanting the new one to have only one. Marcia was not sure why exactly. Part of it was because Haley didn't want it to look like she was just waiting for more to come, but more of it was her general abhorrence of disorganization. She kept each trophy equidistant from the others, moving them closer together as more came in, three inches separating them, then two, then one. Haley was about balance. She was the good girl, and while that was a wonderful thing—a girl who was ambitious, did her homework without being asked, never wanted others to think badly of her, ridiculously competitive—there was a "tightly wound" aspect, a quasi-OCD quality, that worried Marcia.

Marcia wondered what time Haley had gotten home. Haley didn't have a curfew anymore because there had simply never been a need. She was responsible and a senior, and never took advantage. Marcia had been tired and gone up to sleep at ten. Ted, in his constant state of "randy," soon followed her.

Marcia was about to move on, let it go, when something—she couldn't say what—made her decide to throw in a load of laundry. She started toward Haley's bathroom. The younger siblings, Ryan and Patricia, believed that "hamper" was a euphemism for "floor" or really "anyplace but the hamper," but Haley, of course, dutifully, religiously, and nightly put the clothes she'd worn that day into the hamper. And that was when Marcia started to feel a small rock form in her chest.

There were no clothes in the hamper.

The rock in her chest grew when Marcia checked Haley's toothbrush, then the sink and the shower.

All bone-dry.

The rock grew when she called out to Ted, trying to keep the panic out of her voice. It grew when they drove to captain's practice and found out that Haley had never showed. It grew when she called Haley's friends while Ted sent out an e-mail blast—and no one knew where Haley was. It grew when they called the local police, who, despite Marcia and Ted's protestations, believed that Haley was a runaway, a kid blowing off some steam. It grew when, forty-eight hours later, the FBI was brought in. It grew when there was still no sign of Haley after a week.

It was as if the earth had swallowed her whole.

A month passed. Nothing. Then two. Still no word. And then finally, during the third month, word came— and the rock that had grown in Marcia's chest—the one that wouldn't let her breathe and kept her up nights— stopped growing.